MONEYMAKER

Josh Boldt

First paperback edition June 2024
Brown Hound Publishing
Lexington, KY

Cover art by Brown Hound Publishing
Author photo by Sugar Maple Photo

PRINT ISBN 978-1-7359541-2-7
EBOOK ISBN 978-1-7359541-3-4

MONEYMAKER

Josh Boldt

1

In the corner of a rundown strip mall on the east side of Atlanta a neon sign flashed pink letters.

MASSAGE. Blink. MASSAGE. Blink.

Who would come to this shithole for a massage at 11:00 p.m. on Friday night? No one up to any good. The establishment served as a front for a prostitution ring. Any pretense of a legitimate rubdown acted as nothing more than a prelude to the happy ending that followed.

For the second night in a row, Mack Abbott sat in his pickup truck across the street from the massage parlor. Like the previous night, he parked the truck in a nearby motel lot to blend in with the vehicles around him.

Mack faced the tug joint, cautiously aware of his surroundings. His left hand held a pair of tactical binoculars through which he watched the tinted glass door. From time to time, without lowering the binoculars, he reached for the center console and grasped a polystyrene foam cup of black coffee. His right hand slowly raised the cup to his mouth and then lowered it again, settling the coffee snugly back into the vinyl cupholder.

Mack worked on assignment for a client who paid him well. The job was easy: to watch a guy who happened to be inside the massage parlor at that moment getting his rocks off.

Mack had been commissioned to keep tabs on the mark, record his every move, gather whatever he could about the man's daily routine. So far, Mack knew the man was an alcoholic and a pervert. Didn't seem like much to report, but in Mack's line of work digging up that sort of embarrassing dirt might be exactly what his clients had in mind.

The door of the massage parlor swung open. A burly truck driver stepped out on the sidewalk. Mack focused the binoculars on the man's face. A low-pulled baseball cap cast a shadow across his features. The blinking neon sign lit the bearded face with its intermittent flicker.

Not the mark, but Mack watched him anyway. The guy shifted his weight to one foot and removed a can of dip from his back pocket. He scooped the tobacco up with his forefinger and slid it in his lower lip with one quick motion. He sucked the juice into his mouth and spit it on the sidewalk. He grabbed the buckle of his belt and shifted it with an exaggerated motion, before pulling the brim of his hat down further and stepping off the sidewalk.

"Hey, mister, let me get a cigarette."

Mack nearly jumped out of his skin when he heard the voice to his left, just outside his truck window. He lowered the binoculars quickly and turned to face the speaker. His window, lowered about halfway, allowed the night breeze to break the stifling Atlanta humidity.

The interrupter, a worn-out bum with sunken gums,

stood a few feet away. His breath stank of cheap booze. Mack smelled the foul stench through the open window.

"Sorry, pal. I don't smoke," Mack said.

"What you got there? Are them binoculars?" said the bum. He squinted his eyes and pointed toward Mack's lap.

"Nah, don't worry about it."

"You a peeping Tom or something?" the drunk slurred. He wobbled on his legs and leaned forward, placing his hand on the hood of Mack's truck.

"Move along. I'm busy," said Mack.

"You don't have to be a asshole. Lemme have a look through them things."

Mack saw the door of the massage parlor open again. Slowly this time, as though someone peeked out before exiting.

"Take off, guy. I don't have time for this right now," said Mack. He fumbled with the binoculars to regain focus.

"Let me get a dollar then."

Mack reached in his glovebox. His hand passed over a loaded Beretta 92X. He gripped a half-empty pint of Wild Turkey. Mack quickly switched the pint to his left hand and shoved it out the window at the bum. "I'll save you the middleman. Now get out of here."

The bum took the pint of booze without hesitation. He smiled broadly and stumbled off toward the motel without another word.

Mack got the binoculars focused just in time to watch his mark slip out the door of the massage parlor. He wore a black jacket with the hood cinched down tightly over his head.

Mack switched the binoculars for a Nikon camera with

a special lens for taking photos at night without a flash. He snapped several photos of his subject as the man exited the building, making sure to frame the photos so they captured the neon MASSAGE sign in the background.

The guy kept swiveling his head back and forth, watching carefully to see if anyone noticed him. He hustled over to a tan Cadillac and got in. He backed out and gunned the Caddy, making a fast right turn out of the parking lot toward downtown Atlanta.

Mack started the engine of his truck. His headlights flicked on. He reached over and closed the glovebox that held the exposed Beretta. He shifted into drive and pulled out in traffic, following the tan Cadillac.

The mark drove erratically, swerving around cars, sometimes even passing them on the shoulder with his wheels off the road. Mack tried to stay with him, but he could not keep up without being noticed. If he matched the Cadillac's driving style the mark would easily pick him out in the rearview.

Little by little the Cadillac leapfrogged ahead until Mack could no longer see the car. By the time they hit traffic in downtown Atlanta, the Cadillac was gone. Mack strained to see it over the line of cars, but the vehicle had disappeared.

Mack hated to lose his mark, but he knew where the guy was staying. He could circle back to his hotel and watch for him to return. No sense risking exposure. He had the photos. That should be enough for now.

Gripped by the hunger he had suppressed during the long day of surveillance, Mack pulled off at a diner for something to eat.

*

Mack chose a seat near the back of the diner where he could see the entire restaurant. He grabbed a newspaper off the counter and ordered a Coke.

Late night in Atlanta. The all-night diner had an array of patrons. Mack rested his elbows on the cool plastic table. He held the newspaper in his hands but stared over the top of it, surveying the diners nearby.

A group of stoned teenagers giggled in a booth, their eyes red and glassy. A couple truck drivers ate a late meal after a long day. An elderly couple shared a slice of pie.

"Anything good in there today?" asked the waitress as she approached Mack's table.

Mack folded the newspaper and set it on the table next to the menu. "Hardly ever is," he said. He picked up the menu and scanned it quickly.

The waitress stood close to Mack, waiting for him to order. She held a pad of paper and a pen that she had taken from her long, brown hair.

"Let me have," Mack said as he read, "I'll take the flank steak with onions and peppers."

"Hashbrowns?"

"Sure. Can I get them kind of well-done, good and brown?"

"You betcha."

The waitress sauntered off to the kitchen to put in Mack's order.

He picked up the newspaper again but still didn't read it. Just held it in his hands and stared at the words.

What was he doing here in Atlanta? Alone on Friday

night at a hole-in-the-wall diner. Didn't know a soul in town. Had no idea how long he would be there or what he was even supposed to be doing. Just follow some guy and take his picture, report back to his employer everything the guy did. What a life, Mack thought. He drank the Coke and waited for the waitress to bring his steak.

Waiting. That was mostly what Mack did these days. Watch and wait. Wait for something to happen and report back. Hours, days went by with nothing but waiting. In his line of work, Mack had to get good at occupying his time or he could go crazy from all the waiting.

He played games in his head. He would name the state capitals or list the presidents in order. Sometimes he would cycle through the countries in Africa or Europe, picturing the map in his head, trying to recite them contiguously, only moving to countries that shared a border.

Anything to keep his mind busy, to keep from being alone with his thoughts for too long. Sometimes the thoughts wandered too far away, and Mack couldn't bring them back so easily. He focused on concrete details: facts, places, names. Easier to control the thoughts that way, keep them from taking off on tangents that led to memories better left in the past.

Mack had learned how to wait courtesy of the U.S. Navy. Hurry up and wait. In the service, they were always rushing to get ready, and then sitting for hours or days. Bags packed, uniforms crisp, waiting for the next orders.

Now a civilian, Mack had not set foot on a Navy ship since he was honorably discharged from the U.S.S. *Harlan County* in 1994.

A few months after his discharge, he was offered a gig

doing muscle-for-hire work. The gig paid well, and he was good at it.

Three years had passed since that first job. Mack had made a name for himself in the business. He now had clients all over the country that called on his expertise and discretion.

Melting ice shifted in his glass. Beads of condensation formed around the base of the vessel. The beads dripped and spread out slowly on the table in long rivulets.

Mack unrolled the paper napkin from his silverware. He wiped away the condensation. His left hand still held the newspaper, its top edge drooping over at the fold.

Mack stared at the paper. His eyes began to unfocus. The words bled together and swirled in front of him.

He waited.

2

"Yeah, I got some photos of the guy last night. Safe to say he won't want these coming out in the Sunday paper," Mack said into a dingy, yellow telephone. He sat on one of the two double beds in his motel room, facing the window.

Daylight streamed in through the open blinds. Just outside Mack's window, the I-75 on-ramp loomed large, a towering concrete sculpture. The traffic roared loud enough that Mack had to press his finger against his ear to hear the caller on the other end of the line.

"Good. Fax them over this morning," said the voice.

"Is that all you needed?" said Mack.

"For this job, yes. We knew he had a certain, shall we say, fetish. Once he sees the photos, he won't be a problem for us anymore."

Mack said nothing.

"Will you be staying in Atlanta for a while, Mr. Abbott?"

"I guess that depends on you," said Mack.

The voice chuckled softly. "I suppose you're right about that. Why don't you stick around for a little while?"

"I guess I could. I don't really have any other business lined up just yet."

"I'm sure you can find something to do. We may have more work for you nearby soon. I hear the city has grown a lot since the Olympics last year. Maybe you can tour the Coca-Cola plant, visit the aquarium, something nice like that."

Mack grunted.

"We will keep your tab paid. Try to enjoy yourself. Keep your beeper handy. We'll be in touch, Mr. Abbott."

Mack hung up the phone. He didn't care much for sightseeing. He flicked on the television. Flipped channels for a few minutes and then turned it off.

The truth was he didn't have anything better to do, whether he liked it or not. He might as well follow his employer's advice and check out the city.

Mack picked up his beeper from the nightstand. He checked the small LED screen: zero messages. He clipped the device on his belt. He grabbed the manila folder full of photographs and went down to the lobby to send the fax.

The motel lobby teemed with businessmen wearing cheap suits. Mostly traveling salesmen, road warriors who spent most of their lives on the interstate. A motel like this one made a perfect pit stop for that type of traveler. They could pull out of the parking lot directly onto I-75. Next stop Knoxville or Lexington or Cincinnati, take their pick.

Mack watched the men drink coffee and pick at pastries from the continental breakfast displayed on the counter. The room smelled of warmed-over java and cheap cologne.

A television mounted in the corner of the lobby ran the morning news. November 21st, 1997. A chipper news anchor announced the weather. A high of 82 degrees in Atlanta. Less than a week to Thanksgiving, she mentioned more than once during the few minutes Mack stood in line at the front desk.

"Where can I find the fax machine?" Mack asked the desk clerk when his turn finally came.

"I can help you with that, sir," said the clerk, a man in his late twenties who looked like he hadn't slept all night. He reached across the counter for the manila folder in Mack's right hand.

Mack pulled the folder back toward his chest. "I'd prefer to send it myself if you don't mind."

"It's no problem, sir. Just write down the fax number and we will get it sent right away."

The clerk slid a pad of paper and pen across the counter to Mack.

"If it's all the same to you, I would rather do it," said Mack again.

The clerk knitted his brow, slightly perturbed. "Well, the fax machine is back here behind the desk," he said as though that would settle it once and for all.

"Great. It'll just take a second," Mack said, already walking around the side of the counter.

The clerk made a move to stop him, but Mack side-stepped him and kept moving.

"Back here you say?" Mack said as he walked.

"Yes," sighed the clerk. He pointed toward the back office. "Hurry up please. I'm not supposed to let anyone back here."

Mack gave the clerk a quick salute and disappeared into the back office.

Moments later he reappeared, still holding his manila folder.

The clerk waited for him. "Will you be checking out today, sir?"

"Not yet. Think I'll do a little sightseeing."

"Would you like to leave a credit card, or will you be paying cash? I see you are paid up through this morning."

"My employer will give you a call later to arrange for the additional days. Not sure how long I'm staying yet."

"We'll need some form of payment to hold the room."

"Listen, pal, I told you the tab will get paid. Chill out, will ya? Look outside. It's a beautiful day."

The clerk huffed and began typing furiously at his keyboard.

Mack grabbed a banana from the breakfast stand and stepped out into the Atlanta morning.

The air held a slight chill. Mack crossed the street so he could walk in the sun. He followed the sidewalk heading east with the banana in one hand and the folder in the other. After a few blocks, he stopped at a large blue trash can. He ripped the folder and its contents into a dozen pieces and tossed them in the can along with the peel from his banana.

Mack bent over and stretched his arms and legs. He felt relieved to be rid of the psychological weight of the photos. He tightened the laces on his tennis shoes and began jogging. No particular destination in mind, just glad to be a free man again, making his own decisions, working on no one's clock.

Mack jogged until he came to the front entrance of the Atlanta Zoo. He gradually slowed his pace and stopped at the ticket booth just outside the gates. He stood there for a moment catching his breath.

Why not, he decided. He walked up to the ticket booth, paid the admission, and entered the zoo.

3

Mack watched two gorillas peel fruit under a tree. Their dark fingers gripped the yellow skin of the banana and tore the flesh. No different from the way Mack had eaten his own fruit moments earlier. They methodically worked their way through a half dozen bananas each, tossing aside the discarded peels.

The Atlanta sun had fully risen. Heat penetrated Mack's thin cotton shirt. The back of his neck burned. Sweat beaded on his brow. He decided to retreat indoors to an air-conditioned exhibit.

As Mack headed for the amphibian house he unclipped the pager from his leather belt. He checked the tiny screen. Still no messages. When Mack looked down to refasten the pager, a child ran smack into his leg.

The kid backed up a couple steps with a stunned look on his face, trying to decide whether to cry or run.

"Easy there, little fella," said Mack, rubbing his bruised knee cap. "I guess we both could have been paying better attention."

The kid didn't speak. His lip quivered.

Oh no, thought Mack. He looked around for the kid's parents. They couldn't be far.

"Jimmy, watch where you're going!" said a woman's voice to Mack's left.

Mack waved to the boy's mother. She was about Mack's age, maybe a little younger. Thin frame, shoulder-length brown hair, pretty face.

"He's alright, ma'am," said Mack. "I think we share the blame for the collision."

"Well, he knows better than to run like that. We've talked about it many times."

Mack looked at the boy. "Sounds like she's got your number," he said, smiling and shrugging his shoulders in sympathy.

The boy stared up at Mack. He took another step back.

"He's learned not to talk to strangers, I see," said Mack, still smiling at the approaching woman. "That's an important lesson."

The woman put her hand on Jimmy's shoulder. She watched Mack with slight suspicion. "Yeah," she said. Then she looked at the boy, "Let's go find your father."

The smile disappeared from Mack's face. He sensed the woman's judgment. Single guy by himself wandering around the zoo, talking to children. He was a suspicious character.

Just as Mack turned to walk away, he heard someone call his name.

"Hey, Abbott!" said the voice. "Abbott, is that you?"

Mack spun back around to face the man calling his name.

"Mack, I haven't seen you in years, brother. How the

hell are ya?" the man said when Mack turned.

Mack immediately recognized the face of Andy Simpson, one of his old Navy buddies.

"Well, I'll be damned. Andy, what are you doing here?" said Mack. "How long has it been, at least five years?"

"Thereabouts," said Andy. "Man, you got off the boat and got outta there. You couldn't wait for your discharge."

Mack laughed. "Yep, you're right about that."

"What are you doing in Atlanta? And at the zoo of all places? You with your family?" asked Andy.

Mack shook his head. He hesitated to answer, not having a good cover story.

"No. No family for me yet," he said. "Just doing some work here for a, uh, for a client. Killing some time this morning." Mack paused for a second and then added, "What about you? Are you a family man?"

"Yes, sir," said Andy. "Looks like you already met my wife and my son. This here is Jimmy and my wife, Olivia."

"No kidding?" said Mack. "This is your family? What are the chances, of all the kids I'd run into, it would be yours?"

Andy laughed. "Honestly, that boy behaves like a bat out of hell in public. He's probably run into half the legs in this zoo today."

"Takes after his old man then?"

Andy raised his fists in a boxing stance and jabbed lightly at Mack's ribs. "Hey, we're about to go get some ice cream. Why don't you join us?"

"Sure, why not?" said Mack. "I could go for something cold."

*

Mack and Andy took a table in the shade near the giraffes. Andy's wife, Olivia, kept an eye on Jimmy as he wandered near the railing, searching for the best viewing angle, his ice cream cone leaning at a precarious tilt.

"So what are you doing in Atlanta, pal?" said Andy. "You said you're working for a client? What type of work you doing these days?"

Mack lowered his voice. "Not a whole lot different from what we did in the Navy, except less water."

"Oh yeah?" Andy squinted his eyes and matched Mack's tone. "You got something cooking?"

Mack shrugged. "It pays the bills and keeps me out of an office."

"Now you're talking. God, I miss the action. My life is boring as hell these days." He looked toward his wife and son. "I mean, don't get me wrong, everything is good. Got a great wife and kid. Can't complain much," said Andy. He raised his voice, "Isn't that right, honey?"

Olivia's eyes indicated she had heard her husband, but she gave no response.

"Hey, honey, you've heard me talk about Mack before. You remember me telling you about him?"

Olivia took a few steps in the direction of the men, turning occasionally to keep an eye on Jimmy.

"We went all over the world together. We've seen it all," said Andy, still talking to his wife.

"That's nice," said Olivia, patronizingly.

"I'm telling you, I'd trust this man with my life. He's a great guy to have on your side."

"Okay, well, Mack, I'm glad to know you," said Olivia. "But let's try not to have anybody's life in anybody's hands, how bout?"

Mack held up his palms. "No argument here, ma'am. Andy's getting carried away. As far as I'm concerned, my Navy days are over. I'm just a regular old citizen now. No better than the next guy."

"Don't be so modest," said Andy. "I've seen you take out half a dozen dudes before anybody saw you coming."

"Easy now," said Mack, glancing around him nervously. "Let's change the subject, eh?"

The two men sat quietly for a few moments.

Andy fidgeted until he spoke again, "This employer of yours, he ever need any more help?"

Mack sighed. "Andy, you don't want to get involved in this business. You've got a family now. It can get pretty rough."

"Man, that's what I'm craving. Don't you ever need a lookout or some backup or something? I'll stay in the background for all I care. I just need something to juice up my system a little."

Mack remembered his time in the service with Andy, how well they worked together. "I'll let you know," he said. "Do you live around here?"

"Sure do. Not even fifteen minutes from here." Andy handed Mack a business card.

Mack examined the card. "How's the handyman business?"

"Killing it, man. It's like nobody knows how to do anything themself anymore. Or else they're too lazy. I got people knocking down my door to help them install a deck or re-grout their bathtub or whatever else. Good money, too."

Mack nodded. "You always were pretty good with a wrench."

"Pretty good? Ah hell, pretty good. I was the best engineer on our ship, and you know it," said Andy grinning.

Mack smiled at Andy's enthusiasm, glad to see his friend could still take a joke.

"I ain't kidding, though, brother. You need a hand, you call me. I'll pack up my job site and be right there. I'd love to get in some trouble."

Mack watched a giraffe reach high in the air to tear the foliage from a nearby tree.

Trouble…that's exactly what he wanted to avoid.

Mack's pager buzzed as he walked back to the motel. He pulled the vibrating square from his belt and glanced at the screen. The number was unfamiliar. He reclipped the pager and picked up his pace.

The street became gradually rougher the further Mack got from the zoo. Near the interstate, the landscape looked more like a war zone. Trash littered the gutters, drifters wandered aimlessly with dead eyes. Rusted out vehicles and discarded shopping carts.

Mack nodded at the front desk clerk. He hurried into the elevator, hoping to avoid another debate about the bill.

"Your room has been paid for the week, sir!" called the clerk through the closing elevator doors. Mack gave a slight wave to acknowledge he had heard.

His motel room smelled like fresh cigarette smoke. The bed had been sloppily made, the bathroom towels straightened. A thick cigarette ash lay in the bathroom sink.

Sitting down on the bed, Mack lifted the phone from the table. He dialed the number displayed on his pager.

"Hello," said Mack when he heard the line click.

"This is Abbott?" said an unfamiliar voice.

"Who's asking?" said Mack.

The voice laughed slightly. "Our mutual friend said you are a prickly one."

"Which mutual friend are we talking about?"

"The Canadian."

Mack relaxed a little after hearing the code name, but he was still cautious. "Remind me, which province is The Canadian from?" he asked.

The voice laughed again. "There is no need for such games."

"I'll decide that for myself."

"The Canadian comes from further south," said the voice, now sounding serious. "Much further." He paused for a few moments. "Does that satisfy you?"

Mack grunted into the phone.

"I am told that you are good at what you do," said the voice. "I have a very lucrative opportunity for the right person." He sighed a long and exaggerated breath. "But if you are unable to comply, I will find someone else."

Mack watched the cars zip past his window on the interstate. "I'm listening," he said.

"A shipment is arriving tonight in Savannah. I need you to document the delivery and follow the package to its destination. You must not be observed. It is of utmost importance that we learn exactly where the package is being warehoused."

"How's it being delivered?"

"By sea. There is a small island called Tybee off the coast, about an hour's drive from Savannah. The package will arrive on the beach overnight. It will not be, shall we say, declared with Customs."

"Are we talking about a truckload or an envelope? What's the cargo?"

"A large crate. It will likely be received by a standard box truck. It is best that you do not know what is inside the crate."

"How many in their crew?"

"We do not know for sure. Maybe half a dozen. Could be as many as ten. They will be heavily armed, that I can assure you. You do not want to be caught."

"All you want me to do is watch and follow?"

"That is correct. For now. We only need to know where the package is delivered."

"How will I know which boat I'm staking out?"

"I can fax you the details when we hang up."

Mack gave the man the motel's fax number. "I'm at a motel. Give me a couple minutes so I can be waiting at the machine when the fax arrives," said Mack.

"Certainly," said the new employer. "Call this same phone number as soon as you know the destination of the package. If your surveillance is good, there will be more work for you. And, let me say again, you do not want to be caught by these people. It will not go well for you."

Mack hung up the phone. He went downstairs to receive the fax.

The front desk clerk's demeanor noticeably improved once a week's rent had been paid in advance.

"Hello, Mr. Miller. Going out again already?" said the clerk, using the fake name Mack had given when he checked in.

"Not yet. But I may be traveling for work the next couple of days. It's okay if I keep my room while I'm gone?"

"Of course, sir. You are all paid up. It's yours—doesn't matter whether you sleep there or not."

Mack nodded. "I've got a fax coming in a minute. You mind if I get it myself?"

The clerk squirmed. "Well, um, sir, you know the rules."

"Listen, we might as well come to an understanding. As long as I'm staying here, I will be sending and receiving faxes. Some of them will have sensitive information. I need access to that machine. Can we just agree that I'm an exception to the rule?" Mack slid a $100 bill across the counter.

The clerk's eyes lit up at the sight of the cash. "Yes, sir," he said. "I think we can come to that understanding."

Mack released the bill into the clerk's open palm. He slipped behind the desk just as the fax machine whirred awake.

Andy's phone rang four times before he answered. "Hello," he said, sounding half-asleep and confused.

Mack looked at his watch. "Did Olivia send you to bed before dinner?"

"Huh?"

"This how you're gonna be on a job? If so, I may not need you," said Mack, joking with his old friend.

Andy finally recognized Mack's voice. "Nah, the boy

wore me out at the zoo. That kid is hard to keep up with. Just laid down for a few winks."

"Makes me wonder why anyone ever decides to have one of those rug rats," Mack said, still messing with Andy.

"What are you doing calling me already? Didn't expect to hear from you so soon."

"I just wanted to see if you're in the market for a new set of steak knives."

"Get outta here with that."

Mack flicked at a fly that was buzzing around on the bedspread. "Hey, Andy, how are you strapped for firepower these days?"

Andy paused for a second, thinking about how to answer. "I'm not much for going into detail over the phone, but you know who you're talking to," he said.

"That's what I hoped you'd say," said Mack. "You have any interest in hitting up Savannah for a couple days?"

"I thought you'd never ask. How long we talking about?"

"Probably a day. Forty-eight hours tops."

"I think I can do that. Let me make a few phone calls and rearrange my schedule. What's the job?"

"I'll fill you in on the way. Can you pick me up at the Relax Inn by the interstate?"

"Oh, I'm driving? Better add that to your tab," Andy laughed.

Mack smiled. "Don't worry about that, buddy. This line of work is lucrative if it's anything."

"That's what I like to hear."

"I figure it's about four hours to Savannah. That'll put us in town around dusk if we leave now. This job's gonna be graveyard shift. Sooner we get there the better."

"You haven't seen me drive," said Andy. "We'll be fine."

"Meet me out front of the motel in an hour?" said Mack. "And bring along a couple of your little friends. I don't expect us to engage but I want to be armed just in case we need it."

"Roger that. See you in a few."

"Andy?" Mack said.

"Yeah?"

"Thanks, bud."

"You bet, brother."

5

Andy pulled up in the front circle of the Relax Inn an hour later. He drove a black Chevy Tahoe with dark-tinted windows. He lowered the passenger window and leaned across the seat to get Mack's attention.

"You gonna sit there on your butt all night or are we hitting the road?"

Mack, reclining in a broken patio chair near the motel's entrance, looked up and squinted his eyes to see through the dark windshield. He hopped up and strolled over to the SUV, leaning his tanned forearms on the passenger door frame. Conditioned air billowed from the open window.

"Nice ride."

"I told you the handyman business is doing me good. We have a couple cars. Figured this guy would be best for a stakeout with its tint job."

Mack nodded.

"Also plenty of room for stowing the heaters," said Andy, nodding toward the back of the truck.

"Wife didn't give you any trouble?"

"Nah, I just told her we were gonna tie one on for old

time's sake. She's pretty cool."

Mack opened the door and climbed in.

Andy spun the volume knob on the dashboard, cranking Rage Against the Machine through the speakers. He pounded the gas pedal and swerved up the on-ramp to I-75 South.

The sunset had almost completely faded from the horizon when Mack and Andy rolled into downtown Savannah. They took the exit off 16 and cruised down Oglethorpe, soaking in the sites of historic Savannah. Civil War-era buildings surrounded by ancient, twisted trees draped with Spanish moss.

Mack rolled down his window to let in the salty air. Still an hour's drive from the ocean but the smell reminded them they were close to saltwater.

"Damn, it feels good to be away from the family for a bit," announced Andy. "I love 'em but a man needs a breather once in a while."

Mack, half-listening, flipped through the instructions he had received by fax. "You know this town very well?" he asked.

"Never been here in my life," said Andy.

"Me neither. Says here we need to get to an island not far from here. Tybee is what it's called."

"Oh yeah, I've heard of it. Buddy a mine and his wife were telling me about it. Apparently it's kind of a dive—not a whole lot to it but a few motels and a handful of restaurants."

"Sounds ideal for smuggling a shipment under the

cover of night," said Mack.

Andy laughed. "Yeah, I guess you're right."

"Victory Drive is the road we're looking for. Hang a right here. Should be a little ways up. That'll take us out to the island," said Mack.

Andy flipped on his right turn signal. "Let's grab a bite before we head out there. I'm starving."

Mack stuck his head out the window to observe the nearly dark sky.

Andy sensed Mack's reservation. "Hell, they ain't gonna pull up on the beach the instant it turns dark, are they? We got time," said Andy. When Mack didn't respond Andy added, "You ever had Popeye's chicken?"

Mack looked at Andy and shook his head.

"Son, you're never lived then. Wait till you get a taste of their biscuits."

An hour later they were driving along the coast of dimly lit Tybee Island with half a dozen boxes of fried chicken stacked on the back seat of the Tahoe. The smell of grease and butter almost overpowered the acrid scent of surf.

"This place shuts down after dark, doesn't it?" said Andy. "Barely a light on the whole island."

"That's good for us. Easier to blend in," said Mack.

Andy was right. The entire commerce center of Tybee Island consisted of little more than a couple blocks of restaurants, a gas station, and a few bars. The only places showing any signs of life were a small hotel called The Sand Dune and a seafood restaurant that, judging by the neon lights in the window, also doubled as a local watering hole.

"Let's get a lay of the land," said Mack. "Cruise on down a ways, see how far this road goes."

"What are we looking for?" said Andy.

"Not sure just yet. The drop is supposed to happen at a pier on the south side of the island. Says there's a joint called High Tides nearby, so I guess let's look for that."

No sooner had Mack finished speaking than Andy fired back with, "Well, that was easy."

Mack raised his eyes from the faxed instructions and spotted the bar just ahead to their left.

"Looks like they're still open," said Mack. "That's good. We can park in the lot without raising any suspicion."

"Surely these guys won't make a move with people around, would they?" said Andy.

Mack shrugged. "Depends on how much discretion they need. For all we know, the mayor of Tybee Island gave them the okay in exchange for a campaign donation."

Andy sat quietly for a few seconds. He glanced at the flashing neon COORS sign in the window of High Tides. "I could go for a beer or two," he said.

"Better wait until after we're done here," said Mack.

"Yeah," said Andy wistfully. "You're probably right about that."

Andy reached into the back seat and grabbed a box of Popeye's chicken. He set the container in his lap and lifted the cardboard clamshell lid.

"Good lord, that smells delicious, eh?"

Mack had to admit it did. He got his own box and began working on the chicken.

The Tahoe went silent while the two men ate. After a

few minutes, Andy lifted a fried chicken tender in the air. He pointed the tender at Mack and said, "You really think there's a mayor of Tybee Island?"

Mack smiled. He reached across the seat deftly and swatted the chicken tender out of Andy's fingers. It landed with a thump somewhere in the back of the truck.

Avery Calloway propped the heel of her left foot on the coffee table in front of her. She extended her toes and carefully painted neon green polish on each nail, blowing softly across the wet paint. A cigarette smoldered in an ash tray on the coffee table. Wispy smoke swayed erratically with each blow.

The phone in the kitchen rang.

"Shit," said Avery. She took a draw of the cigarette. Standing up carefully, she put her weight on the unpainted right foot and waddled across the soft carpet toward the kitchen. Only the heel of her left foot touched down with each step. She kept the toes pointed up and spread as she walked.

The phone continued to ring.

"I'm coming!" said Avery. She finally reached the kitchen and pulled the receiver off its cradle on the wall. "Yeah?" she said. She leaned against the door frame, shifting all her weight off the left foot.

"Are you coming?" said the caller.

"What do you think?"

"Hell, I never know what to think about you crazy broads. Y'all show up or you don't show up. Nobody ever calls. Half the time you leave in the middle of a shift.

How'm I sposed to run a fuckin' titty bar when I ain't got no titties in it?"

Avery laughed. "Calm down, Leonard. Geez. I need the money. You know I'll be there."

"It's already eleven. Get to gettin' then if you are."

"Me and my titties'll be there in twenty. Go get yourself a drink and chill out."

Leonard hung up without another word.

"Dirty bastard," said Avery. She hung up the phone and returned to the couch to paint her other toes.

The evening news came on the television. The anchor read a series of depressing headlines about increased crime and a rising homicide rate in Savannah. Avery pressed the mute button on the TV remote and turned on the stereo instead. Republica's "Ready to Go" blasted out of the speakers in her one-bedroom apartment. The music blared so loud she jumped, but she made no effort to lower the volume. Within a few seconds, her neighbor started pounding on the wall.

"Fuck off," Avery mumbled. She turned the volume even louder.

When her toenail polish dried Avery walked to her bedroom. She removed a lacy bra and panties from her top dresser drawer. She stepped into the panties and glided them up her long legs, snapping the elastic in place over her ample rear. Her work uniform. Then she rolled on a pair of thigh-high fishnets and clipped them in place with a black garter belt. Next, came a chin-length orange wig and, finally, she stepped into a pair of platform heels.

Avery stood in front of the mirror that hung on the back of her bedroom door. She shifted side to side, examining her outfit. She was ready to become Ava Applebottom, the subject of every john's dreams.

Avery stepped out of the heels, losing about three inches when she stood flat-footed on the carpet. She pulled on a pair of sweatpants with the word PINK stenciled on the butt, discreetly covering her stockings and panties. She added a matching zippered top. She tossed the wig and high heels in her bag and slipped her freshly painted toes into a pair of flip-flops.

Avery switched off the stereo. She gave a quick thump on the neighbor's wall for good measure and left the apartment at 11:30 p.m.

Mack nudged Andy's arm and pointed toward the parking lot adjacent to High Tides. A pair of headlights illuminated the blacktop and briefly lit a large wooden sign that read PUBLIC BEACH PARKING.

Mack and Andy instinctively slouched lowered in their seats. They watched as the vehicle turned off the main road and entered the nearly empty parking lot. A white box truck with a hydraulic lift gate attached to the back.

"Oh, man," said Andy.

"That has to be our guy," whispered Mack.

The box truck pulled into a parking space facing the ocean. The driver killed the engine. The truck's headlights switched off. No one got out.

"What now?" said Andy.

"What time is it?" said Mack.

Andy looked at his watch. "Close to one."

Mack shifted his eyes over to the restaurant. A couple

patrons remained inside, sitting at the bar.

"I guess we wait," said Mack. He leaned back in the seat and extracted his tactical binoculars from a clip on his belt. He raised the glasses to his eyes and zeroed in on the box truck.

"What kind of delivery truck has tinted windows?" asked Mack rhetorically, the binoculars still pressed to his eyes. He swept the lenses across the beach and scanned the coastline.

"See anything?" said Andy.

"Not yet. It's too dark out there to see very far."

"Looks like the bar is closing up," said Andy. "The bartender just shut off the lights. He's heading for the front door now."

"Good," said Mack slowly. "Hey, you brought a piece with you, right?"

"Oh yeah, it's in the back." Andy reclined the driver's seat all the way down, and then slid over it into the back seat. He leaned over the headrest and fumbled around in the cargo area of the Tahoe.

"There you are," said Andy. He picked up the chicken tender that Mack had knocked from his hand. "Thought we lost you." He crunched down on the crispy nugget.

Mack lowered his binoculars. He looked over his shoulder at Andy with disgust. "That's nasty."

"What?" said Andy, pretending to be shocked. "Wounded soldier, man. He had to fulfill his mission."

"His mission for you to eat him?"

"Exactly."

Mack shook his head.

"Here we go," said Andy. He unclipped four locks and

raised the lid of his gun case.

"What the hell you got back there?" said Mack when he heard the elaborate unveiling.

Andy answered by handing the weapon over the center console, barrel first.

"What in God's name?" said Mack when he saw the barrel. "Is that a fucking AK?"

"Yeah buddy," said Andy with pride.

"Are you planning on gunning down an army?"

"Hell, I don't know. You said bring firepower. I figure better to have too much than not enough."

Mack nodded a couple times slowly. "I don't disagree with your logic. But it's overkill. I was thinking like a couple of handguns."

"Oh," said Andy, somewhat disappointed. "I've got those, too." He reached back over the seat and quickly produced a Beretta and SIG Sauer.

"Let me see that SIG," said Mack.

"Careful, it's loaded," Andy said as he handed over the pistol.

"How bout you leave the assault rifle behind and hop back up front?" said Mack.

Andy did as he was told.

Mack stuck the SIG Sauer in the glovebox and returned to his binoculars. First, he examined the restaurant. All the lights were off except for a couple neon signs inside the bar. The bartender had gone home. The Tahoe was one of only three vehicles remaining in the restaurant's parking lot.

Suddenly, a light flashed out in the ocean. The burst lasted less than a second, like the flash from a camera. If Mack hadn't been expecting something, he might not have noticed the light.

Seconds later, the box truck answered with a quick flash of headlights. On and then off. Like one might signal to another driver to turn off his high beams.

"Did you see that?" said Andy.

"Yep," said Mack. He ducked down further in his seat. They were far enough away from the box truck to be inconspicuous, but Mack still felt exposed in the near empty parking lot.

The doors of the box truck opened. Two men got out. The men were dressed entirely in black, including black ski masks. Even with the binoculars, Mack found it difficult to keep his eyes on them in the low light.

The men raised the sliding rear door of the box truck and removed a conveyance that resembled a modified cart. Sort of like a child's wagon complete with handle, but it had extra-large plastic wheels that had been swapped in for traveling across a sandy beach.

Within seconds, the men had pulled the wagon into the darkness of the beach. Once they neared the lapping waves, Mack lost track of them. He could barely make out their outlines if he squinted hard through the binoculars.

"I lost 'em," said Andy.

"Yeah, me, too," said Mack. "Too dark down there to see much."

"Want me to get closer?" said Andy. "I can slip down there in the shadows next to the restaurant."

Mack thought for a second. "No, not yet. I don't think it's worth the risk," he said. "They brought the truck for a reason. They'll come back up once they get whatever they're after."

Andy nodded. He gripped the handle of his pistol tightly. "Just say the word," he said.

"Recon only for now," said Mack. "All we have to do is follow the shipment."

Mack and Andy waited in silence as the minutes ticked by. Finally, they again caught sight of the wagon. The men pulled the wheeled vehicle more slowly on the return trip. The man in front gripped the handle tightly while the other trailed behind the wagon, leaning hard into the load and pushing.

"Whatever they've got, it's heavy," said Andy. "Look at that track the wheels are making in the sand."

"No kidding," said Mack. "That's quite a load."

Once the men were back within range of the streetlamp, the binoculars again became useful. Mack focused his glasses on the wagon. He saw dozens of wrapped packages about the size of bricks, all balanced and stacked neatly in the wagon.

"What do you think it is?" said Andy.

"If I was a betting man, I'd say narcotics," said Mack. "All individually wrapped like that? Coke, heroin, pot—hard to say for sure which."

"Looks like it to me," said Andy. "That'd have to be a couple million dollars' worth of blow or smack, eh?"

Mack didn't answer.

The smugglers made quick work of the load once they reached the truck. They had a system. One man climbed inside the truck and deftly re-stacked the bricks handed to him by the other man. It took the men less than five minutes to load the entire stash and then lift the wagon back in the truck. Thirty seconds later, they backed out of the parking spot as though nothing had ever happened.

"Get ready," said Mack.

Andy slipped his Beretta into a cupholder and stuck the key in the ignition.

"Wait till they're out of the parking lot," said Mack.

Andy watched the box truck until it had returned to the main road. The truck headed back toward Savannah. Andy started the Tahoe's engine. He eased out on the empty road. The box truck's taillights loomed far ahead but they were easy to follow in the pitch darkness.

"That long road back to Savannah?" said Andy. "Them and us'll be the only cars out there. You know they'll be paranoid about being followed anyway."

"That's okay," said Mack. "The good news is we can keep our distance on this deserted road and still see their taillights. But you're right, they will be watching. We stay far enough back, I think we'll be all right.

Andy gave the Tahoe a little gas. The beach road soon came to an end when they hit the long bridge that would carry them back to Savannah. During the entire drive they kept a safe padding between themselves and their target, ever watchful for the truck to make a sudden turn.

Avery nudged aside the sheer red curtain and stepped off the stage after her dance. She shuffled down three stairs and then made a beeline for the small, private dressing area at the back of the strip club.

The room, about the size of a large walk-in closet, typically bustled with girls in various stages of dress. Three vanities lined each wall of the cramped dressing room.

Large mirrors hung behind the vanities, creating an illusion of space while also making it impossible to escape one's reflection.

At the back of the dressing room another small door led to the bathroom—the only place in the club the girls could garner a moment of privacy. Most of the women hung out in the large bathroom between dances.

Leonard hated when the women left the main floor for too long. He always said any girl back there in the can ain't making the club any money.

"How'd you do?" a girl asked Avery as soon as she entered the dressing room. The girl's reflection in the mirror peered at Avery over her shoulder. She held a set of long black eyelashes against one lid, attempting to reattach it as she spoke.

"Not bad," said Avery. "I have a couple regulars down front. I pay attention to them when I'm up there and they tip me good. Every time I take a dollar from them, I look them right in the eye and act like they're changing my life."

The girl with the missing eyelash laughed.

Avery continued. "Those fuckers look around the stage all proud, wanting everyone to know I belong to them."

"I know that game," said the other girl.

"What happened there?" said Avery, nodding at the missing eyelash. "You lose something?"

"Sheeyit," said the other stripper. "I was upside down on the pole getting a nasty friction burn on my inner thighs when that little bitch dropped right off." The girl laughed. "Fluttered down to the stage like a feather."

Avery listened to the story, smiling. "What'd you do?"

"I slid down that pole headfirst and grabbed the eyelash

with my mouth, trying to make it as sexy as I could, considering I was a damn cyclops when I turned right-side up. Lashes like this, you lose one, you look straight-up deranged."

Avery laughed along with the girl. "Gross. You mean you touched that disgusting stage with your mouth?" she said with a look of horror. "Did Leonard see you?"

"Hell no, that old bastard was too busy trying to get into the new girl's panties. Lucky for me, I guess. I got off stage pretty quick, but I saw him over by the bar with his hand on her ass. Fuckin' guy sipping his drink out of a tiny cocktail straw like an asshole."

"As long as he's worked in clubs, you'd think he'd've learned how to drink booze without making a fool of himself by now, wouldn't you?"

The other girl just shrugged her shoulders. She finally got the eyelash to stick. She blinked a couple times to make sure it stayed put. When she was satisfied, she stood up and turned around. "What's your name again, honey?" she asked.

"It's Avery." Avery hesitated for a second. "Or did you mean my stage name?"

"God no. I know your stage name. Everybody in here does. The great Ava Applebottom with an ass like a shelf," said the woman, smiling and affecting a surprisingly deft curtsy in her eight-inch heels.

Both women laughed.

"I'm Gretchen," the woman replied. "I don't work in Savannah much. I'm usually in Atlanta. You ever dance there?"

Avery shook her head. "Not really." She decided not to

mention that Atlanta was her hometown. Or that she had left when she started dancing in order to avoid awkward run-ins with friends and family. "Good to meet you," said Avery. She stuck out her hand and gave Gretchen a quick shake.

"I better get back out there," said Gretchen.

Avery nodded. "Any party favors around tonight?" she asked, thumbing toward the bathroom.

Gretchen winked. "What do you think?"

Avery smiled and headed for the bathroom. Three girls stood at the sink in front of the mirror. Two smoked cigarettes, and the third fidgeted with her hair in the glass reflection. Six lines of white powder were cut out on the counter, carefully cordoned off from any splashing water at the sink.

"It's dead out there for a Friday," said one of the women. She took a long drag from her cigarette and exhaled in the direction of the mirror.

"How many privates you done so far?" asked the girl fixing her hair. She meant private dances, where the real money was made in the strip club.

"Just three so far. Bunch of cheap bastards out there tonight. I can't give this pussy away."

All three girls laughed.

"Jamal is pissed at me anyway," said the first girl.

"The DJ?"

"Yeah, he's playing some bullshit every time I get on stage. How the fuck am I supposed to dance sexy to Alan Jackson?"

"Damn, girl, that was you up there for that?" said the girl in the mirror. "I heard that shit come on and was wondering what the hell they were thinking playing that in a strip club."

"I told you, he's pissed at me. That's how he gets back at you."

"What'd you do to him?"

"Hell if I know. Probably didn't shake my ass at him last week or something. Whatever you do, don't piss that boy off cause he holds a grudge."

As soon as she finished speaking, the woman leaned over the counter and snorted two of the lines. "I'm up again pretty soon. You'll know it's me when you hear Michael Bolton or some other dumb shit come on," said the woman, shaking her head. She brushed past Avery on her way out of the bathroom.

The two remaining girls laughed.

"Hey, can I get in on that?" said Avery.

"Fine by me," said the woman with the cigarette. Her chest and arms were covered in glitter that sparkled in the well-lit bathroom. She tossed her cigarette on the tile floor and stubbed it out under a platform heel. "It ain't mine."

Avery looked at the other girl, but she only shrugged her shoulders in response as if to say "not mine either."

Avery took one of the twenties she had just earned and rolled it into a tight cylinder. She did two of the lines quickly. Then, she tilted her head back and let the cocaine drip down her throat. The effect was immediate. Her eyes lit up, and she brimmed with the energy that she had lacked all day.

"That's what I'm talking about," Avery said.

"Just don't let Leonard see it," said the other girl.

"Leonard is a bitch. He does whatever I tell him," said

Avery, bristling with a newfound sense of power. She leaned over and did a third line. The powder made her cough a little. She turned her head to keep from blowing the final line across the sink. Avery extended the bill to the other girl.

The woman shook her head. "Nah, I don't mess with it," she said.

Avery started to leave the bathroom but hesitated. She tightened the bill again and snorted the fourth line, then got out of there quickly, back into the darkness of the club.

"You ever think about the Navy?" said Andy. He and Mack were still following the white box truck, only a few miles outside of Savannah now.

"Like reminisce you mean?" said Mack.

"Sure. About the other guys, or about what we did. You know, like the time we were in the Caribbean."

Mack nodded. "Or West Africa. That was a shit detail."

"Man, screw that mission," said Andy. "But we did good work though, didn't we?"

Mack thought for a few seconds. "We did," he replied.

"I think about going back sometimes," said Andy. "Re-enlisting."

Mack turned to look at Andy. "Re-enlisting? Why?"

"I don't know. I just miss it, I guess. The action. The brotherhood."

"You need to join a bowling team or something," said Mack.

Both men laughed.

"Seriously, though," Mack continued, "you have a wife

and a kid now. It's not the same as it was back then. You can't be taking risks like that."

"Risks? What do you call what we're doing right now?"

Mack hung his head, sheepishly. "Don't make me regret bringing you along."

"Hell," said Andy with confidence. "You couldn't of done it without me."

The taillights up ahead glowed red when the box truck suddenly braked.

"Lookout, they're slowing down," said Mack.

Andy tapped the brakes to match the slower speed.

The driver of the box truck flipped on the left turn signal. The truck eased off the highway onto a deserted road in a dark warehouse district.

"No way we can follow them inconspicuously," said Andy. "It's dark and empty down on that road. They'll see us coming from a mile away down there."

"You're right," said Mack. "Keep on driving up a ways, and then pull off the road and cut the lights."

As they passed the road where the truck had turned, Mack raised up in his seat. He followed the truck's headlights in the darkness.

"There's not much down there. I can see them still from here. Looks like a couple warehouses and maybe a cemetery or some kind of empty lot." Mack strained to see in the darkness. "I think that's a little canal that leads out to the ocean on the other side of the road. They can't get far."

Andy parked the Tahoe on the side of the road and shut off the engine. "What now?" he asked.

"Now we get out. We're on foot from here."

Mack dug into a black bag he had brought with him.

He withdrew a small camera. He took the SIG Sauer from the glovebox and tucked it in the back of his waistband. Andy followed Mack's lead with his Beretta.

The two men exited the Tahoe. They crept across the road in darkness. After shuffling down the dusty shoulder they quickly landed on the access road below.

The white box truck sat parked at a loading dock about two hundred yards away.

6

Darkness covered the warehouse block. The strip of cavernous metal storage buildings stood far enough from Savannah that the deserted district could not be reached by the city lights.

Mack and Andy crept toward the truck, concealing themselves under the cover of shadows. The two men maintained a state of disciplined vigilance like they had learned in the military. Listen carefully, eyes open, remain as silent as possible. They communicated with head nods and hand gestures only.

About fifty yards from the loading dock a stack of wooden pallets stood tall enough for the two men to crouch behind. From their hiding spot they had a view of the warehouse's open bay door. A gap of several feet separated the rear of the truck from the dock—wide enough to see inside and observe the smugglers entering and exiting the truck.

The criminals behaved less cautiously now. Their footsteps echoed on the metal lift gate as they walked across it. They no longer wore the black ski masks.

Mack raised the binoculars. He saw the men carrying small bricks wrapped in thick brown paper. One of the men was a white guy with scruffy facial hair. Medium build. The other guy was thin and lean, clean-shaven. Looked to be Latin American, although Mack could not tell for sure. Both men were armed. A third man stood just inside the warehouse door with a fully automatic assault rifle strapped over his shoulder.

"Whatever they've got in there, they don't want to share," whispered Mack.

Andy raised his eyebrows.

"They're all packing heat."

"Good thing all we're doing is watching," whispered Andy.

Mack set down the binoculars. He removed his camera from its case. He silently attached a lens. He lined up the viewfinder with the open warehouse door and adjusted the focus. He quickly snapped off two dozen photos, capturing all three of the men's faces along with several shots of the product they were unloading.

"You see an address anywhere around here?" Mack asked as he packed up the camera.

"I got the street name on our way down. Hang on a sec."

Andy dropped back cautiously from the stack of pallets. Mack watched as Andy deftly glided through the shadows along the side of the warehouse.

After about a minute of searching, Andy raised his hand and give a thumbs up to Mack.

Once they had collected the photos and address, neither Mack nor Andy wasted any time retreating. They left the warehouse block and headed for the road where they had parked the Tahoe, reconvening at the base of the offramp. They shuffled back up the shoulder without speaking.

Once they were safely back inside the Tahoe with the engine running, Andy slapped his hands together with excitement.

"Hot damn, that's what I'm talking about, man!" he nearly shouted.

Mack smiled. "That was an easy one."

"Like hell. More fun than I've had in years."

Mack's shoulders began to relax once the truck started moving again. By the time they entered the outskirts of Savannah he was celebrating along with Andy.

"I always get the nerves when I'm in the heat of the moment. Doesn't matter how many times I do it," said Mack.

"That's the point, ain't it?"

Mack laughed. "I guess that's part of it. Definitely makes you feel alive."

"Damn right, buddy," said Andy. "Speaking of feeling alive, there's no chance I'm going to bed with this adrenaline. What's next?"

Mack looked at the dashboard clock and frowned. "At two a.m.? I figure we could get a case of beer and a cheap motel room."

"Nope. You aren't getting off that easy. You know the last time I had a guy's night out?"

"I'm not even sure we can find a bar open at this hour."

"That's okay cause we aren't looking for a regular bar."

Mack turned to Andy, his face a mix of confusion and

apprehension.

Andy raised his eyebrows mischievously. "Where do you go when the bars close?"

"Oh no," said Mack.

"Oh yes. What's my cut on this job anyway? I'll spend the whole thing on lap dances," roared Andy, sounding like he was already drunk. "I saw a strip club on the way through town. That be where we're headed!"

Mack shook his head. Andy seemed to have his mind made up. Mack shrugged, granting Andy some leeway for his help on the job.

"Lap dance. Lap dance. Lap dance," Andy chanted, tapping the steering wheel for effect.

"I get the impression I'm not gonna talk you out of it."

"Yessss!" said Andy, sounding like a child who had received a new toy. He gassed the Tahoe and retraced their path into town, navigating straight back to the club from memory.

Avery's brain buzzed with energy as she swept the red curtain aside and stepped out on the strip club floor.

The electronic drumbeat of "Closer" by Nine Inch Nails thudded through the club's speakers. Avery strutted to the beat, swinging her hips from side to side, grazing her fingers across the shoulders of seated patrons as she passed above them. She felt good. Damn good. She could do anything she wanted.

"Hey, baby, let me know when you're ready for a dance, okay?" she leaned over and whispered in the ear of one of her regulars.

The guy was dumbstruck, speechless. He nodded his head. Avery playfully slid a finger under the guy's chin and lifted as though she was closing his mouth for him. She smiled and swaggered off.

"You let me violate you," she mouthed along with the song lyrics using exaggerated lips as she walked.

Every head in the club turned to follow Avery as she made her way across the room. She placed a hand on the bar, and slid her ample rear end up on a stool.

"Who you think you are?" growled Leonard to Avery. He sat three stools down with his back against the wooden rim, surveying the club. He wore a pair of yellow-tinted aviators and a patterned silk shirt, open to his belly button. He raised his voice over the music so Avery would hear him.

"I'm the best girl in this club and you know it," said Avery. "So you can just sit your ass back down."

Leonard's eye twitched but he forced a smile.

"That so?"

"Yep."

Avery stared Leonard down, daring him to disagree with her. He held her gaze for a few seconds and then turned his head slowly back to the stage.

"Girls ain't supposed to sit at the bar when they're working," Leonard said, but his words held no power after he had caved in to Avery's challenge.

"Yeah, well. Make an exception."

Avery ordered a Diet Coke from the bartender. After a few seconds passed she turned back to Leonard and smiled. She recognized the difference between challenging the boss and humiliating him. She did not want to push him over the edge, just mess with him a little. She slid her Diet Coke down the bar and scooted over two stools toward Leonard.

"How many customers in here tonight? Looks pretty full," Avery said, knowing the question would bring Leonard back. He loved talking about money.

"More than two hundred last time I checked. We're making bank."

"That's what I like to hear. Hope they're big tippers," said Avery. She leaned over and reached across Leonard's shoulder, tracing her fingers around a thick gold chain that rested on his bare chest. "This new?"

"As a matter of fact, it is. Cost me five grand."

"It's heavy," said Avery, lifting the necklace with her fingertips and letting it come to rest on Leonard's hard pectoral muscles.

Leonard sat up a little taller on his stool. He straightened his pants and flattened them with his palms. He sniffed hard and exhaled through pursed lips like he was lifting weights or having sex.

It's so easy to work him, thought Avery. Just as bad as any other rube in this joint.

Leonard cleared his throat. His yellow lenses did not hide his eyes as they swept over Avery's body, pausing too long on the thin bikini straps that barely covered her chest.

"You're not gonna make any money sitting here with me," he said.

"I was just thirsty. I'm about to go give a lap dance. To that guy right there."

Avery pointed to the front row of chairs. A balding man with a paunchy belly protruding from his unflattering polo shirt sat with his head tilted up toward the stage. His face held the dazed smile and glazed eyes of a man who had had one too many.

"That fuckin' guy?" said Leonard. "No way. Too cheap. What is that, a Casio?" he said, referring to the man's wristwatch. "Hundred to one he uses that thing to calculate his tip on every drink. And it never tells him more than a buck."

Avery laughed slightly, then got serious. "Three songs minimum," she said.

"You gonna get that skinflint to go three rounds with you? Ain't no way."

"Twenty bucks says I do."

Leonard shook his head. "You're crazy."

"Scared?"

"No way. I'll take that bet. Fine," said Leonard. "And if you do get him, you might as well go to his house and take the braces off his kid's mouth while you're at it."

"Hey now," said Avery. "Don't be nasty. I can't help it if his wife don't have an ass like mine." Avery hopped off the stool. She still felt good from the cocaine, but the drug's euphoria was starting to wear off.

"Get that twenty ready," she said, and then she sauntered down the aisle toward her mark.

Rap music pounded in Mack's ears as he and Andy entered the club through a set of heavy double doors. The beat reached down his throat and gripped his guts. It rattled his chest and his nerves.

A bouncer with a wired earpiece in his left ear nodded when they entered. He raised a hand to stop them and signaled for them to lift their arms to their sides like wings. The bouncer quickly patted Mack and Andy down, checking their waistbands and pockets for weapons.

The bouncer said something Mack couldn't hear over the music. He cupped his hand to his ear. The bouncer repeated his request, but Mack still didn't catch it.

"My cover's on this guy," shouted Andy to the bouncer. He slapped Mack on the shoulder. "Twenty-five each," Andy said into Mack's ear.

Mack raised his eyebrows, shocked by the cost of entry. He took a $50 from his wallet and forked it over to the bouncer.

The bouncer waved them in.

"Thanks, brother," said Andy when they were inside. In the spacious club room, the music became less overwhelming. The two men could hear each other once more.

"For that price we ought to get a free dance."

"Hell, you know better than that. Ain't nothing free in a strip club." Andy scanned the crowd in the nearly full room. Neon lights spun and refracted through a layer of hazy smoke that hung above the stage. "Speaking of which, how bout you give me an advance on the payment for tonight's work, eh?"

"How much you want?"

"Enough to get covered in tit glitter. I want to walk out of here smelling like stripper snatch."

Mack shook his head. "You aren't right in the head, are you? When's the last time you smelled stripper snatch?" He handed Andy a wad of cash discreetly, so every girl in the place didn't swarm them on the spot.

"Mexico," said Andy, only half paying attention. He had his eyes on a redheaded stripper currently dancing on stage.

Mack knew exactly which time in Mexico Andy was referring to. They, along with a handful of other Seabees, had to fight their way out of a shady Mexican joint at dawn. It was a miracle nobody got stabbed.

"Check out the rack on that broad," said Andy, referring to the redhead that had caught his attention.

Mack had definitely noticed the woman, but he didn't respond to Andy's statement. Instead, he followed Andy through the crowd toward the stage. Andy pulled two chairs together in the front row and motioned for Mack to sit down in one of them.

Before Mack could take his seat, a burly drunk next to him surged into the walking lane and nearly knocked Mack over. Mack braced himself and caught the guy's weight with his shoulder. "Easy there, fella," he mumbled.

"What'd you say?" said the man. He stood up tall, a few inches higher than Mack, and stared down his nose aggressively.

Mack felt a twinge of rage flash through his body, knowing he could put this guy on his ass, but he swallowed it down. He looked for Andy and found his partner deeply engrossed in the acrobatics of the naked redheaded woman on stage.

Mack showed his empty palms to the bully to indicate he meant no threat.

"That's what I thought," said the drunk.

Mack held eye contact until the guy turned to walk away. The drunk swerved once again and nearly fell across the back of a stripper wearing an orange wig who was working a john in the front row.

The drunk steadied himself against the girl's back and then slid his open palm up her thighs and between her legs like a credit card.

"What the fuck?" said Avery, standing up straight like someone had poured cold water down her back.

"You like that?" slurred the drunk.

"Absolutely not," said Avery. "Don't touch me."

"I'll touch you anywhere I want, you bitch."

Avery snapped. In one quick motion, she swung her knee up and nailed the drunk in the groin. He doubled over in pain. She kneed him again, this time in the face.

The guy fell forward and hit the floor hard, blood pouring from his nose.

"That bitch broke my nose," he whined, trying to catch the flow of blood before it dripped on his shirt.

Security guards swarmed the scene in seconds. They grabbed everyone who hinted they might join the melee. Someone ushered the injured drunk to the bathroom to clean him up.

Mack barely moved during the entire scuffle. It happened so fast. He stood still, a few feet from the stage, now facing Avery. She was close enough for him to touch. She seemed fine, not a scratch on her.

Avery looked at Mack. "That motherfucker had it coming," she said.

"Looked to me like he tripped on his own feet and fell over," said Mack with a wink.

Avery smiled. "Yeah. That's what I saw, too." Her brown eyes locked with Mack's, and she smiled even broader. "I'm gonna go get myself together, and then how about a dance, hmm? What do you say?"

Something about this woman captivated Mack, how she had switched from hand-to-hand combat to instantly being cool and collected. He liked it. The girl was something else. Sure, a dance…why not? He nodded slowly in response to her invitation.

"Good lord," said Andy over his shoulder. He watched Avery walk away. "Get a load of that tail. I'd follow that into a minefield."

"Yeah," said Mack, still slightly dazed. He sat down next to Andy, who had somehow been completely unaware of the fight that had broken out a few feet away from him. When Mack tried to recount the events, Andy just shrugged and continued laying out dollar bills on the lip of the stage, watching intently as the object of his attention collected them and stuffed them in her string bikini bottom.

When the redheaded dancer exited the stage, Andy made a beeline for her. Mack didn't see Andy again until an hour later when the DJ announced last call.

While Mack waited for Andy to return, he withdrew to the bar where he sipped a beer slowly. He scanned the audience, casually observing the girls on stage with mild interest. Avery never came back out on the floor. Mack was sure of that. He had been watching for her.

7

Mack's pager buzzed on the nightstand with the force of a jackhammer. At least that's how it sounded to Andy's hungover ears. Andy rolled over in bed. He grabbed a pillow and held it on his ear to dull the vibrating clatter. The white cotton pillowcase smelled like bleach and stale cigarettes. Mack's pager continued to buzz.

"Turn that damn thing off, will ya?" groaned Andy. "What time is it?"

The toilet flushed in the motel bathroom. Seconds later, the door opened. Steam and the scent of cheap shampoo filled the room. Mack stood in the doorway with a towel wrapped around his waist and another one in his hand drying off his wet hair.

Andy opened one eye. "How are you up and moving already?" His voice cracked as he spoke.

Mack smiled. "I didn't try to drink the entire world last night, for starters."

"I was only going for all of Georgia. Think I almost got there, too." Andy propped himself up. He put a second pillow behind his head. "My mouth tastes like a litter box."

Mack pulled up his jeans under the towel. He tossed the wet cloth in the bathroom. The towel slapped on the tile floor. Mack towered over the foot of the bed, his bare chest lean and hairy.

"Your thingie's been going off for half an hour," said Andy. "I was about to smash it to pieces for you."

Mack suddenly realized what Andy meant. He stepped quickly across the small room and picked up the pager. He sat down on the bed opposite from Andy and lifted the phone, already dialing as he brought the receiver to his ear. He raised a finger to his lips, signaling for Andy to remain quiet.

"You were supposed to call as soon as you witnessed the delivery," said the caller. The voice was terse and irritated.

"Yeah, I remember you said that," said Mack. "It was two a.m. I figured it could wait until morning."

"You figured?"

"I'm guessing that was the wrong assumption," said Mack. The lack of sleep made his head feel groggy, less confident in himself.

"I should say so. That was six hours ago. It is very possible the package has already been relocated."

"Nah, I don't think so. It's in a warehouse here in Savannah. They unloaded the whole shipment and restocked it inside the place. It's still there." A tinge of apprehension entered Mack's mind as he began to question his decision to wait until morning.

"For your sake, I hope you are right. If we lose track of the package, it will be your fault."

Mack bristled a little at the accusation but swallowed his

pride. "I'll drive back over there this morning and check it out."

"What is the location?"

Mack gave the address of the warehouse. He offered to send the photos and was given a P.O. Box with instructions to overnight the roll of film.

"You want me to stay in town? What am I doing next?" said Mack.

Andy, still lying in his bed, mouthed the words "bloody mary." He tilted an imaginary glass to his lips.

Mack slung a pillow from his bed at Andy. Andy rolled to duck and the pillow hit him in the back with a dull thud.

"First, I want you to make sure the package is still at the address you gave me. If all is well, stay in Savannah. I want to know immediately if the package moves."

Mack did not respond. He pondered how he could manage continuous surveillance of the warehouse.

"Did you hear me? The instant it moves I want to know."

"I got it," said Mack. "I may need to invest in some equipment," he added.

"Whatever is necessary," said his employer. "I will reimburse. Do not lose that package."

Mack hung up the phone.

"Boss man pissed?" said Andy.

"Seems that way."

"Shit. That ain't the way you want to wake up after a night like we had."

The room was quiet for a few seconds before Andy spoke again. "That gets me thinking, I better call my boss lady. Make sure I stay out of the hot seat myself."

---

*

Two hours later, Mack sat in a dark green Dodge Caravan in the parking lot of an Avis car rental. He watched the late morning traffic inbound to Savannah.

Andy had dropped Mack off at the car rental office on his way out of town. There must have been something in Andy's voice that Olivia detected when he called from the motel room earlier that morning. She had cut Andy's vacation short and demanded he head back to Atlanta to spend Saturday with the family.

Mack hated to lose his partner. On the other hand, the job might be easier going it alone. Andy's energy certainly livened things up, but a surveillance gig was not always meant to be lively. Sometimes on a stakeout, you just sit still for hours without speaking, and that was fine with Mack. He missed Andy's company, but after the previous night's antics he welcomed a little solitude.

Mack adjusted a switch on the Caravan's dashboard, and ice-cold air conditioning blasted his face and chest. The freezing wind quickly dried the sweat beads on his forearms, sending a welcome chill shivering through his body.

The Dodge did not look like much, but it was perfect for Mack's needs. One of a thousand other boring minivans on the road with plenty of room for stowing gear. Not to mention a spacious cargo area in back for stretching out.

A weathered phone book lay open on the passenger seat. Mack flipped through the yellow pages until he landed on a section that contained a handful of listings for military surplus and survivalist stores. He recognized one of the street names. They had passed it on the way out of town. Mack shifted the minivan into drive and eased into the traffic, turning left back toward Savannah.

It was 9:00 a.m. before the last person left Avery's apartment. The sun forced its way through the cracks of her tightly drawn blinds. Beer cans littered the coffee table. A gold-rimmed mirror about the size of a cafeteria tray nestled among the empty cans. Pressed into the corner of the mirror was an exposed razor blade for cutting and separating cocaine. Wet fingertips, eager to collect every remaining bit of dust, had streaked and smudged the mirror's reflective surface.

Avery sat slumped on her black leather couch. Her heart pounded in her chest. Both nostrils were useless. She breathed through her mouth like a fat middle-aged slob, aware of how dumb it made her look but unable to do anything about it. She stared at the carnage in her apartment.

After a few seconds, she roused herself from the couch to get a drink of water from the sink. She swallowed the cool water down her raspy throat and refilled the glass. She carried the glass to her bedroom and closed the door.

The dark bedroom resembled a cave. A blanket hung over the only window in the room, carefully tucked into the blinds to block the maximum amount of light.

Avery made no effort to remove her clothes. She simply lifted the blanket on her bed and slid under it. She pulled the bed sheet around her eyes, leaving a small gap at her mouth for breathing. She closed her eyes and prayed for sleep to come as soon as possible.

"Where'd you serve?"

The question came from somewhere deep within the military surplus store seconds after Mack stepped inside the building.

The lighting in the store was dimmer than Mack had anticipated. He blinked a few times, allowing his eyes to adjust. The large warehouse smelled like machine oil, like an industrial lubricant, slightly sweet and pungent.

Mack took a few steps into the warehouse. He peered around a rack of antique gas masks, searching for the man who had greeted him.

A head of gray hair popped up suddenly to Mack's left from behind a white counter. The gray hair was cut so closely to the scalp that the clerk appeared nearly bald. A pair of thick, black eyeglasses covered half of the person's face. The lenses looked like telescopes, magnifying the eyes to nearly double their actual size behind the glass. The clerk dressed head-to-toe in camouflage, complete with insignias and patches. He even had a beige canteen strapped to his waist with a Velcro loop.

Mack suppressed a smile at the clerk's clichéd appearance. Something about the guy seemed slightly off, not what Mack would expect. He quickly scanned the clerk, trying to identify the idiosyncrasy. Then it struck him. The clerk's chin had a light dusting of whiskers, but the throat contained no Adam's apple. Mack's gaze traveled down the clerk's camouflaged body.

"Yep, they're taped!" bellowed the clerk. She slapped

her chest with both palms.

The dull thud knocked Mack out of his focused examination. "Oh, uh, I didn't," he stammered. "I wasn't sure if, um…"

"S'matter, ain't ya ever seen a female soldier before?"

"Soldier? Well, uh, sure. I have," said Mack, still trying to find his footing in the conversation.

"Alright then, quit your yammering and let me know how I can help you."

Mack finally gathered his wits. "Your voice is what threw me. It's so…deep."

"Just blessed I guess!" shouted the woman. She sounded like she had lost most of her hearing, her voice excessively loud given the proximity of her listener.

Mack took a step back. This time he did crack a smile.

"Navy," he said, answering her initial question.

"Say again?" shouted the woman.

"Navy," Mack repeated, louder this time.

"See any action?"

Mack nodded. "A little."

"Army myself," said the woman. "12B, Combat Engineer."

"That so?"

"You'll have to excuse me. Damn near lost my hearing blasting a bridge."

"Thanks for your service," said Mack.

"Glad to do it and I'd do it a hundred more times if they'd let me," said the woman. She slapped her hands together. "Now, what can the Army do for the Navy today?"

Mack explained he was looking for a discreet tracking

device that would alert him when it moved.

"What are ya, a P.I.?" asked the woman.

"Something like that."

"Reason I ask, is I'm not supposed to sell that kind of thing to civilians. They say some might use it for following people. I say, well, what in the hell else would ya use it for? Course you use it for following! That's the whole point of a tracking device, you ask me. But don't nobody ever ask ol' Conrad," said the clerk. "Nope, they jus' tell, they never ask. I don't give a good goddamn, personally, what you want to do with your own life. You know why I don't?" Conrad didn't wait for Mack to answer. "I'll tell you why. Cause it ain't none of their business. You want a tracker, I can get you a tracker. Sit tight for a minute, Navy. I got something in back gonna blow your tits backward when you see it."

Mack couldn't help smiling at the clerk's boisterous rant. "I'd appreciate that, Conrad," he said.

"Call me Connie!" shouted the clerk as she disappeared around a display of empty artillery boxes.

Mack browsed through the dusty shelves while he waited. He could hear Connie in the storeroom moving boxes and cursing to herself.

Mack grabbed a bundle of paracord and some zip ties and tossed them on the counter. He was fingering a set of hemostats when he heard Connie's voice over his shoulder.

"Roach clips!" she shouted with a proud smile, aware of the common civilian use for hemostats.

Mack smiled and put the clips back on the shelf.

"This here is what yer looking for, young man," said Connie. She slapped a small metal box on the counter.

Removing the lid, she withdrew a device about the size of a textbook. Connie turned a knob on the side of the box, and a green LED screen came to life.

"Now take this and walk over to the other end of the warehouse," Connie instructed Mack. She handed him the tracker.

Mack did as he was told. When he reached the back wall, he raised a hand to signal to Connie.

Connie fidgeted with the tracking beacon and then gave a thumbs up to Mack. The screen in Mack's hand displayed in blinking text the words 150 FEET. Mack took a few steps toward the counter and saw the number steadily decrease. He walked rapidly back to Connie until the screen displayed 2 FEET.

"Not bad," said Mack. "I like it."

Connie beamed. "Range goes up to ten miles."

Mack whistled.

"Ain't cheap though."

"Not my dime," said Mack with a wink.

"That's the best kind of dime," said Connie. She rung up the tracker along with the paracord and zip ties, giving little more than an eyebrow raise at the combination of purchases. "Best grab them clips, too, eh? On the house," Connie said, smiling. "Never know when you might need 'em."

"Sure," said Mack. "Why not?"

Half an hour later, Mack and the Dodge Caravan were parked down the street from the warehouse where he and Andy had watched the delivery the night before.

Lucky for him, the warehouse district was more active during the day. Workers milled in and out of the various buildings on the block. The parking lots were filled with cars. Plenty of action to keep Mack well-disguised.

Mack figured if he could watch the loading dock all day, he should be able to sneak in after dark and place his new tracking device. From then on, the job would get easier. He had about six hours to kill before dusk. He settled in with his binoculars for a long day of surveillance.

The loading dock stood vacant, with the overhead door shut and secured by a padlock. Mack observed no activity around the building. A metal staircase with eight rusted steps led to a small landing onto which opened a steel door. A sliver of window above the doorknob glinted a reflection in the sun.

Mack's high-powered binoculars allowed him to see inside the small window, although he quickly established there wasn't much inside worth observing. A row of vents near the roof permitted enough sunlight into the warehouse to reveal a lack of occupancy. Mack watched the window for close to an hour but saw no movement inside the building.

Satisfied that no one was coming or going, Mack lowered the binoculars. He ate a turkey sandwich he had picked up at a convenience store. He washed down the soggy lettuce and slimy lunchmeat with a cup of lukewarm coffee.

Mack cracked the minivan's window. Salty, humid air rushed into the vehicle. He surveyed his surroundings. A wide canal of brackish water surged along at the end of the warehouse block. A rowboat drifted past, manned by a fisherman seeking to harvest his evening meal from the water.

Mack's watch chimed. Two p.m. He stuffed the last of the sandwich in his mouth. He leaned back in the van's cloth captain's seat and pulled the plastic lever to his left. The chair reclined a few inches. He watched the loading dock door and waited.

Avery awoke with sweat beading on her face and arms. A fly buzzed somewhere in the dark bedroom. The annoying vibration reached through her ears and dug into her brain. The buzzing rattled within her skull.

From the way the sun peeked through the cracks in her blanket-covered window, Avery sensed late afternoon. It wasn't the first time she had hidden from daylight.

Avery extended her hand from under the blanket. She felt carefully in the dark for her water glass. Her fingers clasped the plastic cylinder. She slowly raised it to her lips. She dipped her fingers in the cool water and splashed some on her face to clear the sweat. Her head pounded and her body ached. She rolled over and tried in vain to fall back asleep. Her mind had other plans. Like a movie screen, the backs of her eyelids replayed the events of the night before.

How did she get back to the apartment after leaving the club? That's right, she had ridden with Liam, both of them doing bumps from her fingernail the entire way home. How many people had been in her apartment? She had no clue—at least a dozen at one point. Several of them complete strangers. She hoped nothing was stolen.

Avery climbed out of bed. She checked her underwear drawer and found the wad of cash still intact. Her stack of tips, mostly small bills, had grown to nearly double the size of her fist. Nothing appeared to be missing.

Her temporary relief was quickly supplanted by a wave of anxiety. The cocaine was gone. She remembered doing the last of it shortly before everyone had split that morning.

After a night like she'd had, Avery would need a little help to get moving. It wouldn't take much—just enough to clear her head and motivate her to clean up the mess in her living room.

She headed for the phone in her kitchen, cringing when she opened the bedroom door. She braced to face the sunlight that streamed in her apartment.

"Ohhh," she sighed. She found a pair of aqua-framed sunglasses on her counter and slid them on. She picked up the phone and dialed a number she had long ago memorized.

"This is Liam," said the voice that answered.

"Hey, Liam. This is, um, this is Avery."

"Oh man, glad to see you're alive. Hell of a party last night."

"Yeah," said Avery. "Listen, do you have anything on you?"

Liam paused for a second before answering slowly, "Yes."

Avery's voice picked up with excitement. "Can you come over?"

"You going for another round already?"

"No. I mean, it's just that I'm out," said Avery. "And

I'm working again tonight. I just want to do a couple bumps before I go in."

"Okay," said Liam, still sounding a little reluctant. "You want half a gram or what?"

Avery thought for a second. She remembered the stack of cash in her dresser drawer. "Make it a whole and that way I'm set for the weekend."

"Riiight. I've heard that one before."

"Can you come soon?" said Avery. And then she added "Please."

"Give me an hour. I'll be over."

"Thank you!" said Avery. She was smiling now, already feeling the relief that would come from having the powder in her possession.

Avery hung up the phone and did a little shuffle step on the linoleum floor. The quick motion reminded her about the pounding sensation behind her temples. She opened the freezer door and basked in the cold air until chills ran up and down her arms. She withdrew a box of popsicles from the freezer. She reached her fist inside the box and came out with a purple freezer pop.

Avery tore the plastic package with her teeth. She spit the ripped top on the floor. Her fingers stuck to the icy sleeve. She sucked on the popsicle until all its sugary juice was consumed. Then she ate the remaining ice in small bites, savoring each piece.

When she finished the popsicle Avery surveyed her disheveled apartment with a sigh. She pulled a new trash bag from the roll under the sink and shook it open. First into the bag went the empty popsicle sleeve. Then she began collecting beer cans, bottles, cigarette butts, and all the other trash that littered her living room and kitchen.

Still wearing the sunglasses, she walked from window to window, opening the blinds. She pulled her vacuum from the hall closet and swept up the crumbs and ashes from her carpet and linoleum.

With the apartment clean, Avery felt a little bit better. She lit a scented candle and got in the shower.

Liam knocked on the apartment door just as Avery stepped out of the hot water.

"Just a minute," she yelled through the open bathroom door. She quickly dried off. She wrapped the towel around her torso and headed for the door.

Liam's eyes traveled down Avery's nearly naked body when she answered the door. He tried to focus on her face, but the exposed flesh kept pulling at his attention.

Avery noticed Liam's preoccupation with her bare legs. Being ogled by men was nothing new to her.

"Hang on a sec. Lemme get dressed."

Liam entered the apartment. "I like you just the way you are," he said, plopping down on the couch.

"Don't be nasty," said Avery from the bathroom.

"You got this place cleaned up quick." Liam leaned to his left on the couch, straining to see through the cracked bathroom door, trying to catch a glimpse of Avery's naked body.

Avery threw the door open, catching Liam looking. He tried to pretend he was stretching.

"Careful there, you might pull a muscle." Avery crossed from the bathroom to her bedroom wearing only a bra and panties. "I don't like living in filth," she said once inside her bedroom.

Liam took out a scale from his pocket and placed it on the now-spotless coffee table. He tared the weight of a tiny plastic baggie and used a small spoon to add white powder from a larger bag until the scale's display read one gram.

"One G did you say?" Liam said to the open bedroom door.

Avery appeared in the doorway, fully clothed in a cotton skirt and t-shirt, barefoot with the green toenail polish she had applied the night before.

"Unless you're offering a special?" she said with a smile.

Liam sealed both plastic bags and dropped them on the coffee table. He took another long look at Avery's legs, now smooth and silky from her hot shower. His hand rested in his lap. He cupped his palm and shifted himself in his pants to deal with the growing reaction therein.

"You ever do anything extra at the club?" he asked, still staring at her legs.

"Extra?"

"Yeah, you know, like a customer wants a little something more, so you meet him after for cash or whatever."

Most of the dancers at the club had done what Liam was suggesting, including Avery from time to time. But she didn't want to start down that path with her dealer. Better he not know.

"Nah," was all she said.

"Bet you could make a lot of money if you did." Liam did not want to drop the topic.

"Maybe, but I'm not a whore, so give it a rest."

Liam got quiet. "Just sayin'," he mumbled.

"What are you up to later?" asked Avery, trying to

change the subject.

"I'll be around. Supposed to be some new shit coming in town this weekend. Straight from Columbia."

"Oh yeah?"

"Super pure apparently. I've got an order in for a half key. And for the price I'm paying it better not be stepped on."

Avery listened with interest. "If you get it, let me know. How much for a G of it?"

"Twice the usual," said Liam. "But I might make you a special deal. Don't tell anybody else though."

Avery made a "lips are sealed" gesture. She tossed some cash on the coffee table and picked up her small baggie.

"You sure you don't want to, you know, *earn* this one?" said Liam.

"What did I say about being nasty?"

"Fine."

"Let me know about that new stuff when you get it, okay?"

Liam nodded.

"Now buh-bye," said Avery, making a shoo-ing motion with her hands.

"Damn, you're cold."

"I got stuff to do. Need to get to the bank before it closes."

Liam stood up and started for the door.

"Give me a hug before you go, boo," said Avery. She scooted across the carpet and caught Liam before he opened the door. She hugged him close, feeling his manhood press against her hip.

"Thanks, baby. I appreciate you," Avery said. She patted

Liam's butt before closing the door behind him.

"All day, I ain't seen nothing. No cops, feds, junkies, nothing. It's quiet out there," said Jerry Musen into a black telephone that sat on a desk just inside the warehouse's loading dock door.

Jerry perched on the desk, the phone cord spiraling down his tattooed forearm. There were no lights on in the warehouse other than a single emergency bulb near the back of the building. Afternoon sunlight streamed in from the vents near the roof. A small floor fan oscillated in front of the desk, blowing Jerry's linen shirt against his tan chest with each pass.

"Juice, I'm not suggesting you did anything wrong. I'm just being extra careful," said the voice on the other end of the line, using Jerry's nickname. Juice the Moose, to his close friends.

"Yeah, well, quit asking me then. I done told you it's all clear."

"Hey, next time you smuggle two hundred keys of pure Columbian into the states, you tell me if you aren't a little paranoid. You know how much money I got tied up in this deal?"

"It may be your money, but I'm the one doin' all the heavy lifting out here!"

"Sit on it for another day and keep watching. You see anything fishy, you let me know. If we're still clear tomorrow, I'll come down there myself with a couple guys and help you break it down."

"I ain't trying to rush you. I know, better safe than

sorry," said Jerry. "But you promised me my cut. I need that cash. And, anyway, I'm getting bored sitting on my ass. Least you could have put a TV in here."

"Juice, in a couple days you'll be able to buy as many TVs as you want. Be patient."

"Patient, my ass, man. You ain't the one sitting on enough blow to put you away for life. I'm risking my balls here, Lucas."

Lucas went silent for long enough to make Jerry second-guess his aggressive tone. "I mean, sir," Jerry added.

"Watch the parking lot. Tell me if you see anything suspicious. I will be there in the morning," said Lucas, and then he hung up the phone.

"Fuck you, too, pal," said Jerry to the dial tone. He slammed the phone down on the cradle. Jerry took a deep breath and exhaled. He gripped the hem of his shirt tail and rippled the fabric over the fan so the air would blow underneath and cool his skin.

Jerry slapped the desk with his open palm.

"If I'm gonna sit here like an asshole all day, I'm kicking things up a notch."

Jerry slipped a pocketknife from his pants and folded open the blade. He made a small incision in one of the packages and then dug the blade of his knife into the contents. He carefully withdrew the blade, balancing a neat pile of white powder as he lifted it to his nostril. He inhaled violently and cleared the cocaine from the knife blade.

"Whew!" said Jerry. He cleared his throat and spat on the polished concrete floor. "Now we're talkin'," he said to the empty room.

*

Ever since Avery had started dancing, she always felt a little weird going out in public during the day. She couldn't help wondering if the men she encountered recognized her from the club. Had she given a lap dance to the bank teller? Did the grocery clerk know the curves of her naked body? If the gas station attendant looked familiar, did that mean she had sat in his lap, felt his excitement pressed against her thighs?

And the women…could they tell by looking at Avery that she made her living seducing their husbands and boyfriends? All around Avery, other women's eyes seemed to judge her, interrogate her motives, critique the way she walked and talked. Was it only in her head, or did she really see the sneers and stares she imagined?

Avery fought to suppress the critical inner monologue that sometimes challenged her confidence. As a result of her perceived judgment, she overcompensated, often deliberately trying to de-sexualize her daytime appearance. When she left the apartment to run errands, she dressed casually in baggy clothes. She wore sweatshirts with hoods, and she avoided eye contact.

It wasn't fair the way she had to hide herself from the world. She had just as much to offer as anyone else. Regardless of the way she made her money, she was not a bad person. Her profession did not define her. There was no reason for her to feel shame, but sometimes she did, nonetheless.

Sitting in the parking lot of the bank at 3:55 p.m., Avery did a quick bump to steady her nerves. She checked her nose for residue and then hustled inside the building to deposit the thick wad of small bills that bulged in her pocket.

Later that afternoon, shadows crept across the concrete floor of the warehouse. With the sun almost down, the office where Jerry sat had grown dark. The small incision he had made in one of the kilos was wider now. Jerry had returned to the well several times. His pocketknife lay open on the desk, covered in white powder. Under the desk Jerry's knee bobbed up and down rapidly.

"Fuck am I supposed to do here all night long?" said Jerry to the empty room. He lit a cigarette and paced the warehouse.

After a few minutes, Jerry picked up the phone and dialed a number he had memorized from a local radio commercial.

"Old South Pizza, where the dough always rises again," a teenage kid answered.

"I'm hungry," said Jerry. "Gimme a large pepperoni and a two-liter of Coke. Ya'll got two-liters?"

"Yes, sir, we do."

"Alright, gimme two of 'em."

"Anything else, sir?"

Jerry thought for a minute. "Are any of your drivers girls?"

"Excuse me?"

"I said do you all have any female delivery drivers?"

"Um, yes, a few," said the kid, sounding uneasy.

"How bout you send one of 'em on this run. I'll tip her

real good," said Jerry.

"We usually just send whoever is next in line," said the kid.

"Well, make sure the next driver in line is a girl," said Jerry. "And beer. She brings a case a beer with her I'll make it worth her while." Jerry let out a sick laugh, waiting for the kid to catch his drift but he got no response. He stopped snickering and gave the address of the warehouse.

"Okay, sir, that's gonna take us a little while to get all the way out there. Maybe an hour?"

"That's fine. Don't forget what I said, though, huh?"

"Yes, sir."

"Good boy," Jerry said, and he hung up.

When a green Toyota Corolla with a lighted pizza sign on the roof turned into the warehouse parking lot, Mack sat up straight. He had been waiting in the minivan for close to six hours with no movement. His legs and back felt stiff.

Mack slipped between the two front seats of the minivan. He knelt down in the back of the vehicle. He unzipped his bag and felt around until his fingers touched a long infrared scope, which he uncapped and raised to his eye.

The warehouse lot was dark now except for a lightbulb at the top of the landing above the door. Mack used the scope to follow the Toyota Corolla up to the loading dock.

The delivery driver parked and hopped out. She checked the address on her delivery ticket, and then dove back into the open car door to retrieve the pizza bag.

Mack watched the woman carry the pizza bag in one

hand with the receipt in the other as she bounded up the steps to the warehouse door. She wore a baseball hat with her ponytail sticking out the back hole.

A few seconds later, the door opened. Mack saw a barrel-chested man, late thirties with a bushy mustache, greet the driver. The guy wore a tight pair of blue jeans and a loose tank top that exposed a pair of large, hairy arms.

Mack cracked the window of the minivan. He listened but he was too far away to hear anything. He gathered up the tracking device that he had purchased earlier from the surplus store. He popped open the lid and rifled through the contents until he found the transmitter, a small, thin disc about the size of a nickel. Mack pressed a button on the bottom of the transmitter and heard a single beep indicating it had been activated. The distraction from the delivery driver could be his chance to make a move. He wanted to be ready just in case.

The delivery driver stood on the landing. Mack watched the discussion between the driver and the mustached man, trying to read their lips. There appeared to be some kind of debate about the price. The mustached man leaned against the door frame casually with an arm raised, exposing a thick mass of underarm hair. He smiled at the driver, evidently talking about more than just the cost of the pizza.

Mack pocketed the tiny transmitter. He quietly slipped out of the van. Staying in the shadows, he covered the distance to the warehouse in a matter of seconds. He settled against the same stack of pallets where he and Andy had hidden themselves the night before.

Only a dozen yards from the metal staircase, Mack was now close enough to hear music coming from the speakers of the Corolla's open door. He strained his ear to catch the conversation on the landing above.

"Pretty girl like you, driving around listening to music all night, I bet that's a sweet gig," said Jerry. His words drawled out slowly. He smiled as he spoke, trying to seem harmless but having the opposite effect.

"Yeah, it's okay," said the driver. "You got that nineteen —" she paused and squinted at the bill, "nineteen seventy-seven? I gotta get back to the restaurant."

"Busy tonight, eh?" said Jerry. "You ever need a little pick-me-up, something to get you moving faster?"

The girl frowned. "Coffee helps."

"I'm sure it does, but how bout something a lot better? What I got's a hundred times better than a cup a coffee. You ought to come in for a minute and try it."

"What I need is nineteen dollars and seventy-seven cents." She checked the bill again as she spoke. "You got your pizza. Time to pay for it."

"Aw, you're no fun. Relax a little. The boss man ain't gonna miss you. Come on in and have some fun."

"Fuck this shit," said the driver. She rolled her eyes and started back down the stairs. "I'll just report you for stealing when I get back."

Jerry turned submissive and apologetic at the threat of police paying him a visit. "Now, hold on," he said, following her down the stairs. "Just hold on. I got your money. Geez, don't get your panties in a bunch."

The driver had already reached her car. She tossed the empty pizza bag into the backseat. She got in the Corolla, started the engine, and backed out of the parking spot.

In his rush, Jerry left the warehouse door wide open. Mack's heart pounded when he saw the unguarded door. He tensed his muscles and prepared to make a run for it.

Jerry took long strides across the parking lot to head off the driver before the Corolla reached the exit of the fenced lot. He placed both hands on the hood of the car and worked his way toward the driver door, one hand at a time, always keeping contact with the vehicle.

Mack stood up. Jerry and the Toyota were far from the open warehouse door now. The vehicle pointed away from the warehouse. Jerry had his back to the door.

Mack heard the car's stereo in the distance, recognizing the faint notes of Sublime's "What I Got."

Now or never, he thought. He made a break for it.

Mack ran up the metal staircase as quickly as possible and slipped inside the warehouse. The room was empty and dark except for a desk and a light toward the back of the warehouse. The pizza box lay on the desk, along with an open pocketknife that was covered in white powder. Next to the desk sat the neatly stacked pallet of individually wrapped kilos.

Mack took a quick peek out the door. He saw Jerry still yammering away at the delivery driver, oblivious to Mack's presence.

The kilo Jerry had been sampling lay open on top of the pallet. Mack licked his finger and dabbed up a trace amount of the powder. He touched it to his tongue and tasted the bitterness of the raw cocaine.

Without hesitating, Mack slid the tracking device into a tight fold of packing paper a few levels down in the stack of bricks.

Mack crept across the polished floor. When he reached the door jamb he pressed his back against the cinder block wall. He peered around the side of the frame.

The Toyota Corolla edged forward toward the opening in the tall chain-link fence. Jerry's hand dragged along the car as it passed him.

Mack darted down the stairs. He concealed himself behind the pallets just as Jerry turned around.

Jerry stomped through the parking lot, huffing loudly.

"That broad doesn't know what she's missing," Jerry muttered as he passed the stack of pallets where Mack hid.

Mack watched Jerry climb the stairs. The same stairs on which he had just stood. Jerry entered the door without bothering to close it. Mack heard two loud sniffs from inside the warehouse, and then Jerry reappeared in the doorway.

"I don't even want this goddamn pizza," growled Jerry. He took a step forward and tossed the pizza box like a frisbee into the parking lot. The box popped open when it hit the ground. The pie skidded across the concrete, leaving a trail of cheese and grease.

Jerry watched the pizza slide. He let out a sneering laugh. A second later, the emotion faded from Jerry's face. He stepped back in the warehouse and slammed the door behind him.

Mack waited a couple minutes. He hid behind the pallet stack, his heart beating in his throat. When he felt confident, he retreated from the warehouse parking lot. He followed the shadows back to the minivan.

Once inside the van, Mack powered up the tracking

device's monitor. He took a deep breath and closed his eyes as he flipped the switch and turned on the screen. He smiled and exhaled when the screen lit up. The display said 286 FEET.

Mack flipped through the instruction manual until he found a setting that would alert him if the transmitter moved. He used the handheld console to engage the setting. It beeped a confirmation once he completed the steps.

"Easy enough," Mack said. His work could now be done from anywhere. He was still on call, waiting for a signal from the tracker, but at least he didn't have to sit in a hot minivan and kill time.

Mack drove the van back to his motel, glancing occasionally at the tracker as he drove. He watched the number climb higher as he got further from the warehouse. When he pulled into the motel parking lot the screen said 6.8 MILES.

Mack parked the van and got out. He felt relieved to be free of surveillance work, but now he had a new problem. What to do in a city where he had no friends and no plans? Mack was stuck in Savannah until either the cocaine shipment moved, or he heard from his employer.

Mack tossed his bag on the motel bed. In the corner of his eye he spotted a scrap of color on the small dining table by the window. He walked over for a closer look.

On the table lay a small box of matches. Andy must have picked them up the night before. The matchbox displayed the silhouette of a topless woman clinging to a gold stripper pole. Pink lettering below the image said:

The Fuzzy Peach
Gentleman's Club
Savannah, GA

Avery recognized Mack the moment he walked in the club. Second night in a row. Clean-cut, decent build, nice smile. He looked out of place under the neon lights.

She remembered him as the guy who had watched her kick the ass of the handsy customer, how he had smiled and pretended not to notice. She liked how casual he was about the event, as though he saw guys kneed in the balls by a stripper every day.

"Hey, honey, what you looking over there for?" said the sweaty customer in whose lap Avery currently sat. "I'm right here in front of you."

Avery answered the customer absentmindedly. "I know, baby. My neck's sore. I'm stretching it out."

She turned her head back to watch Mack as he cautiously entered the main room of the club. Cute enough, she thought. She remembered her promise to the clean-cut stranger: a lap dance. She had not followed through on the promise.

Avery tried to recall the hazy details of the previous night. She had kicked the creep's ass—that's when she met this handsome stranger. Then she had gone backstage. Worried about the unruly patron or his friends, she had decided not to return to the floor—just in case they were still around. Sometimes drunk guys can get rough at a moment's notice. Not long after that, the coke came out in the dressing room. Next thing Avery knew, the club had closed, and half the dancers were en route to her apartment for the after party.

Avery turned her attention back to her current mark.

"Seems like you kinda like me, hon." She smiled broadly, showing her teeth. She shifted her hips on the guy's lap, waiting for the inevitable sign of his stimulated affection.

"Maybe I do," said the customer. He stared up at her dumbly, his eyes glazed and cloudy.

Avery turned her head slightly when the guy spoke. His breath smelled like sour dog shit. She tried hard not to react to the repulsive smell.

"How bout we go to a private room then? Get away from the crowd a little," said Avery. She paused, letting the words drip out seductively, and then added, "I can make you feel real good."

"How much?"

"I bet you can afford it." Avery rubbed her hand along the guy's flabby bicep.

"How much?" said the guy, sounding irritated.

"Eighty."

"Eighty *dollars*?"

"Well, it's not eighty cents." Avery got a little snippy. She braced herself for rejection.

"What's 'at get me?"

"What do you want?"

"Head."

"Shit, for eighty bucks? No chance."

Avery started to stand up, but the guy pulled her back down on his lap.

"How much you want for some head then?"

"I couldn't do that here in the club even if I wanted to," said Avery. "The bouncers watch." Avery traced a finger down the guy's unbuttoned shirt. "But you give me eighty plus a good tip, I bet I make you bust with your pants on."

"Oh, you think you're that good?"

"I know I am."

"You gonna make me finish in my pants?"

"If that's what you want."

"You got a money back guarantee?"

"Fuck no."

The guy thought for a minute. He thrust his hips against Avery, lifting her from his lap. "Aight, let's see what you can do."

Avery took the guy's hand. She led him toward the private rooms. She threw a quick glance over her shoulder, looking again for Mack, but she couldn't spot him in the dark room.

Mack watched the girl from last night lead another man away from the stage toward the back of the club. He caught a glimpse of her backside as she walked away. The view was as stunning as Mack remembered.

After buying an eight-dollar Budweiser at the bar Mack

took a seat near the back of the club. Within minutes, two dancers accosted him, hoping to pick him off before the other girls got to him. Mack politely refused their advances, suggesting maybe later he would take them up on the offer.

A black woman dressed in a leather bikini and a pair of thigh high boots strutted on the stage, using the pole as a prop. Mack sipped his beer and watched her dance. He kept an eye on the private rooms at the back of the club, waiting for the woman from last night to come out.

Fifteen minutes later, Avery reemerged from the private room. She headed straight for the bar, where she yanked a small, white towel off the brass railing by the bartender's entrance. She glanced around to make sure no one was watching and then quickly wiped the towel along her inner thigh down to her shin.

"Hey!" said the bartender.

Avery balled the towel up in her fist and tossed it at the bartender. "I'd pull that one out of rotation, if I were you," she said.

The bartender swerved his hip to avoid the sailing ball of cotton. The towel landed on the rubber mat by his feet. He carefully lifted the cloth with the toe of his boot and deposited it in the trashcan as though it were contaminated with nuclear waste.

"Get out from behind my bar," the bartender shouted at Avery over Bell Biv DeVoe's "Poison."

Avery saluted the bartender ceremonially and strutted away. Two men at the bar smiled and watched her leave.

In the corner of her eye, Avery again spotted the guy from last night. Sitting at a table by himself, sipping a Budweiser. She slipped into the dressing room to wipe off the stink from the last guy.

Staring at herself in the mirror, Avery smoothed her hair back from her face. She touched up the dark mascara on her eyelashes, applied a few squirts of perfume.

Something wasn't quite right. She examined herself, trying to discern what was missing. Tonight's outfit was a low-cut halter top with sheer sleeves paired with a tiny plaid skirt that only covered the top half of her butt.

She looked good but felt her confidence slipping. Was she nervous? She never felt nervous to talk to a customer. Her left index finger pressed the tiny, zippered pocket inside of her skirt. She flicked the baggie she knew was hidden there. Maybe just one bump to get over the nerves.

Mack's eyes hadn't left the backstage curtain since he watched Avery pass through it a few minutes prior. When the curtain swept open again and Avery stood in the doorway, Mack's heart jumped to his throat. He fought the urge to stand up and wave her over. He played it cool and sipped his beer.

Turns out, he didn't need to wait long. She immediately began walking in his direction. Mack tried not to make eye contact until she came within a few feet of his table. Finally, he looked up and nodded in her direction like some kind of cowboy. Stupid, he thought. What would he do next, tip his hat and say howdy?

"Hello, there, pardner," said Avery, bending at the waist and leaning over Mack's table.

Great, thought Mack, she noticed it, too. He pulled out a nearby chair with one hand, trying to be suave.

"Do you remember me?" he asked.

Avery slid effortlessly into the chair, wasting no time in touching Mack's leg.

"You think that asshole's balls remember my knee?" said Avery. She winked at Mack and smiled.

Mack laughed. "You got him pretty good it looked like."

"Yeah, well, somebody needed to teach him some manners."

Mack raised his hands innocently. "Don't worry. I'll be on my best behavior."

"I sure hope not," said Avery, switching to her sexier voice. She allowed her fingers to slide up Mack's thigh until they almost crossed the line, and then she quickly shifted her touch to his shoulder.

A shudder of pleasure spread through Mack's chest and back. The hair on his neck stood at attention.

"Did you get in trouble last night? I didn't see you come back out again," said Mack.

"You were watching for me, huh?"

Mack felt his face redden. "I, um, yes, I guess I was," said Mack, his voice gaining confidence as he spoke.

Avery smiled again. She pulled her chair close to Mack's, so their legs touched. "Nah, I didn't get in trouble. It was late. I decided to go home," she said. "These heels start to wear on you after a while."

Avery gestured down at her feet in the tall heels.

"I would imagine."

"I'm glad you came back, though," said Avery. "I owe you a dance."

"You don't owe me anything."

"Don't argue. I said I would come back out and give you a dance for not telling on me. So you're getting a dance. Like it or not."

Mack laughed. "Okay then. But to be clear, I'm pretty sure I'll like it."

"You will."

Avery took Mack's hand. She led him deftly through the tables in the dark room, dodging half-naked women and slurring drunks.

They came to a wall toward the back of the club with several doorways, each covered by black curtains. Avery slid one of the curtains aside. Metal rings jingled on the curtain rod above Mack's head. He stepped inside the room. Avery pulled the curtain back across the doorway behind him.

The private room was about the size of a large walk-in closet. A wraparound, cushioned bench seat lined the perimeter. Mirrors covered the walls above the seating. The reflective surfaces created a funhouse-like atmosphere where Mack could see himself reflected infinitely smaller and smaller over his own shoulder. A disco ball hung in the center of the room, casting flecks of light on Mack's arms and legs. The only other light in the room was a pink neon sign above the door that said YOUR FANTASY in cursive lettering.

Mack sat down on the cushioned seat. He raised his arms and placed them on the top of the bench, opening his chest to face Avery.

Avery approached Mack, still smiling but all-business now, her eyes slightly squinted in the dark room. She slipped a knee in between Mack's legs and eased them open. She leaned forward until her thigh grazed Mack's crotch. As she slowly undid her top "The Rhythm of the Night" by Corona played on the speakers.

The beat of the song pounded in Mack's chest. He felt Avery's legs gently caressing his inner thighs. Her breasts grazed his chest as she swayed slowly with the music. Her perfume, strong and sweet, filled the air.

Mack leaned his head against the mirror behind him and closed his eyes. The glinting disco ball danced across his eyelids.

"Don't you fall asleep on me," Avery whispered in Mack's ear.

Mack opened his eyes. He watched as Avery turned around. Her supple flesh, covered by only a thin strip of cloth, lowered onto Mack's lap. He watched her move to the beat of the music. He felt the pressure and friction, sensed the warmth coming from her inner thighs. He leaned into the pressure and allowed it to build.

Avery spread her legs and straddled Mack's thigh. She swerved her hips, dragging herself up and down over Mack's lap until she also grew aroused by the motion. The two pressed firmly against each other. Mack gripped Avery's hips and held them tightly. She covered his hands with her own and froze in a state of ecstasy, her quivering thighs wrapped tightly around Mack's leg. She sighed and fell back against his chest.

"How many times a night do you do that?" Mack asked when he and Avery were seated back at the table.

"That?" said Avery. "I don't usually."

"Bullshit. I'm sure you tell every guy that."

Avery's face looked hurt. Mack couldn't tell if she was pretending.

"I'm serious!" she said. "You think that happens every time I give a lap dance? I'd be exhausted by the end of the night."

Mack scrutinized Avery, trying to decide if she was putting him on. "Why am I the lucky one then?" he asked.

"You know how many pieces of garbage come in here every day? I'm talking about disgusting men. Dirty, smelly, foul human beings. And I have to pretend to like them, every one of them, like they're the one I've been waiting for all my life."

Mack listened to Avery speak. The words flowed so easily from her mouth. They sounded good, no matter what she was saying. It felt to Mack like he had known her for years. She crossed one of her leg's high on her thigh. Her dangling foot wagged softly beneath the table. As she spoke, she casually surveyed the room, but always shifted her gaze back to Mack's eyes.

"Half those assholes are so gross I don't even want to touch them. Feels like I need to be wrapped in latex to come near them," Avery continued. "So a guy like you comes in, clean-cut, handsome, not speaking to me like I'm scum, it can happen. All that rubbing, I mean, things can happen. Sometimes you get *into* it."

Avery stopped talking. She lowered her eyes to the carpeted floor. Her cheeks seemed to be slightly flushed.

"All right then. Good to know." Mack smiled. "Do you want a drink or something? I'm having another."

"I'm supposed to be asking *you* that."

"Well, in that case, sure, I will have another drink.

Thanks for asking," said Mack. "And put one on my tab for you, too."

Avery laughed. "Will do. It's better if I get them anyway. The drink girls around here'll screw you on table prices."

"I'll have a High Life if they've got 'em."

Avery stood up. "I need to circulate for a little bit. They get mad if I stay at one table too long."

Mack nodded. "Do what you have to."

Two steps away from the table Avery turned and said over her shoulder, "Don't you go anywhere."

"Yes ma'am. Thank you," said Mack. He watched Avery walk up to the bar and put in their drink order.

Avery leaned against the bar. She poked her butt backward and rested her breasts on the wooden surface, so flesh spilled over her tight halter top. She imagined Mack was watching her posture, and she tried to pose in a manner that would garner his attention.

"Lemme get two High Lifes," Avery said to the bartender. "Please."

Without waiting for the beers, Avery left the bar. She sauntered over to a nearby table and flirted with three college boys for a while. When it became clear they were broke she moved on to other tables. She touched the men's arms, sat in the occasional lap. She steadily laid the groundwork for return visits later in the night when she would sell them on a dance.

Avery wanted to talk more with Mack. He was one of the few people in here not trying to grope her or scam her. Get the beers and head back to his table, she thought. As long as Mack was ordering drinks, she could justify it to

Leonard why she was sitting with him.

But she had to do one thing first. She slipped briefly into the dressing room and dug out the tiny pouch from her skirt pocket.

"Where are you staying anyway?" Avery said over Mack's shoulder when she returned from the dressing room. She approached him from behind, placing her hands on his shoulders. She spoke softly into his ear.

More than an hour had passed since they left the private room. Avery had spent as much time as she could at Mack's table. She used him as a kind of home base to which she always returned after giving a lap dance or performing on stage. Each time she returned to Mack's table she carried another High Life with her. A few beers deep now, Mack felt less inhibited.

"Not far from here. It's nothing special. A little motel off Victory."

"Oh man, I know that place. I better check you for bedbugs."

"It's not *that* bad."

"You don't want to know how many hoes from this joint meet johns at that motel after closing time."

Mack raised his eyebrows.

"Not me," Avery added with a smile. "I'm a good girl." She traced an imaginary halo over her head with a finger.

"Yeah, I bet you are."

"I am!" Avery protested, laughing.

They were quiet for a few seconds. The DJ cut in and announced the next girl on stage would be Lola Starr.

"That's my girrrrl," exclaimed Avery. Let's go down front." She grabbed Mack's hand and pulled him toward the stage where they took a seat in the front row.

Avery poked an elbow into Mack's ribs. "Get your money ready. This gal deserves it."

Mack obeyed. He took a money clip from his pocket and peeled off some ones and a couple fives. It was the first time all night any of his money had changed hands.

A tall redheaded woman with long legs and milky white skin stepped on stage. The crowd erupted when Warrant's "Cherry Pie" blasted through the speakers. Mack smiled. A little on the nose maybe but it fit.

Avery folded a twenty-dollar bill in half lengthwise and set it on the stage in front of her and Mack.

Lola saw Avery and winked at her. She dropped her backside to the stage with the velocity of a zero-gravity rollercoaster. She leaned forward on all fours and crawled across the stage. She gave Avery a long, slow kiss and then rolled on her back, spreading her legs above her in a V-shape.

Avery watched Lola move with rapt attention. She tucked the twenty neatly into Lola's g-string.

"Thanks, baby," said Lola.

Then it was Mack's turn. Even with the alcohol lubricant he still felt shy. He could feel the other club patrons' eyes on him. They all wondered what he had done to win Avery's attention, why he was being treated like a VIP by these two beautiful women. In fact, Mack kind of wondered himself.

Lola rolled over once until she lay directly in front of Mack. She extended her long, freckled legs and rested her heels on Mack's shoulders. In one quick and surprisingly strong motion she bent her knees and pulled Mack's face between her thighs.

Mack's butt left his chair. He almost fell forward onto the stage. Avery laughed and swatted the seat of Mack's pants with her open palm.

Caught off guard, Mack dropped the stack of cash from his hand. The bills landed smack at the bottom of the V-shape made by Lola's legs.

"Well, that was too easy," Lola smiled. "Thank you, hon."

Mack sat back down in his seat, his face burning red with embarrassment. He managed to flash a good-natured smile, nonetheless.

Lola Starr was the last dancer of the night. The club began to thin out quickly once the girls left the main floor.

"What now?" said Avery.

Mack repeated her question slowly, trying to decide if the words meant what they seemed to mean.

"You tell me. I'm not from around here, remember?"

Avery stared Mack down for a few seconds, waiting to see if he would speak again. "Well," she finally said, "I'm not sleepy yet. I don't really want to go home."

"I know how much you've been wanting to see the motel where I'm staying," said Mack with a laugh. "I mean, all your friends have seen it already. Wouldn't want you to miss out on such an opportunity."

"I thought you'd never ask."

"Do we just walk out of here? Is that allowed?"

"Hmmm. Not really," said Avery. "There's a door around back. Pick me up there in like five minutes?" Then, thinking about the pouch in her skirt pocket, she added, "make it ten."

"Will do. Keep an eye out for a very cool green minivan."

An hour later, Avery lay on the motel bed next to Mack. The white sheet was peeled back and kicked down at their feet due to the heat generated by their bodies. Both Mack and Avery breathed heavily. Beads of sweat stood on Mack's forehead.

Avery's bare leg covered Mack's. Her soft, smooth skin contrasted with the dark hair that covered Mack's lower body. Her head rested on his chest. She felt his elevated heart rate beating against her cheek. Her hair, still wet from the shower she took first thing, felt cool against her back.

"I did not expect that to happen tonight," said Mack. He stroked Avery's shoulder blade softly.

Avery leaned up. She looked into Mack's eyes. "What are you trying to say?"

"Nothing," said Mack, sensing unease in her voice. "Nothing at all. Just that I'm glad you're here." He tilted her chin up and kissed her. "I mean, I wanted it to happen—I just didn't have any expectations."

Satisfied, Avery laid her head back on Mack's chest. "I'm not a whore," she said quietly into his ribs.

"That wasn't what I meant."

"I came here cause I wanted to. Cause I liked you. It was my choice."

"I know," said Mack.

"I don't know what you think this is."

Avery sounded melancholy. The confidence she had earlier in the night faded with her dwindling supply of cocaine. She considered doing another bump but decided to ride it out. Sex always helped with the comedown. No sense going right back to where she started.

"I don't think this *is* anything," said Mack. He quickly realized the error of his implication. "Let me rephrase that…what I mean is, I don't have any particular expectations or notions about what this is. I'm glad you came back here with me. I enjoy your company. There's no need to stress. It's all good. I know what you do, and it doesn't bother me. You can stay with me tonight or leave. It's your decision entirely."

"You say that, but you don't know anything about me."

Mack pondered that for a second. "I guess that's true. It doesn't bother me, though. No reason to put any pressure on anything. We're both grown adults." He looked down at Avery and waited for her to return his gaze. "But if you want to know my thoughts, I hope you stay here with me. I hope I get to see you again. That's my opinion."

Avery didn't answer.

"Is that okay with you?" said Mack.

Avery sighed. "Can I ask you one question?"

"You can ask me ten if you want."

"Are you married?"

Mack smiled. "That's an easy one. No, I'm not."

Avery studied Mack's face. Her wet hair lay in a fan across his chest and stomach. "That's what they all say. And how do you explain the minivan? You're probably married with three kids. Here on a business trip, figured you'd get laid while you're at it. I don't care if you are, just be honest about it.”

“Avery, come on. I’m not lying to you. Stop looking for ways to wreck a fun night, will you?” Mack grabbed her backside with both hands and pulled her body tight against his side.

“Okay,” said Avery. She nuzzled into Mack’s ribcage. “We’ll see.”

9

Rafe Lucas turned into the warehouse parking lot in a black Range Rover SUV. He took his time, driving slowly through the open gate to keep from scraping the bottom of the vehicle on the bump where the sloped exit met the road. The car windows were tinted so dark even he had trouble seeing out. He pressed the automatic switch, lowering the passenger side glass to get a better look at a pile of something mounded in the center of the parking lot.

"What the fuck is that?" said Lucas to the man in the passenger seat. Lucas leaned forward to see around the passenger's broad shoulders.

"I dunno. Looks like a pizza box to me."

"Complete with a rotting pizza," said another guy in the backseat.

"It's Old South, too, man," said the first guy. "Waste of a good pie."

Lucas frowned. "Why's there a pizza laying in my parking lot?" he asked.

The passenger shrugged.

"That stupid bastard," Lucas cursed under his breath.

He parked the Range Rover by the door and got out. "Wait here a second," he told the two men in the car.

Lucas had only taken one step on the staircase when the warehouse door swung open so hard it slammed against the concrete wall with a thud.

Lucas dropped back and braced himself for whatever was coming. The two men in the car instinctively reached for their weapons and held them at their sides just below the SUV's open windows.

Jerry appeared in the doorway, blinking his eyes rapidly and licking his lips. Just as quickly as he appeared, he then vanished back into the dark warehouse. A few seconds later he reappeared, smiling coyly and shielding his eyes from the sun.

"Lucas, good to see you!" Jerry shouted. He clenched and unclenched his fists rapidly and worked his jaw like he was chewing gum. Dark circles surrounded his eyes. White powder dusted his nose.

Lucas shook his head. "Juice, what in God's name did you do?"

"Huh? Whaddya mean?" said Jerry, still grinding his jaw.

"Get back inside before somebody sees you."

Lucas ushered Jerry inside the warehouse and closed the door.

"What time is it?" said Jerry. He began nervously pacing the warehouse floor.

"It's almost seven. Have you been up all night?"

"In the morning?" said Jerry, sounding surprised but quickly realizing it was a dumb question.

"Are you stupid or something?"

Jerry looked hurt.

Lucas glanced around the warehouse. He spotted the slice in one of the kilos and the knife lying open on the desk.

"You sat in here and snorted blow all night? How are you supposed to be doing a job when you're cracked out?"

"Cracked out?" repeated Jerry.

"Jesus. Look at yourself in a mirror, will ya? You look like shit."

Jerry took a few steps toward the bathroom where he knew there was a mirror.

"Nevermind that," said Lucas. "What the hell is that heap a' garbage laying out there in the lot? Is that a fuckin' pizza?"

Jerry hung his head.

"Tell me you didn't order a pizza to this address."

"I was hungry!"

"Doesn't look like you were hungry to me. The whole damn thing is smeared on the driveway. Anyway, that's beside the point, whether you were hungry or not. You ordered food delivered here in the middle of the night, knowing it would bring extra attention, knowing you're sitting on two hundred keys of cocaine? Let me ask you again, are you stupid or something?"

Jerry cringed. "I messed up."

"Hell yes, you messed up. You might've blown the whole thing. I knew I shouldn't of left you here alone."

"It was just a girl driver. She don't know anything," said Jerry.

"You don't know what she knows."

"I'm sorry, Lucas." Jerry looked like he was about to

cry.

"Shut up for a second and let me think. We got a buyer for most of this shipment but now I can't have them coming here. For all I know, the feds are already watching us, thanks to your dumb ass."

Jerry paced over to the small window in the door. He looked out nervously, watching as though he might see DEA agents swarming the parking lot at any minute.

"Sit down, will ya? You're making me nervous."

"Who's that out there in the car?" said Jerry, ignoring Lucas.

"Don't worry about it."

Jerry's eyes flashed. He swung wildly away from the door as though he wanted to shout something at Lucas, then he quickly pivoted and pressed his face back against the glass.

"I'm not splitting my cut with anybody else. I already told you, I need it all. You can't be bringing more guys in."

"First of all, I'll do anything I damn well please. You need to think about who you're talking to. That powder's got you running your mouth too much." Lucas waited until Jerry's body language wilted. "And second, you get us busted, nobody's gonna get nothing. Only cut you'll get is when I have your eyes stabbed out in prison."

"I didn't mean anything. I just need that cash. It's real important." Jerry tapped his fingers against the concrete wall slowly, still watching the Range Rover in the parking lot. "Who are those guys anyway? I don't recognize 'em."

"They're the ones gonna help you move all this shit to the bar."

"The bar? I thought you didn't want to move product

through the business."

"That was before some coked-up dumbass went and ordered a midnight pizza to the stash house. Anyway, we're not moving it through the business—just using it for temporary storage."

Jerry stuck out his jaw, pissed off but trying not to show it. "When?"

"Right now."

"Right now?"

"What did I just say?"

Jerry sighed. The long night was starting to weigh him down. His shoulders felt heavy.

Lucas ignored Jerry's protests. He brushed past him and opened the warehouse door. Standing in the entry, he signaled to the two guys in the Range Rover. They got out and quickly ran up the short staircase.

"I want you three to move this product to the bar. As fast as possible. But don't do anything stupid like get pulled over for speeding." Lucas looked at Jerry and shook his head in disgust. "Jesus, Juice, do another line or something before you get started moving. You look like you're about to fall over."

Lucas watched as Jerry headed straight for the pallet of cocaine. He snorted two large bumps from the tip of his knife.

"Bull, you drive," said Lucas, looking at the guy who rode shotgun in the Range Rover. "The box truck is on the other side of the lot. Jerry, give him the keys."

Jerry, who looked more alert after his bump, fished the truck keys out of his pocket. "They call you Bull?" he said, handing over the keys.

Bull grunted assent.

"All right then, Bull. My name's Moose."

"What is this, the National Geographic?" said the third man. "I'm Steve but you can call me the spiny fuckin' anteater if it makes you feel better."

"Now that everybody knows everybody, let's get to work," said Lucas. "You three load up the truck and bring the stash to the bar. It's seven-thirty now. I better see you pull in by nine. First buyer is coming this morning."

Bull nodded and left to get the box truck in position. Jerry and Steve started breaking down the pallet and stacking keys in front of the large garage door.

Lucas watched the men work for a couple minutes. They carefully loaded the cocaine back into the box truck.

"Ninety minutes," said Lucas, glancing at his watch. He got in the Range Rover and drove away, taking a wide berth around the remains of the obliterated pizza.

"Hey," said Avery, gently poking Mack in the ribs. "Hey, what is that?"

Mack opened his eyes. Both sets of curtains were pulled tightly across the window in the dark motel room. A thin strip of light framed the shrouded glass like a picture.

"What's what?" said Mack, opening his eyes.

"That beeping noise. You don't hear it?"

The beeping finally registered in Mack's brain. He sat up quickly, bumping his head on the wooden headboard. He tossed off the blanket and jumped out of bed.

Mack took a couple seconds, hovering above the bed, completely naked, to gain his balance. Then he darted across the room to the table that held his bag.

"Easy there, tiger," said Avery through the darkness from under the covers.

Mack quickly pulled the tracking device from the bag and set it on the table. The screen said 5.9 MILES. Mack grabbed his jeans from the floor and slid them on. He fumbled around in the dark for his t-shirt. He glanced back at the screen. 5.7 MILES.

"It's coming this way at least," he muttered.

"What is?"

"I have to go," Mack said, sliding on his shoes.

"What's coming this way?" Avery pulled the blanket down around her chin and squinted to see Mack in the low light.

"Huh? Oh, it's nothing. Just a job I'm working on." Mack had the keys to the minivan in his hand. He stood with one hand on the doorknob. He cradled the tracker under his other arm. "Listen, sorry I have to run out like this. It can't wait."

Avery groaned. "It's way too early for me."

"You can stay here. Do you want to? Stay in bed?"

"I hate to break it to you, but that was gonna happen, with or without your permission."

Mack managed a tight smile. "Okay, good. I shouldn't be long, but I might be. It's hard to say. Do you want some money for a cab or something?"

Mack pulled the door open. Morning light and the sound of traffic invaded the small motel room.

Avery slid a bare leg out from under the blanket. "Do *I* need money? You know how much cash I made last night? Don't act like you're my sugar daddy."

"Okay then, moneybags, sorry to offend you."

"You didn't offend me." Avery smiled. "And you can leave cash on the dresser."

"I thought you said—" Mack smiled and shook his head. He tossed a $50 on the dresser. "Use it if you need it. Where can I find you later?"

"I'll be around."

The tracker beeped. 5.1 MILES.

"Gotta go."

Mack blew a kiss to Avery and closed the door.

Mack slammed the Caravan in reverse and peeled out of the parking spot. He hit the highway and turned toward the ocean, in the same direction as the warehouse that he had staked out the night before.

The tracker lay on the passenger seat, beeping steadily. He thumbed the buttons of the device until the screen displayed a pixelated rendering that resembled a treasure map. A green dot blinked on the screen showing his own location, and a blue square indicated the location of the object he was tracking. The unscaled map made precise locations hard to decipher but it seemed like the green dot and the blue square were heading directly toward each other.

Mack pressed buttons until the screen returned to the distance display. 3.8 MILES…3.7 MILES…3.6 MILES. It was ticking down fast now, almost a tenth of a mile per beep. At this rate, they would collide in less than a minute.

The bridge loomed up ahead. Mack jammed the brakes and pulled over on the road's shoulder, angling the Caravan to execute the U-turn he knew was coming.

Within a few seconds the white box truck appeared on the road ahead, westbound toward Savannah. Three guys rode side-by-side on the bench seat up front in the cab. Mack recognized the mustached man in the middle from the night before—the dude who had ordered the pizza.

Mack leaned over and pretended to fiddle with the contents of the glovebox as the truck drove past him. He watched in the rearview mirror until the truck was almost out of sight and then he gassed the van and flipped it around. He retraced the route he had just driven, keeping the display of the tracker screen to within a tenth of a mile.

The box truck slowed down when it hit Savannah traffic. Mack followed steadily behind the truck. He kept a car or two between him and his mark at all times.

The truck entered downtown Savannah. Morning activity bustled in the streets. Lawyers and business folk milled about on the sidewalks.

They passed a city park near the river. The truck took a left turn down a narrow alley that dead-ended across the street from the Savannah River.

Mack parked the van on the street near a stretch of greenery. He shut off the engine. The tracker screen held steady at 418 feet.

It took a second for Mack to get his bearings, but he soon realized he wasn't even half a mile from his motel. If he shouted loud enough Avery could probably hear him from the bed where she lay.

10

"Morning, Rafe, I think you've got a delivery around back there. Saw a truck pull in the alley just now." The mailman tapped a stack of envelopes on his palm to straighten them and then handed them through the open door.

"Yeah, thanks. Beer truck. We had a good night last night," said Rafe.

"Good to hear. Good to hear," said the mailman. He stood on the patio, waiting for Rafe to say more. Rafe gave a terse nod and started to shut the door.

"In case you're wondering, we got behind on our work this week. The city offered overtime to any carriers who wanted to pick up a shift," continued the mailman. His expression seemed to suggest a 'thank you' was in order.

"Ah," said Lucas, anxious to rid himself of the mailman's inane chatter.

"You know, cause it's Sunday."

"I hadn't noticed," said Rafe. He slammed the door in the mailman's face. "Idiot," he muttered under his breath.

Lucas flipped through the mail while he walked across the dark bar. He liked to leave the lights off in the morning, let the early sun stream in from the patio windows that overlooked the Savannah River. The quiet bar seemed strange with no customers. The smells and sounds more acute, the ambience more innocuous.

Lucas's footsteps on the wood floor echoed in the dark hallway as he passed the bathrooms. He reached the back door where he unlocked two deadbolts and raised a metal crossbar. He swung the door open to the alley.

The smell of rancid garbage from a nearby dumpster rushed into the hallway. Lucas squinted in the sunlight. Bull backed up the truck to within a few feet of the bar's door.

"Any trouble?" Lucas asked Bull when he slid out of the driver's seat. The morning sun framed the henchman's stocky silhouette.

"Nah, unless you count the trouble your coked-out boy is about to be in if he don't quit running his mouth a mile a minute."

Lucas shook his head. He gritted his teeth and spat out the door into the filthy alley.

"Do you trust that dude? Juice or Moose, or whatever his name is?" said Bull. "He seems like a liability to me."

"He'll be alright once he sobers up. He's the one put the deal together on the other end. Talks too damn much but he's in as deep as we are."

Bull grunted.

"Grab me one off the top of the stack, will ya?"

Bull walked over to the back of the open box truck and said something to Jerry and Steve who were standing in the truck's cargo area.

Steve leaned down from the truck bed and handed Bull one of the kilos. Bull carried it back to Lucas and offered it to him like a librarian lending a library book.

"Now hustle up. Get them all stacked in my office behind the desk," Lucas ordered. "There's a tarp in there you can cover 'em with once you're done."

"Will do."

"I got a guy coming here in a minute to take this one." Lucas raised the package in his hand and held it like a pizza above his head. "Once you finish up, take Juice next store and get him drunk. See if you can make him pass out. Put him to bed somewhere, I don't care where, a motel if you need to. There's one down the street. He needs to sleep it off. I want him out of the way until he sobers up. Whatever it costs, I'll cover it."

Bull nodded.

"You get him passed out, come on back here with Steve. We need to figure out what to do with this shit until we unload it. My bartender'll be in around five this afternoon. I'd like to have it stashed and organized by then."

Bull listened to Lucas's orders. He wasted no time grabbing a stack of kilos from the neat pile that Steve and Jerry had built at the tongue of the truck bed. Bull turned sideways to squeeze past Lucas in the hallway. He carried his stack to the back office.

"That's about eighty grand you got in your hands right there. Precious cargo," said Lucas. His voice resonated in the small hallway.

Once he felt satisfied that Bull knew the plan, Lucas returned to the front of the bar. He poured a shot of scotch in a rocks glass and took a corner barstool that allowed him to watch the sun reflecting off the river that flowed outside.

From the minivan, Mack snapped a few photos of the bar's exterior. He jotted down the address on his notepad. He slipped out of the van and jogged across the street to a payphone in the park. Mack wiped both ends of the phone on his shirt and then dialed the number of his contact.

The phone rang a couple times before the familiar voice picked up.

"This is Abbott."

"Yes?"

"I've got some news for you on the, uh, package."

"Proceed."

"It moved."

No response. Mack cleared his throat and continued.

"It's in downtown Savannah now. At a bar on the river."

"All of it?"

Mack swallowed. He realized he didn't know for sure if the entire pallet had been transported or just the kilo that held his tracking chip. He pondered the question for a split second. Three guys in the truck. They wouldn't all be involved to move just one or two keys. Mack felt pretty confident the whole shipment had changed locations.

"Yeah. Same truck from Tybee. They just pulled in back of a bar. I'm out front, got a good view of the place. They're in the back alley now. Only one way out. That's the way they went in."

"Good. We expected this. At the Irish bar, correct?"

Mack lowered the phone to his chest. He craned his neck around the side of the payphone so he could see the road. "Looks that way. Got a tricolor hanging out front." Mack squinted to read the lettering above the dark wood door. "McCarthy's or McCarty's maybe? Can't quite read it from here."

"McKearney's," corrected the voice. "That's the one."

"There you go." Mack heard a sound in the background on the other end of the line, possibly hounds baying. "So what'm I doing here? Staying with it? I could be a lot more helpful if I knew the plan."

"You have been plenty helpful, Mr. Abbott." Muffled voices spoke in a low tone as if the receiver had been covered by a hand. Mack waited.

After a few seconds of unintelligible discussion, the voice returned. "We would like to know the security posture at the bar. Do they seem prepared for defense?"

"Like an ambush or something?"

"Correct."

"I can tell you they had three guys in the truck. Typical goons from what I could see. Probably packing heat but I doubt they have any special training."

"Good."

"You want me to go in there and gather more intel?"

"If you can be discreet about it. We do not want to raise even the slightest suspicion they are being watched."

"Hey, I'm not sure who gave you my phone number, but I can bet you that it came with a glowing endorsement. I'm good at what I do."

"Indeed it did."

Mack let that sink in for a moment. "What do you want to know?"

"The usual, I suppose. Number of exits, how many

men, what time they close and how they lock up. A layout of the building if you can get it."

"Shouldn't be a problem."

"By tomorrow would be preferable."

Mack exhaled through his nose. "Tomorrow? That only gives you one day of data. Not exactly a dependable pattern."

"We do not have time to wait. Do the best you can. Call me tomorrow when you have the answers."

The line clicked dead before Mack could respond. He hung up the phone and returned to his van.

Not even ten minutes after Mack resumed his surveillance, a scrawny white kid with baggy jeans approached the door of McKearney's Irish bar. Mack watched as the kid glanced over his shoulder repeatedly, his eyes darting side to side. If the kid was trying not to draw suspicion, he was failing miserably.

The kid pulled the handle of the large wooden door and almost fell sideways when the door did not give. He cupped his hands around his face and peered inside the glass. He knocked a couple times, his knuckles covered by sweatshirt sleeves that were too long for his lanky arms.

The door opened. Mack couldn't see into the dark building. The kid slipped inside. The door slammed behind him, vibrating the large panes of glass in the front windows of the bar.

Liam slouched into a chair near the front of the bar. The hood of his sweatshirt flopped back against his thin shoulders, revealing the crest of a neck tattoo that started deeper down on his chest.

Rafe Lucas hovered above Liam, surveying his disheveled appearance with disgust. "I told you not to come here dressed like a bum anymore."

Liam shrugged. He stared out the front window.

"It's too obvious. Somebody sees you walk in here before we're open, looking like…like…well, like a drug dealer. That's what you look like."

"Man, chill out. Nobody's watching your bar at—," Liam glanced at his wrist but realized he had no watch, "at whatever time it is."

"How do you know? Did you even bother to look around?"

"Dude, what are you, my dad? Get off my back. Last time I checked I'm the customer. Haven't you ever heard the customer is always right or whatever?"

Lucas took a seat across from Liam. If anyone asked, he would say Liam was the new dishwasher.

"How much do you want?" Lucas asked, his tone quickly becoming serious.

"That's more like it, man. Shit, I was starting to think you didn't want my twenty G's."

"Twenty? What are you buying for twenty?"

Liam squinted, looking confused. "A half key, like I told you."

"A half key is a waste of your time with this stuff. It's the real deal. As soon as your people get a taste of it, they will clean you out. It's nothing like what they've been getting on the street lately—better than anything we've had before."

Liam seemed suspicious. "Even if I believed you, I only

have twenty on me."

Lucas thought for a second, debating whether he could trust Liam. He weighed any trepidation against his desire to limit the number of meetings he had with the scruffy dealer.

"I'll tell you what," Lucas said, "I will float you the other half on credit. I know it will go fast."

Liam perked up. "You'll float me fifteen thousand dollars' worth of blow?"

"It's eighteen. This shit is thirty-eight a key."

"It better be good for that price."

"You want to taste it?" Lucas asked, standing up.

"Sure."

Liam followed Lucas to the back office. On the desk lay a perfectly wrapped kilo of cocaine that Lucas had set out in anticipation of the meeting.

Liam picked up the package and hefted it in his hand. "I've never held this much blow at one time before. How much you got altogether?"

"Don't worry about that. You need more, I've got it."

Lucas took the kilo from Liam. He set it back on the desk. From a drawer he extracted the package that Jerry had already dipped into. He shook a large, yellowish rock out and laid it on the smooth glass surface of the desktop. He crushed the rock with a letter opener and formed the powder into a line, which he offered to Liam with a nod.

Liam wasted no time. He pinched one nostril with a finger and snorted the pile directly off the glass.

"Holy shit, man. That's fire." Liam squeezed his nostrils together and sniffed hard. He made a guttural sound in the back of his throat. "Wow, you weren't kidding, bro. I feel incredible."

Lucas smiled. "I told you." He handed the wrapped brick of cocaine back to Liam. "Remember, you still owe me eighteen. Don't start putting this up your nose and forget."

"Dude, if I snort half a key of coke, I'd have a lot more to worry about than getting you your money."

Lucas remained serious. He showed no sense of humor to his customer.

Liam tossed a tight roll of cash on the desk. He slipped the package of drugs in the front pocket of his hoodie. His mind raced as he crunched the numbers. A key was 1,000 grams. About 300 eight-balls. He knew he could unload half of it that weekend to regulars. The other half would go faster once word got around how good the shit was. He figured he could double his money in a week. Pay back Lucas and still have at least fifty G's left over.

"What are you waiting for, a kick in the ass?" said Lucas.

Liam realized he had been staring into space, fantasizing about his profits. "Nah, I'm good, bro." He turned toward the front of the bar, preparing to leave the way he had come in.

"Use the back," Lucas said from behind his desk. "It's open."

Liam pivoted and headed for the back door. He shoved the heavy steel door hard with his shoulder. The door thudded against something solid.

"Hey, I'm standing here!" said a deep voice on the other side.

Liam winced. He nudged the door open slowly. Three

men stood in the back alley smoking cigarettes. A few inches from the door, a brawny guy with slicked back hair and a navy-blue work shirt glared angrily at him. The guy rubbed his shoulder with a meaty fist.

"Sorry about that," mumbled Liam. "Didn't think anybody was out here."

"Yeah, well next time maybe don't throw all your weight into a door until you know there ain't somebody on the other side, eh?"

Liam didn't recognize these men, and he had no interest in chatting with them. For all Liam knew, these guys were delivering a new dishwasher in the white box truck that was backed up to the door. Judging from their tough appearances, though, the men did not seem much like typical nine-to-fivers.

"My bad, bro," said Liam as he slipped past the men and cut into the alley.

The three men stared at Liam. They held their ground, forcing him to turn sideways to avoid them.

"That's alright, *bro*," the injured man shouted after Liam as he turned the corner in the alley.

Liam heard the other two men laugh. He picked up his pace, anxious to get back to his apartment where he could split up his haul. And, maybe he would cut out one or two more lines for himself while he worked.

Mack watched as the scruffy kid appeared again in the side alley. In through the front door and out through the back. Certainly suspicious.

For a moment, Mack wondered if he should follow the

kid, but he decided against it. Instead, he snapped a few quick photos, trying his best to capture the kid's partially obscured face under the gray hoodie.

Mack thought about Avery for the second time since leaving her that morning. He wondered if she was still in bed. The Dodge's dashboard clock said 10:04 a.m.

With his binoculars, Mack scanned the front window of the bar. The glare coming off the Savannah River reflected on the dark glass and made it impossible for him to see beyond the first few tables. The place was obviously still closed.

Mack checked the screen of his tracking device. The distance reading had not changed. After a few more minutes of uneventful surveillance, Mack decided to return to the motel, knowing it was less than a mile from where he currently sat. Maybe he would pick up some donuts on the way. He hoped Avery would be there waiting for him.

11

Balancing a box of donuts on his forearm and a cup of coffee in each hand, Mack turned the handle of the motel room door with his fingertips.

Inside, the room was dark and quiet.

"Hello? Anybody home?" Mack said into the darkness.

He got no response.

Mack stepped into the room. He closed the door behind him with his foot. Steam from a recent shower left the air humid. The room smelled like shampoo and body lotion.

Mack set down the two coffee cups. He tossed the box of donuts on the dresser by the television. He glanced at the bed. The sheets were twisted and unmade. An imprint was pressed into the blankets where Avery had been lying.

Mack pulled the cord that dangled next to the window. The curtains zipped opened. Late morning light streamed into the dark room.

Mack stood at the window. He looked out at the depressing cityscape. He watched a woman push an empty shopping cart down the sidewalk until she vanished from sight.

When Mack stepped away from the window, he spotted a note on the small table next to the discarded donut box. He picked up the piece of paper, feeling a rush of excitement as he read Avery's handwriting.

"Had to run. Thanks for last night," said the note, followed by a heart, the letters XO, and her phone number.

Mack smiled. He flipped open the donut box and selected a large, glazed donut. He returned to the window with his donut and coffee. He bit into the sugary dough, chewed it slowly, and watched the morning unfold.

"It's about time you answered," said Liam when Avery picked up the phone at her apartment. He spoke fast, his voice full of excitement.

"Huh?" said Avery.

"I've been calling you. I left like five messages."

"Already this morning?"

"Yes! Where have you been?"

"I've been out," said Avery. "It's none of your business where I've been. Chill, will ya? What's the big emergency?"

"Remember that shipment I told you about?"

Avery thought for a second. "Yes," she said slowly.

"The one with the good stuff I mean? Like the really good stuff?"

"Dude, it's too early for all that chattering. I need you to take it down a couple notches."

Liam forced a nervous laugh. "Sorry, I'm just excited. I mean, it's good. Real good."

"Okay," said Avery. It finally dawned on her what Liam

was talking about. "Did you save me some?"

"You have no idea. You've never seen this much. It's like Scarface."

Avery perked up a little more. "Yeah?"

"You want me to come over there?"

"Right now?"

"Sure, I'm heading out anyway."

"You sound like you're about to leave the ground and fly away."

Liam made the sound of fake laughter again. "Feels that way. You need to try this."

Avery scratched the back of her leg with her toe. She leaned her butt against the kitchen counter and twisted the curly phone cord with her fingers.

"Hello?" said Liam.

"I'm here."

"You want me to come over?"

"If I start that shit now my whole day is gone. I need to work tonight."

"Just do one bump with me. I need someone else to try it."

Avery sighed. "Fine," she said.

Liam was still talking when she hung up the phone.

Jerry Musen rattled the ice at the bottom of his empty bourbon glass. Not even noon and he was already halfway to drunk. Not that he had much choice with the way Bull had been pouring drinks down his throat.

But Jerry wasn't arguing. Once Lucas cut him off from the blow, he started feeling bad quick. He knew firsthand that the morning sun could burn a hole right through his head when he'd been up all night snorting uppers.

"You need a refill there, Moose?" said Bull.

After unloading the shipment, the two men had ducked into a dive bar a few blocks down from McKearney's—one of the only places in town they could get a drink at 11:00 a.m.

"Yeah, I guess," Jerry answered. His whole body hurt. His mind terrorized him with memories of his behavior. The way he had acted with that poor pizza girl. She was just trying to make a buck. She didn't need him getting all creepy on her.

"Stupid," Jerry muttered under his breath.

"What'd you say, pal? Didn't hear you," said the bartender.

"Nothing."

Jerry stared at the bar. His confidence from the previous night had evaporated. "Make this one a double, okay?" he said. He spoke louder but still directed his voice downward at the dark lacquered wood of the bar top.

"Thirsty, fella?" Bull laughed sadistically. He slapped Jerry hard on the back.

Jerry winced at the impact of Bull's open palm.

"Did Rafe give you any for the road?" Jerry asked.

"Any what?" Bull played dumb, messing with Jerry's head.

"You know…"

"Naw, I don't fool with that stuff myself. Makes people act stupid, and then it makes 'em feel lousy." Bull stared at the side of Jerry's head. He sipped from his own glass. "Don't it?"

Jerry didn't answer.

"I said, don't it make you feel lousy?"

Jerry looked up. He would have given one of his fingers for a pair of sunglasses right then. "Yeah," he mumbled.

Bull laughed again. "Drink up. It'll all be over soon."

Jerry wondered what Bull meant by that statement. It'll all be over soon? Were they going to kill him? That's just the paranoia talking, he told himself. Anyway, would it even be so bad if they did? A dead man has no problems.

Jerry took the double bourbon down in two swallows. He wiped his mouth with the back of his hand.

"I need to go home," said Jerry. His speech had begun to slur. His vision was cloudy. "My wife's gonna kill me."

"Alright, Moose. We can get you home. Juice the Moose," said Bull, sounding too jovial for their current circumstances. "How'd you ever get a nickname like that anyway?"

Jerry heard the question, but he couldn't find the energy or the confidence to answer it.

"That'll make three days in a row if I do it. I don't think I want to," Avery groaned up at the ceiling of her apartment. She pressed her back into the round papasan chair and tucked her knees against her chest. "Three days in a row is, like, a problem. I don't want to have a problem."

"Suit yourself," said Liam. "You'll be missing out. I'm telling you, you've never had coke like this."

Liam reached into the large pocket of his hooded sweatshirt. He took out what was left of the kilo—about two pounds. He still had a lot left, even after selling a couple ounces to a smaller dealer that morning.

Avery heard the bag thud on her coffee table and opened her eyes. Her jaw dropped when she saw the plastic bag.

"You're a dumbass for walking around with that much on you. That's just asking for trouble. And bringing it here is putting me at risk, too."

"Relax. Nobody knows I bought a whole key except you."

"Thanks, I guess."

"Look at all this yey!" said Liam. He hoped to impress Avery, maybe get her loosened up enough to make a move on her.

"I bet your momma's real proud."

"You don't get excited about anything, do you?"

Avery flicked a piece of lint off her knee. "I do. Just not about scrawny little coke dealers bringing enough powder to my house to put us both in jail for life."

"Hey, now. You know you love me."

Avery flashed a smile in Liam's direction. "Of course I do, baby. I just haven't been sleeping well lately."

Liam dipped the tip of his car key into the bag and produced a small bump of cocaine. He sniffed it quickly and dipped the key back into the bag. This time, he held the key out to Avery. "You sure?"

"Fine, motherfucker," sighed Avery.

"Yesss!" exclaimed Liam.

"Will you bring it over here? I don't feel like moving." Avery wiggled her backside into the oversized chair, partially to get more comfortable and partially to entice Liam.

"Okay, queen. You want me to give you a back rub, too?"

Liam stood up carefully, balancing the powder on the end of his key. He walked over to Avery's chair.

Avery considered Liam's offer of a back rub for a second. She did the bump and looked up at him, her eyes at his waist-level. "You'd probably get a boner or something if I let you."

"If you *let* me? Oh my god, please. If you *let* me." Liam flopped back down on the couch.

Avery laughed. "I'm just playing with you, hon, you know that."

"Whatever."

"Oh, come on now. Don't be mad."

Liam sulked. "Do you want to buy any of this or not?"

When the bump hit Avery's nasal passage her neck and shoulders began to tingle. Her mind cleared instantly. She felt like she could do a cartwheel right there in the living room.

"Damn, that is pretty good," she said.

"I told you."

"Why don't you lay out a couple lines for me. I'll call you later for more. I don't want the temptation laying around here all day."

"When has anyone in the history of cocaine ever stopped at only a couple lines? You're just delaying the inevitable and making me work harder."

"Don't you want to see me again later?"

Liam pursed his lips. She had him there.

"Just cut out a few lines and leave them for me. Look how much you have. A few lines won't even make a difference in that bag."

Liam lifted the large bag of powder. He shifted his eyes over to Avery, surveying her soft pajama pants and the vintage My Little Pony t-shirt that stretched tightly against her chest. "Show me your tits and I will."

Avery rolled her eyes. "Dude, are you serious?"

"What's the big deal, you show them to guys, like, every night at work."

"Fine." Avery gripped the bottom of her t-shirt and lifted the thin cotton hem to her shoulders. She held the shirt up for three seconds and then lowered it. "Are you happy?"

Liam blinked. "Yes," he whispered. He poured a small pile of cocaine out on the coffee table. "Call me later when you want more."

"What if I don't want more?"

"You will."

Liam stood up quickly. He looked once more at Avery, and then let himself out of the apartment.

Avery tucked her t-shirt down behind her, covering her exposed skin. She stared at the door that Liam had just exited.

Out in the parking lot Liam's car started, backed out, and drove away.

"Where the hell do you think you've been?" Jerry's wife screamed from behind the screen door.

Jerry slid out of Bull's truck in front of his rundown house on the northside of Savannah.

Billie Musen swung the thin metal frame of the screen

door open by kicking the base of it with a dirty pink slipper. The door banged hard against the exterior of the house, adding to the already deep indentation in the rotten wood siding.

Billie took one look at Jerry's slumped shoulders, the way he wavered in his drunken stupor. "You got some nerve bringing him home like this!" she shouted into the open door of the pickup truck.

Bull peeled out before Billie could lay into him. The truck kicked gravel against the back of Jerry's legs.

"Jesus, Jerry. What have you done?"

Billie stood with her hands on her hips, facing her husband, her robe opened enough to expose the top of her sun-damaged chest.

"I'm trying to make us some money."

"By staying out all night drinking? Looks more like you're spending money than making it."

"Them drinks didn't cost me a dime," said Jerry, continuing to stare at the dusty yard as he spoke.

Billie squinted her eyes, more suspicious than ever. "Who paid for 'em then? What kind of crap are you getting mixed up in now?"

"Don't worry about it."

Billie shook her head. "Tell me not to worry about it. I'm flushing the toilet with water from the neighbor's hose. How'm I gonna not worry about it?"

Jerry's legs wobbled. He felt the acid in his stomach churning.

"You need to go in there and tell your daughter why the faucet doesn't run anymore, is what you need to do."

Jerry's head started to swim. His vision darkened. He

fell to his knees in front of his wife and vomited on her pink slippers.

12

A little after nine o'clock that night, Mack returned to McKearney's, only this time he went inside and took a seat at the bar. Following his employer's instructions, Mack planned to stake out the bar, gather as much intel as he could. One day of surveillance wasn't near enough time to get a good read on a place, but he resolved to do his best.

Mack sipped slowly from a glass of bourbon mixed with water and ice. About thirty people were spread throughout the large, dimly lit bar. A mix of college kids and middle-aged drinkers, with a few other seasoned boozers sitting at the bar near Mack. Through the front windows of the bar was visible a walkway along the Savannah River, lit by streetlamps.

Mack casually turned to survey the clientele behind him. Nothing seemed out of the ordinary. The night was just getting started. So far no one looked like a drug dealer or hired muscle.

"Refill?" asked the bartender.

Mack shook his head. "Not yet."

The bartender nodded. "I don't recognize you around

here. Just visiting?"

"Passing through."

The bartender's eyes held a glint of suspicion.

"I'm supposed to meet someone here actually," said Mack, trying to deflect attention from himself.

"Oh? Lady friend?" pried the bartender.

Mack hesitated to commit one way or another. He didn't want to lock himself into a story yet. He rattled the ice in his glass and pretended not to hear the question.

"Which way is the can?" Mack asked after a few seconds.

The bartender nodded toward a dark hallway at the end of the bar. Mack slid off the barstool and walked slowly across the room. He listened to snippets of conversations as he passed each table. Nothing stood out as suspicious.

The back hallway stretched into darkness. Doors flanked the corridor on either side with the bathrooms being clearly labeled on the right. The first door on the left was marked STORAGE. The second door on the left, further back—almost to the rear exit—stood slightly ajar. Mack looked over his shoulder to see if anyone was watching him. He crept up to the last door.

"Don't worry about that, we can handle any quantity," a voice said inside the room.

Mack leaned closer.

"Just bring the cash on Tuesday and we'll work it out," said the same voice.

"Are you lost?" asked a man behind Mack.

Mack straightened up quickly. He turned to see a stocky fellow with a crew cut wearing a tight black sports coat.

"That's not the bathroom," said Mack, playing dumb.

"No, it ain't, pal. Bathroom's the one with the big sign says "MEN" on it, has a couple pissers mounted on the wall in there." The guy extended a thick finger from his meaty hand and pointed across the hall.

"Thanks, big fella. They ought to see about getting a light back here in this hallway. Hard to see anything."

The stocky guy grunted. He pulled the office door shut with a click and took a post in front of it. His shoulders nearly touched both sides of the door frame.

When Mack finished in the bathroom, the stocky guy had disappeared from his post. The office door remained closed.

Returning to his seat at the bar, Mack felt exposed. He worried he might have blown his cover by getting caught snooping.

"I'll have another one of these," Mack said, touching the rim of his glass. He waited for the bartender to start pouring and then added, "It is a lady friend supposed to meet me tonight. Maybe she got her wires crossed. You mind if I use your phone?"

The bartender lifted the phone from its perch near the cash register. The phone's long cord allowed him to place the cradle on the bar in front of Mack.

Mack withdrew from his pocket the note with Avery's phone number. He took a deep breath and dialed.

The phone rang four times before Avery answered.

"Not working tonight?" said Mack.

"I'll be there in a little bit," Avery said, sounding pissed off, assuming it was one of Leonard's guys calling to harass her about being late.

"Could I convince you to take a night off?"

"Huh? Who is this?"

"It's Mack. You know, from, uh, last night. You left your number at the motel."

"Oh shit, why didn't you say so? Man, a girl in my line sometimes gets weirdos calling up."

Mack laughed. "I'm at McKearney's downtown. Come have a drink with me."

Avery hesitated. She thought about Liam's visit earlier that day, and about the lines that were long gone from her coffee table.

"I'm supposed to go in tonight. They're expecting me."

"Come on, it's Sunday night. The day of rest."

"Right," said Avery with a laugh, "the day God tells all the strippers to climb down from their poles and relax."

"Exactly."

"Are you buying?"

"I owe you."

Avery rested the back of her head against the yellow wallpaper in her kitchen. The television in her living room said something about The Bedazzler and how it could add sparkling rhinestones to any item of clothing.

"Yeah, okay," she finally said. "Lemme see if I have any clean clothes that aren't crotchless."

"I'll save you a seat."

Mack hung up the phone with a smile on his face. He glanced in the mirror behind the bar, checked his teeth and combed his hair with his fingers.

"Did you get ahold of her?" said the bartender as he retrieved the phone.

"Yes, I did. She's on the way."

13

Avery recognized the Irish bar. Liam had mentioned it. Something about how the owner of the place was involved with his drug connection, although Avery wasn't sure whether the bar owner was a buyer or a seller. Either way, she figured drugs would be around if she got hard up.

She was glad Mack had called. He seemed like a pretty good guy—maybe a little bit boring compared to her usual type. But he was fun to be around. And, so far, he had treated her with respect. More than she could say about most men.

She spotted Mack at the bar when she entered the dim building. His muscular back stretched the fabric of his shirt. His left boot lightly tapped the gold metal railing that ran along the bar's base.

Avery reached a hand under each shoulder of her blazer to straighten the straps of her loose-fitting cami. She checked to make sure the rip in her jeans sat just above her knee, and that her pant legs stopped high enough to expose her ankles and the straps of her shoes. She took a breath and strutted across the room like she owned the place.

"Hey, stranger. Miss me?"

Mack turned around. He did a double take when he saw Avery.

Avery smiled. "I clean up nice, don't I?"

"I barely recognized you," said Mack, still taking her in. "I mean, not in a bad way," Mack stammered. "You look good is what I'm trying to say."

Avery slid her fingers down the lapel of her blazer. "It's not too much? I wasn't sure about the jacket."

"Not at all. It's a good look on you."

"Why, thank you. What are we drinking?"

"I have bourbon. What do you like?"

Avery scrunched up her nose. "I'd like a Paloma. With Patrón."

Mack turned to the bartender. "Did you catch that?"

The bartender already had the clear bottle of tequila in one hand and a metal shaker in the other.

"It's sweet and sour with a bite," explained Avery as she sat down next to Mack.

"Just how I like my women," Mack laughed. He reached his arm across the barstool and hugged Avery. She leaned into his chest and squeezed his thigh. Neither of them could decide if a kiss was in order, so they stopped at the hug.

"Did your boss give you any trouble about missing work?"

"Nah, they owed me a day off anyway," said Avery, choosing to omit the part about Leonard whining and then calling her a bitch before hanging up on her. Office politics at the strip club go a little differently than they do at most workplaces.

"That's good."

The bartender served Avery's Paloma. She and Mack touched glasses. They each took a long swallow.

"Did you get your business taken care of this morning?" Avery asked. "You rushed out in such a hurry."

"Yeah, sorry about that. I didn't want to leave."

"Where'd you go anyway?"

"Had to meet a client."

"Ah," said Avery, reflecting suspicion about Mack's vague response. "Must have been an emergency."

"Yeah…" Mack trailed off. He didn't want to lie to Avery, but he couldn't tell her the whole truth. "What did you do today?"

"Um, went shopping," said Avery, thinking about her visit from Liam and the gift he had left on her coffee table, and also how she had earned it.

The pair fell silent for a few seconds, both thinking about the partial truths they had told each other.

"So are you sticking around town for a while?" said Avery. She tugged at the sleeve of her blazer. The outfit made her feel more formal than usual. She struggled to feel comfortable. It didn't help that her last real date had been, well, she couldn't even remember how long it had been. Talking to men at the club was easy—she knew exactly what they wanted and how to give it to them. Conversation on a Sunday night in a bar with a man who wasn't a client proved to be less easy. She knew what would help, but she fought against the urge to call Liam.

"For now," said Mack. "I'm still working."

"You never told me what you do."

"Well, hmm." Mack stalled. He took a sip of bourbon.

"It's kind of private."

"Oh, man. Now you *have* to tell me." Avery flashed her eyes at Mack, prodding him. "Anyways, you know everything about what I do for a living. Like, *everything* everything."

Mack blushed. He looked down at his hands. "I suppose that's true."

"So?"

"What would you think if I told you I'm working right now? Like, as we speak."

Avery looked at the bourbon glass in Mack's hand. "I knew it. You're a professional alcoholic."

Mack laughed. "Not quite." He scooted his stool over to Avery until their thighs touched. "If I tell you, you can't say anything. Keep it a secret."

"Oh boy. You're starting to get weird on me. They always do eventually."

"I'm serious. Promise me."

"Fine. I promise."

Mack glanced over his shoulder before answering. "I am staking out this bar."

Avery looked sideways at Mack, trying to decide if he was joking. Or worse, if he was crazy. "You better not be a fucking cop."

"No, definitely not that. People hire me to do…things."

"Well, that's vague as hell. What kind of things?"

Before Mack could answer, a commotion started at the back of the bar. Raised voices projected down the hallway, near the office where Mack had been snooping.

Avery and Mack both turned to see what was happening. Each of them saw one familiar face and one stranger.

The stocky henchman that Mack had encountered outside the office guided Liam forcefully toward the door with one arm behind his back.

"Liam!" exclaimed Avery.

Liam shook free of Bull's grasp. He paused to straighten his shirt. "Hey, Avery. How you doing?" he said once he collected himself.

"What are you doing here?" said Avery.

"Other than getting manhandled by this asshat?"

Bull stared at Liam. He realized people in the bar were watching them and listening. The scuffle was garnering unwanted attention.

"I was just about to leave," said Liam. "But I think I might have a drink now. A drink with my friends sitting there at the bar." Liam glared at Bull as he spoke.

"Do stay for a while," said Avery. Then she addressed Bull, turning on her club voice, "He won't cause any more trouble. I promise."

Liam was already halfway to the bar. He leaped the last few feet and climbed on a stool next to Avery. "Sierra Nevada," he said to the bartender.

The bartender looked at Bull for confirmation. Bull nodded slightly before slipping back into the dark hallway.

"Jesus, what was all that about?" said Avery when Bull had gone.

"I've told you about this place before, haven't I? Just negotiating some business back in the office. It's nothing, he'll be fine. Only a disagreement on price."

"Price?" said Mack.

Liam squinted his eyes, looking at Mack for the first

time. "Who's this guy?" he asked.

"He's okay," said Avery. "He's with me."

"*With?*" Liam sounded hurt.

Avery laughed off Liam's reaction. "Calm down, boo. What, you didn't know I have a social life?"

Liam and Mack stared at each other suspiciously.

"Boys, relax. Have a drink." Avery continued using her club voice with the men to disarm them. She raised her own glass and took a long swig. Liam and Mack cautiously obeyed.

"I'm glad you're here, anyway," continued Avery. "I was just about to call you."

"I knew you would," said Liam, starting to relax a little. "You'll never believe this, but I'm almost out. That's why I'm back here."

Avery shifted in her seat. She didn't want Mack to know the nature of her relationship with Liam. "Can we smoke a cigarette or something?"

Liam shrugged. "If you got one for me."

"We'll find a couple out front." Avery placed her hand on Mack's leg. "I'm gonna go outside for a minute, hon. Get me another one of these drinks, will you, please?"

Avery did not wait for Mack to respond. She grabbed Liam by the arm and pulled him toward the front door.

After bumming a couple cigarettes from a group of smokers outside, Avery leaned against one corner of the brick building. Her back faced the alley that ran alongside the bar.

"Dude, keep the drug talk on the D.L., will ya?" she said out the side of her mouth as she lit one of the cigarettes. She handed it to Liam and lit the other one for herself.

"What? I thought you said he was cool?"

"Cool in general, but I'm not trying to share all my secrets with the world, you know what I mean?"

Liam exhaled a breath of white smoke. "Whatever, man. He a john or something?"

"No," said Avery quickly. "Well, kinda, I guess. Not really."

"Glad you have that so clear in your mind."

"It's none of your business anyway," Avery snapped.

"Geez. Just asking. Don't get in a tizzy about it. You can screw any dude you want. It's your life."

"Says the guy who sells cocaine for a living."

"You wouldn't be talking shit if you saw the wad of cash in my pocket right now."

"You're lucky I'm not the criminal type with the way you brag about yourself. I could put a knife to your throat right now and rob you, couldn't I?"

"You wouldn't do that."

"Keep tempting me, I might someday." Avery took a drag on her cigarette. "So what were you doing back there in the office? You got kicked out or what?"

"That fucking guy, Lucas, he's a pain in the ass sometimes."

"Is he where you get all the stuff from?"

Liam hesitated. He shifted on his feet, glanced around nervously. "Yeah, and he has a lot more back there in his office, I think. But he wouldn't give me anymore tonight."

"What does he care who buys it as long as you've got the cash?"

"Who knows. He said something about a big buyer was

coming and he had to wait to see what was left over."

"I can't believe you already unloaded that whole bag you had this morning. That's nuts."

"It's good stuff. You tried it. Told all my regulars it was a special occasion, and they bought extra."

"They're probably stepping on it and reselling."

Liam sniffed with disdain. "I wouldn't be surprised. Shame if they do, though. To ruin something pure like that."

"If I've learned anything working at the club, it's that people will do some crazy shit to earn a dime," said Avery.

Liam nodded. "Mm-hmm."

A small boat passed them on the water, cutting a dark shadow through the Savannah River. Voices with no words reached the patio and faded as the boat vanished from sight.

"Can you do a gram?" Avery broke the silence.

"Yeah, probably. Not much more. I don't want to be out completely. That tool Lucas better hook me back up tomorrow."

Liam lifted a tiny baggie from his pocket. He examined it against his palm by the neon light.

"That may be a little light, I can't tell for sure. I don't want to get out my scales right here." He handed it to Avery. "Let me know tomorrow if it's straight and pay me then, okay?"

Avery nodded. "Stand over here for a sec." She tugged Liam's shirt until he blocked the view of the other smokers. Then, she quickly dipped a fingernail in the baggie and gave herself a lift.

---

*

"Sorry about that. I'm back," Avery said when she hopped up on the barstool next to Mack. She leaned into his shoulder and nudged him playfully.

Mack observed her through squinted eyes. "Who was that guy?"

"Oh, just a friend. I don't know him that well."

"A friend who was about to get kicked out of this bar for reasons unknown, and who you suddenly decided you needed to talk with outside?"

"Don't get jealous on me now. I stepped outside for a minute, and now I'm back." Avery leaned forward, craning her neck over top of the bar. She carefully placed the stirring straw from her fresh drink in her mouth. She batted her eyelashes at Mack while she sipped, trying to distract him.

"I'm calling bullshit."

Avery sat back, feigning surprise. "What do you mean?"

"I mean my bullshit meter is going off the charts right now. I think you're laying it on thick." Mack took a beat before continuing. "Remember how I told you I was casing this bar for a client?" Mack paused to let his question sink in.

Avery gave no indication of anything being amiss. She hid it well. She took another sip from her drink and allowed Mack to continue.

"I know what's in that back office," said Mack.

"I'm so confused." Avery knitted her brow, keeping up the ruse.

"Oh, please. I think you know, too." Mack smiled

slightly. "I don't care. Believe me, I'm no angel. You want to do some blow, that's your business. I'm fully aware what goes on at strip clubs. And I know I'm on a date with a stripper."

Avery frowned. "Fine. If you want to be that way. But we prefer the term 'dancer'." She lowered her voice, finally dropping the pretense of innocence.

"Sorry about that," said Mack. "Dancer. Anyway, like I said, I got no issue. Matter of fact, if you have a connection to what's happening in that back office, that makes you even more special in my book."

"Yeah?" Avery looked up. Her eyes lightened. "I thought you might get mad if you knew. You seem kinda straight edge."

"I'm not gonna use the stuff personally, but to each their own. And if it makes you behave like you did last night, then by all means, go for it." Mack laughed, taking the edge off the conversation. He took a drink of his bourbon.

Avery looked into Mack's eyes, searching them for trustworthiness. She relaxed her shoulders and smiled. "Okay," was all she said.

Mack didn't want to let it go so easily. "Now that we have that established, how about you share what you know concerning the owner of this bar? And maybe anything you can add regarding your friend who I just met?"

Avery hesitated for several seconds. She liked Mack and wanted to help him but not at her own expense. If word somehow got out that she had told secrets she would be in trouble.

"I don't really know anything," Avery mumbled.

Mack shook his head slightly. He pushed a little harder. "That guy, what's his name?"

"Liam. I don't know his last name," Avery lied.

"He's a dealer of some kind?"

"You swear to me you're not a cop?"

"I swear. I have no interest in getting these guys in trouble. I don't even know a soul in the police department here."

Avery sighed. "He gets me coke sometimes. I think the guy who owns this place sells it to him. That's all I know. For real. Please don't ask me any more about it."

Mack nodded. "I don't want to put you in a bad spot. My client is paying me a lot of money to learn what I can about this place."

Mack stared into the mirror briefly. He watched people mill about the bar behind him.

"Matter of fact," he continued, "I'll tell you something, too. Just for fun. Since we're sharing. I watched this very shipment come in off the water a couple nights ago, over on Tybee Island. The guy you're talking about—the owner of this bar—he's no small timer. That back office is full of enough blow to supply all of Georgia."

Avery's eyes widened. She remembered the large bag Liam had brought to her apartment that morning.

"It's good shit, too," she said. "Best I've ever had."

"Really? That's interesting."

"Yep. And if you don't mind, I'm about to go to the ladies and remind myself how good it is."

"See if you can get a look in that office while you're back there."

"Seriously?"

"Absolutely. I'll put you on the payroll."

"Well, why didn't you say so? I'm gonna hold you to that."

Mack winked. "You got it."

Avery opened the bathroom door slowly, hoping the hallway was as empty as when she had entered. She felt invincible with a head full of drugs, like nothing could hurt her.

Across the hall, the office door stood ajar. Avery saw a light on inside the room. She decided her best play was to go straight at her objective. Sneaking around like a spy was not her style.

She shed the blazer, neatly folded it, and hung it over her bare arm. The thin camisole showed every curve of her upper body. She ran her fingertips over her nipples to make them visible.

Avery affected a tipsy walk as she approached the office door. She placed her hand on the knob and pushed.

"Who's back here?" Avery said into the widening doorway. She spoke with an exaggerated drunken slur.

The man behind the desk sat up quickly. He had been leaning over the desk with his face down.

"This is private!" he shouted. He raised a hand to stop his unknown intruder. "No one's allowed in here."

Avery stumbled forward, catching herself with her palms on the desk across from the man. She arched her back, making sure her breasts bulged forward between her forearms. "Oh, excuse me. I thought I was supposed to meet someone here."

Rafe Lucas recovered from his temporary surprise. He realized the woman in front of him was exceptionally pretty and more than a little drunk.

"Who are you looking for?" he said. His voice was warmer now, more coaxing.

Avery took a chance. "Um, my friend. Liam? Do you know him?"

Rafe sat back in his chair. He crossed his fingers over his stomach. "What's a girl like you doing hanging out with a guy like him?"

"So you do know him?"

Rafe paused. "Yeah, I know him."

"Is he here?" Avery kept up the drunken act.

"Not anymore, but maybe I can help you. What are you looking for?"

Avery spotted a large stack of something behind the desk covered by a green tarp. She took three quick steps and, before Lucas could stop her, she got a hand on the tarp and started to pull it back. "What you got under here?" she asked innocently.

Lucas slapped her hand away from the pile. "You're a fast little thing, aren't you?" He encircled Avery's waist with his arm and pulled her backward until she fell into his lap.

"Hey!" said Avery coyly. "I don't know you!"

"I bet I know why you're looking for Liam. And whatever arrangement you had with him, I can do better."

"Oh yeah?"

Lucas lifted an overturned tray from his desk and exposed a mound of cocaine. "Hmm?" he purred.

"For me?" Avery did not need to feign excitement.

Lucas laughed. "Not all of it. Cut yourself out a big

one." He slid a business card across the desk.

Avery used the card to separate out a line. She snorted it and slipped the card in her pocket.

"Very good. You've done this before," said Lucas.

Avery smiled. She bounced slightly on Lucas's leg.

"Run along out to the bar and have some drinks. Tell the bartender that Rafe said it's okay." Lucas tapped Avery's thigh and rested his hand above her knee. "In a little bit, come on back here, and you can have some more. How does that sound?"

"Fuck Liam. That's how it sounds."

"Oh my, she has a mouth on her, too," said Lucas. He patted Avery's butt when she stood up. "Come back and see me when you're ready."

"It's back there," Avery said when she returned to the bar.

"What's back there?" asked Mack.

"What you're looking for. He's got it under a tarp in the office."

Surprised at Avery's quick success, Mack stumbled over his words. "You mean you got in the office? Who? What are you saying exactly?"

"That creepy fucker who owns the bar." Avery fished the business card out from her pocket and tossed it on the bar top.

"Rafe Lucas," Mack read from the card. "You talked to him?"

"I could have screwed him if I had wanted to. He let me right in."

Mack shook his head slowly. "You're something else,

you know that?"

Avery smiled briefly, and then frowned. A cold shudder rippled through her body. "Something's off about that guy. He's shady."

"Thanks for doing that," said Mack. He placed a hand on Avery's shoulder to steady her.

"Yeah. It's okay," she said, but her face contradicted her words.

Mack said nothing. He kept his hand on her shoulder. They were silent for a few seconds until Mack asked, "You want another drink?"

"Nah, I don't think. Can we just go back to the motel? Are you still staying there tonight?"

"Sure, of course we can."

Mack took out his wallet to pay for the drinks.

"Rafe said these were on the house," Avery told the bartender. She didn't wait for a response. She jumped off the stool and headed for the door.

Mack stood up and followed her.

14

Jerry Musen opened his eyes on Monday morning face to face with a naked Barbie doll. He blinked and rolled sideways, lifting his cheek off the piled carpet. He massaged his forehead to stop the pounding throb that pulsed with each heartbeat. He ran his fingers across the palette of deep indentations that the carpet had made on his unshaven face.

"Daddy, wake up," said Jerry's daughter.

He heard her voice, but he could not see her. He rolled over further and was greeted by a pair of pointed knees colliding with his rib cage.

"Mommy said to wake you up, Daddy." The girl rolled off her father's chest and landed on the floor with a soft thud.

Jerry gasped for air. "I'm awake," he exhaled roughly, clutching at his stomach. He fought the urge to vomit. "Go tell her I'm awake. I'll be in there in a minute."

"Okay, Daddy. Why are you sleeping on the floor?"

Jerry wished he knew the answer. "I was playing with

Barbie and took a nap," he said.

The girl seemed satisfied with that explanation. She skipped out of her parents' bedroom. Jerry felt the floor shudder with each of his daughter's dainty leaps.

"What's for breakfast?" Jerry said when he entered the kitchen, still holding his bruised ribcage. He stopped in the doorway to take his wife's temperature. His daughter had joined her baby brother at the kitchen table. The baby sat in his highchair and pounded his hands on the tray in front of him.

"Frosted Flakes!" shouted the little girl.

Jerry patted his daughter on the head. He lifted the box of generic brand Frosted Flakes off the table and shoved his hand into the open top. He grabbed a fistful of the sugary cereal and tossed it in his mouth.

"Hey!" said his daughter.

"You have a whole bowl there. You can spare it," Jerry answered.

Jerry cautiously approached his wife. She had not turned away from the stove since he entered the room. He placed a hand on her waist and whispered in her ear. "What you got cooking over here? Smells good."

"Don't you dare," said Billie.

"Aw, come on, you're still mad?"

"A whole day and you barely left that bedroom except to pee."

"Has it been that long?"

Billie turned to glare at her husband over her shoulder.

"I was tired," he whined. "I told you, I been working on something."

Billie shook her head. "My sister said she's ready for me

and the kids anytime. She said take the car and come on, that's what she told me last night."

"Hell, Billie. You talked to your sister? You know I don't want her knowing our business."

"It ain't up to you anymore. One of these days you're gonna come home and there ain't gonna be nobody to cook your food and wash your drawers. What do you think about that?"

Jerry leaned his hip against the counter. He watched a pancake slowly brown on the griddle. "Don't do that to me, honey. You know I love you and the kids. Don't talk that way, will ya? It hurts me."

Billie flipped the pancake. Her body language softened. "You're gonna make me do it, Jerry."

"Make you do what, Mommy?" said the little girl.

"Go visit Aunt Janet," said Billie. "How would you like to visit Aunt Janet?"

The girl looked at her father. She seemed unsure how to answer. "Aunt Janet has a doggie," she finally said.

"Yes, she does," said Billie. "We can go see the doggie."

A bucket of hose water sat on the counter by the kitchen sink. Jerry leaned over the bucket and observed his ragged reflection. He dipped his head into the water until it reached the tip of his upside-down nose. The cool water soothed his aching head. He ran his palms over his scalp and slicked his hair back from his forehead.

"What is today? Monday?" Jerry asked his wife. His wet hair dripped on his shoulders and ran down his back.

Billie rolled her eyes at her husband. "You want one of these or not?" She gestured with her spatula at the stack of pancakes.

"Yes, ma'am, I do." Jerry took a plate from the cupboard and held it out like a beggar. She transferred two pancakes to his waiting plate.

"Tuesday is the day," said Jerry. "That's tomorrow. I'll have our water back on and all our problems will be solved."

"What happens on Tuesday, Daddy?" said the girl with a mouthful of cereal.

"Tuesday is Daddy's payday," said Jerry, looking at his wife while he answered his daughter's question.

For the second morning in a row, Mack woke up next to Avery's warm body. Her head rested on a pillow in the crook of his arm. She breathed through a small gap in her lips and each time she inhaled, the soft palate in the back of her throat vibrated slightly, creating a mini snore that Mack found more cute than annoying.

Mack lay awake in bed for a few minutes listening to Avery breathe and to the occasional horn honk outside the motel window. He heard the maid's cart roll past his door on its squeaky wheels.

The intel Mack had gathered should be enough to appease his employer, especially on such short notice. He had a mapped layout of the building, a cursory headcount of the key players, and a good idea of how the business operated late at night. Add to that, Liam's news about a big buyer coming in on Tuesday—a detail Avery had let slip while she and Mack lay in each other's arms the night before. Mack felt he had a pretty good report to pass along.

Mack carefully lifted his arm from behind Avery's head

without nudging her pillow. He carried the phone over to the table and sat down, wearing nothing but a pair of boxer shorts. A light dusting of cocaine covered part of the table's surface. Avery had ceased hiding her habit once Mack was aware of it.

Mack tore a sheet of paper from the motel's complimentary notepad and did his best to clear the powder from his workspace. He dialed the number of his employer and let it ring while he flexed and relaxed his bicep.

"Yes?"

"It's me," said Mack. "Hope it's not too early your time," he added, prompting his conversant to tip off his location.

"We've been waiting for your call."

"We?" said Mack. He wanted elaboration but got none. "I've been thinking it's time for me to know more about you. Like, your name would be a good start."

"That information is not essential to this job."

"Not essential for whom?"

The voice seemed to sigh. "What is the update?"

Mack gave up his prying. "I got what you wanted."

"Yes? Tell us please."

Mack was again put off by the use of a plural pronoun, but he ignored it and continued. "The stash is in a back office of the bar. Looks like the owner, guy by the name of Rafe Lucas, is sitting on it. He keeps a bodyguard of some kind nearby, big dude with a square jaw and a bad attitude. My guess is the other two delivery men aren't far away." Mack took a breath and continued. "The bartender may or may not be in on it, I'm not sure yet. That puts the total at five guys tops, if he has all hands on deck."

Mack could hear the smile on his employer's face when he replied, "Very good."

"Two ways in—the front door and the back door that opens into the alley. The back door is only a few feet from the office, which would be on your right when you enter. Two bathrooms across the hall that could pose a problem since they're unpredictable. One of those doors opens, you lose your view of the hallway. And it's already dark back there—good for the element of surprise but bad for visibility once you engage."

Mack heard the voice relaying his report to someone else in the room.

"One more thing," Mack said. "If you want to make a move you better go tonight. According to a local source, Lucas is planning to unload the stash on Tuesday to a big buyer. If you wait, you might miss the boat."

The muffled voice again passed along Mack's information to the third party.

"Tonight will be the night then," said the employer when he returned to the line. "One a.m."

"Alright. Well, good luck with that," said Mack.

"We would like your help."

"Unh-uh." Mack shook his head as he spoke. "That's going to be a no for me. I'm not getting mixed up in some cocaine shootout. No, sir. I'll pass."

The line went silent.

"Hello?" said Mack after a few seconds of dead air.

"We will triple your fee and give you a cut of the score."

Mack hesitated. "What kind of cut?"

"We need a man on the inside who knows the building. We want you to signal from inside the bar when the time is right."

"Be a lookout and give a signal? Then I'm gone?"

"That would be our expectation. In exchange, you can expect a quarter million once we clear the area and procure the merchandise."

"Two hundred fifty K?" Mack nearly choked on the question before he could finish asking it.

"Correct."

Mack held the phone to his ear. He lifted the window curtain with a finger and peered out through the exposed glass. Two teenagers rollerbladed around in the parking lot, chasing each other and laughing while their parents packed suitcases into a station wagon.

"One a.m.?"

"Wait in the bar until then. If all is well, stand up, walk to the front window, and look out at the river. We will take it from there."

"Shit," said Mack. "Okay."

Mack hung up the phone. He watched the rollerblading kids for a few more minutes until the station wagon was fully packed. The kids took off their skates and climbed in the backseat.

Mack let the curtain drop. The motel room returned to near darkness.

Behind him in bed, Avery quickly closed her eyes and pretended she had not heard the entire conversation.

*

Jerry finished his pancakes. He set his plate in the sink and poured out a splash of water from the bucket to loosen the sticky syrup.

He watched his daughter twirl her spoon in the leftover cereal milk. She sang a song to herself softly. Jerry could not make out the words. He figured they were made up, something the girl had taken to doing lately.

"What are you learning at school today?" Jerry asked his daughter.

She stopped singing. "I don't know."

"Making a turkey with your hand?"

"Huh?"

"Didn't you ever do that? Put your hand on a paper and trace your fingers to make a turkey?"

The girl scrunched her face in confusion.

"You know what holiday is coming up, don't you?"

The girl thought for a few seconds before answering, "Thanksgivings?"

"That's right. When I was a little boy in school we made hand turkeys for Thanksgiving."

The girl looked at her hands, turning them from front to back, trying to understand her dad's words.

"I'll show you this week. Remind me. We'll make hand turkeys."

"Okay, daddy."

Jerry tried to kiss his wife's cheek, but she swerved away from him. He frowned and moved on, swinging open the screen door. He went outside to smoke a cigarette.

Carefully stepping over glass from a broken beer bottle,

he shook a Kool Mild from his soft pack and held it between his teeth while he fished in his pocket for a lighter. His hands came up empty.

"Damn it." Jerry spat on a lone patch of driveway that had not been overtaken by tall weeds. Going back inside for a lighter would open the door to more berating from Billie if her mood turned. It was hard to know what might set her off these days.

Jerry shuffled across the broken driveway that separated his house from the neighbor's. He took each step gingerly to avoid cutting his feet on hidden objects in the tall grass.

The neighbor's fat coonhound began thumping its thick tail when it saw Jerry approaching. The dog lay on her side in the morning sun. She lifted her head a couple inches and yawned, then laid back down, still thumping her tail slowly on the packed dirt next to a rotting deck under which she retreated when the afternoon sun reached peak heat.

"Hey, girl, don't get up for me. I don't have anything for you," Jerry said to the dog, his teeth still clamped on the cigarette.

Jerry took a few more steps into his neighbor's yard. "Roy, you in there?" he hollered in the direction of a cinder block garage behind the house.

"Yep," answered Roy from within the garage.

"That dog ain't worth a shit, is she?" Jerry said when he reached the open garage door.

"Nope."

"You got a light on you?"

"Over here on the workbench somewhere, if you can find it."

Roy was hunched over his workbench wearing a welder's mask. His torch sent sparks cascading on the dirt floor.

"What are you up to in here?" Jerry asked when Roy straightened up and lifted the mask. The dark visor hinged and locked above Roy's head.

"Building a yacht."

Jerry cracked a smile. He located the cigarette lighter on the work bench and lit his smoke. "Do me a favor and put my wife on there when you get done. Send her on down to Cuba or anywhere else, long as I can't hear her talking."

"Already this morning, huh?"

"Brother, it never ends."

"You get your water back on yet?"

Jerry pressed his toes into the cool dirt floor. "Nah. Listen, Roy, I meant to thank you for letting us use your hose for a little while. I'm working on something that'll get us back in business in a day or two. It won't be long."

Roy raised his eyebrows. "Do I want to know?"

"It's a sure bet this time. Once it comes through, first thing I'm gonna do is stock your fridge full of Keystone for you. Hell, I'll get the good stuff. Coors Banquet. Imagine a fridge full of those golden beauties."

"That'll be the day." Roy coughed. "Go ahead if you want to," he said, knowing what Jerry was driving at.

"You sure?"

"Might as well make room for one more Banquet to fit in there."

Jerry opened the garage fridge and took out a cold can of Keystone Light. The amber liquid cooled his throat. He drank the beer quickly and got another one.

"Roy, you're a damn good neighbor, you know it?"

"I know it."

Avery opened her eyes when Mack got back in bed. She lifted her head so Mack could slide his arm under her neck and pull her closer. Faint traces of his fading deodorant mixed with the smell of bleached bed sheets.

"Where'd you go?" she asked. Her voice rasped from raw sinuses.

"Nowhere. Just had to make a phone call."

Avery traced a finger along Mack's pectoral muscle. "Your boss?" she said.

"I'd rather call him my client, but yeah, I guess so."

"What does he want you to do?" Avery feigned naivety, pretending she had not heard the phone call.

Mack didn't answer for several seconds. The shower turned on in the next room over, low water pressure trickled in the porcelain basin.

"Something I don't want to do," Mack finally said.

Avery exhaled a long sigh across Mack's chest. "I know that game."

Mack tilted Avery's chin up and looked in her eyes. He kissed her long and sensually. She felt a warmth growing in her stomach, a tingling that spread lower, into her waist and thighs. She slid a bare leg over Mack's knee and caressed his calf with her foot. Mack slipped his strong hands around her hips. He tightened his grip until her warm skin pressed against his. He kissed her deeply, and then he slid her over his lap until she straddled him.

*

Minutes later, they lay in each other's arms, hearts pounding, beads of sweat running down their backs in tiny rivulets.

Avery, still out of breath, stared at the ceiling, listening to her heart beat in her ears. She felt relaxed and energized at the same time.

"Are you gonna take the job?" she asked without looking at Mack.

Mack stroked her hair, his fingers brushing back the dampness that had formed on her brow.

"It's a lot of money…" he trailed off. "More than I've ever been offered."

"I don't want you to get hurt."

Mack smiled. "Does that mean you like me?"

"Come on, I'm being serious. Drug people, they're not like normal people. You can't trust them. They're too unpredictable."

Mack wondered if Avery counted herself among the "drug people" but decided not to press it. "I know," he said. "I'm out of there before the shit goes down, that's what they tell me."

"Is it tonight?"

"You don't need to worry about it. It's my problem to deal with."

"Don't patronize me. I can worry about anything I want to." Avery took a breath and calmed the anger that was rising inside her. "What about Liam? I don't want him to get hurt or arrested or anything. I shouldn't have told you so much. Liam is my friend. He's not a criminal like those other guys."

"There's no reason for Liam to be involved. My client doesn't know anything about him."

Avery exhaled, feeling her body relax again.

"If you want to be sure he's safe, see to it he doesn't come around the bar for a few days. That's all it would take," Mack added.

"Okay," said Avery. "I need to pee."

Mack laughed. "You're gonna have to solve that problem on your own."

Avery gave him a mock glare, pretending to be offended. She flipped the bed sheet off their naked bodies. Standing on the mattress, her head nearly touching the ceiling, she strutted to the foot of the bed, glancing back dramatically to catch Mack staring at her butt, which is exactly what he was doing.

"Busted," she said and jumped off the bed. She landed on the thin carpet with a vibration that surely confused their neighbors. "I need to pee!" she shouted with urgency and then skipped into the bathroom.

Mack waited until he heard the shower running before getting up. He put on his pants and returned to his post at the table, where he lifted the phone and dialed Andy Simpson's number.

"Yello?" said Andy's voice after a few rings.

"Long time, no talk," said Mack, a little cautiously, not sure how Andy would receive his second request for assistance.

"Damn, when I said we should keep in touch you really took that literally, didn't you?" Andy laughed. He sounded surprised to hear from Mack again so soon.

"Yeah, well, I've got one more night in town. Not sure when I will be back down this way in Georgia. Thought maybe we could have one last beer together."

"By one last beer, I'm assuming you mean you have another project you want my help on?"

"Yes and no. The beer *is* the project. We sit in a bar and have a drink. Then, at a certain point, we get up and walk out. Project over. And you go home to Atlanta with very heavy pockets."

"Riiight. You think I'm stupid? It's never that easy."

Mack chuckled. "Maybe I'm overselling it a tad."

"If all we're doing's drinking a beer, why do you need me to be there with you? Hell, I'll drink a beer in my living room, and you can send me a check. How's at sound?"

Mack could not help smiling at Andy's brash humor. He paused for a few seconds to think. He would feel a lot better knowing someone had his back in McKearney's, just in case anything did go sideways. Plus, he genuinely wanted to help his old Navy buddy. Andy had been by his side through some tough times in the service. Mack knew this job could be a chance to hand Andy a life-changing sum of money that would make a difference to his family.

"What would you say to one hundred?"

"Come on, Abbott. A hunnerd bucks? You pulling my leg, man? I know they're paying you a lot more than that," said Andy, sounding more than a little perturbed. "Anyway, Olivia would never let me leave for another day, even if I wanted to."

"A hundred grand," said Mack.

Andy swallowed. "You serious? Don't joke about that kind of money."

"I'm serious. Drive to Savannah. Drink a beer. Make six figures."

"Jobs don't pay like that unless they are very illegal or very dangerous."

Mack could not deny Andy's point. He'd had the same thought himself. The work was certainly illegal. He wondered if the danger level was higher than his employer led him to believe.

"I won't bullshit you, it's very illegal. Could be dangerous, too. But not if it goes like it's supposed to. The money is designed to make up for the risk, though."

"That's more than two years' salary for me," said Andy.

"I could use your help, old friend. But I understand if you can't."

"You kidding me? I'd be an idiot to turn down a payday like that. I trust you."

Mack bowed his head. He felt a twinge of guilt for involving his friend in a dangerous job, especially considering Andy had a family.

"Thanks, Andy. It will be fine. We will both walk away with a pile of cash." Mack wondered if his words of reassurance were intended more for Andy or for himself.

In the motel bathroom, the shower turned off with a squeaking noise followed by dripping water. Mack heard the shower curtain slide on its rings along the metal bar.

"I gotta run, Andy. Tonight, about eleven. Meet me at the motel room. Bring those heaters."

"They're still in the Tahoe. See you then."

Mack hung up the phone just as Avery exited the bathroom wrapped in a tight towel that barely covered her wet body.

15

Rafe Lucas paced his office, walking from wall to wall, straightening items on his shelves and desk. He periodically lifted a corner of the tarp that concealed the bricks of cocaine behind his desk, checking compulsively to see that nothing was out of place. A loaded shotgun leaned against the desk, in addition to the pistol Rafe carried in his jacket pocket. When he could no longer stand the cramped room, he examined both weapons once more, and then gave up the office for the open floor plan of the bar.

Rafe's nerves were bothering him more than usual. Sitting on several million dollars of pure cocaine for the last few days had done a number on his mental health. He had a huge chunk of money invested in the stash. The deal he had arranged for the following day could not fail, or else he would be screwed.

"Bankrupt or in prison for life," Rafe muttered to himself as he locked the office door. A third option crossed his mind, but he pushed the finality of that outcome from his head.

The bar was about half full. A typical crowd for a

Monday night at—Rafe checked his watch—ten p.m. Rafe nodded at the bartender as he passed the row of stools.

Alonzo the bartender wiped the bar down with a damp, white cloth. He nodded back at the bar's owner.

Rafe wondered how much Alonzo knew about the contents of the back office. Surely, he had an inkling that something was happening—Alonzo wasn't stupid. Rafe never spent this much time in the bar. Alonzo himself had commented earlier on how frequently he had seen the boss lately. Rafe watched Alonzo's forearm tighten as he swept the cloth along the shiny wood bar top.

"How's business tonight?" Rafe asked his bartender.

Alonzo shrugged. "Nothing special so far. It's a Monday." He wrung out the towel into a red bucket behind the bar and hung it up on a brass handle to dry.

"Have you seen anything," Rafe chose his words carefully, "weird at all tonight?"

Alonzo squinted, trying to interpret his boss's question. "Weird?"

"You know, like out of the ordinary or anything?"

"I don't think so," said Alonzo, still trying to make sense of Rafe's implication.

"Good. That's good." Rafe tapped his knuckles on the bar. "Nobody who seemed shady or out of place?"

Alonzo's face brightened. He nodded, thinking he finally understood. "Oh, no, sir. That was just a one-time thing, I think. The guy with the stolen credit card? I don't expect he'll be back. Shame he got through half a fifth of Johnny Blue before we caught him. I'm real sorry about that. I should have called in his card first so the bank could flag it."

Rafe nodded. "Good. Yes, that's right. It's okay, Alonzo. Like I told you, it happens. Some people are real pieces of shit. You never know for sure who's who until they show you."

Alonzo poured a martini from a metal shaker. He carried it to the end of the bar for a woman with glazed eyes and a rumpled dress. She looked like she had been drinking since happy hour.

"Just be on the lookout, though, will you?" said Rafe when Alonzo returned to his end of the bar.

"For shady people?"

Rafe coughed, realizing that he sounded a little paranoid. "Right, I'm sure it's fine. Nothing to worry about. Let me know if you see anything. I'm going outside to smoke a cigar."

Alonzo shook his head slowly as he watched through the large front windows while his boss glanced repeatedly from side to side and then walked to the alley where he squinted into the darkness for several seconds.

Alonzo tilted a pint glass under the Guinness tap. He pulled the lever that released the dark beer. Watching the black liquid fill the clear glass, he said under his breath, "Dude needs to quit sampling his merch."

A Monday night at the strip club was always unpredictable. It could be completely dead because all the men had burned their cash over the weekend and had to spend Monday at home with their wives. Or, on the other hand, the club could be jammed full of guys blowing off steam to take the edge off a shitty start to the week. So far, this

Monday was shaping up to be the slow kind at The Fuzzy Peach.

Avery bounced around the handful of occupied tables, trying in vain to convince the Monday cheapskates to part with some of their cash. She tried all her regular moves—lap sitting, sexy eyes, dirty talk—but had little luck.

No sense getting on stage on a night like this one. It would be a waste of her energy. Instead, Avery let the newer girls and the traveling dancers from out of state take turns. She had only performed once so far, and that was because the DJ had called her out by name and coaxed her up on stage. Best to stay on the DJ's good side so he doesn't make her job any harder than it needs to be.

Taking a break from the fruitless circuit, Avery sauntered up to the bar. She leaned her elbows on the dark wood. She wore large hoop earrings that dangled nearly to her jawline.

"Rum and Coke, hold the rum," she said to the bartender with a smile.

The bartender glanced over Avery's shoulder and scanned the club. "I don't see Leonard around. You want me to put something in it?"

Avery smacked the gum in her mouth. She blew a bubble and sucked it back in. "Naw, not right now. If it stays this dead in here, I may hit you up later though."

Avery sipped the fizzy drink. The carbonation burned her nose as she tilted the glass. She considered calling it an early night when, out of the blue, Liam entered the club with a group of rowdy-looking college guys.

"There's my payday," Avery said to the bartender. She nodded at the door. "Look at all that fresh meat."

The bartender shook his head. "Go in for the kill, girl."

Avery winked at him and smiled. She set her glass on the bar and headed straight for the group of young men. She caught them just as they sat down at a row of tables near the back of the club.

"Y'all picked a good night to come in," Avery greeted the college guys, making a point to engage each one of them physically in some way.

"Why is that?" asked one guy wearing a Savannah State sweatshirt.

"Cause I'm here," answered Avery with a smile. "Obviously."

"She's the one I told you about," said Liam to the Savannah State guy. "Watch out for her."

"I don't know what Liam told you about me but I'm sure it's all true."

Avery nudged her way into the group. With a quick motion, she swung one of her bare legs high and straddled Savannah State. She sat down with her legs around his waist, facing him, her mouth only inches from his. She leaned forward and whispered in his ear, "Yes, you better watch out for me." Then she gave the kid a quick peck on the cheek and stood up. "What are you boys drinking?" she asked the group.

After a few stunned seconds during which the college guys gathered themselves, they managed to put in drink orders.

Avery strutted off to relay their requests to the cocktail waitress. She had done her part. Now, she only had to swing back by later, after they'd had a few rounds. Get a couple drinks in them and she would have no trouble picking them off.

Andy pounded on the motel room door and shouted, "This is the police! Open up!"

Although Mack knew Andy was coming, his raucous greeting still made Mack jump. He clicked off the television. Mack opened the door, saying, "Officer, I'm glad you're here. There's a crazy man pounding on the door of my motel room at eleven p.m."

Andy laughed when he saw Mack. "Hey, if you don't want me here, I can drive back to Atlanta and get in bed with my wife."

"Get your ass in here," said Mack, giving Andy a slap on the shoulder. "Don't worry, we'd all rather be in bed with your wife right now."

Andy shot a look at Mack. He stepped inside the motel room. "You didn't say what to wear. I've got blackout gear in the truck if we need it."

"Let's hope we don't need that." Mack glanced at Andy's dark blue jeans and Atlanta Falcons t-shirt. "You'll be fine. But how are you planning to carry a piece with just a t-shirt?"

Andy shrugged. "I brought a shoulder holster and a jacket to wear over it." He hoisted a duffle bag from the floor with both hands and tossed it on one of the beds. The sound of the thick, black zipper sliced through the silent room.

"What are you thinking we need?" Andy asked as he began laying firearms on the bed next to the duffle. He unloaded several handguns, a couple shotguns, and the

AK-47 assault rifle he had from the other night.

"I knew I could count on you to go completely overboard with weapons," Mack laughed.

"That's what I do, baby." Andy dug around in a corner of the bag until his hands found a hard cylinder, which he extracted from the bag and promptly displayed like a waiter showing a bottle of wine.

"You gotta be kidding me," said Mack. "A grenade? Is that live?"

"What do you think?"

"Do not bring that damn thing. It's awesome, but do not bring it."

"Got some flashbangs, too. Those be better?"

Mack thought for a second. "This is supposed to be pretty low-key. I can't imagine we would need anything like that but, what the hell, bring one. Non-lethal. Could come in handy if things get hairy."

Andy grinned, glad to know his excessive firepower was appreciated.

Mack picked up one of the handguns. He released the clip and checked it for ammo. Satisfied, he slapped the clip back in place and tucked the weapon into the back of his pants to see how it fit. He removed the gun and laid it on the table.

"Do you want to know the plan?" Mack asked.

"I'm all ears."

Mack took a seat at the table. "There's an Irish bar about a mile down the road by the river. Remember the delivery we staked out the other night?"

Andy nodded.

Mack continued, "Well, the stash got moved."

"Moved from the warehouse?"

"That's right. It's sitting in a back office at this Irish bar I'm telling you about."

"Must be a big office to hold that much blow."

"From what I can tell there isn't much in the office except for a small desk and a big stack of drugs."

Andy whistled and shook his head. "Man, I knew this was gonna be more than just getting a beer."

"It's not as bad as it sounds. We aren't doing any of the heavy lifting. Our part is kind of like a lookout. We take a seat in the bar for an hour or so till they're about to close. Then we give the all-clear to somebody outside. After that, we get the hell outta there."

"And collect our giant paychecks."

"Exactly."

"The guys in this bar, they have no idea what's coming?"

"They better not, is all I can say about that."

"You're not exactly exuding confidence about the plan here, bub."

"My employer says it's a complete surprise attack. They will never see it coming."

"Guess we'll see about that."

Mack shared Andy's suspicion but did not want to stoke the fear.

"On top of that, a source says these guys are planning a big drug deal for Tuesday night. So tomorrow they'll be on high alert," said Mack. "As long as we hit them tonight, we should be catching them off guard."

"Ah," said Andy solemnly. "Just for my own peace of mind, let's specify that *we* ain't hitting anybody. Lookouts only, right?"

"Right. That's what I meant."

Andy racked a Beretta and laid it on the bed. "I don't mind these M9s, but I think I still prefer my SIG."

Mack nodded, remembering the handgun they had used in the service. "It's a reliable weapon," he said.

"When do we go?" said Andy.

"We have about an hour before we need to be at the bar. I don't want to sit in there too long and draw suspicion."

"Fair enough," said Andy. "Want to go over the plan again, think through some alternatives just in case?"

"Good idea. I'll make us a pot of this shitty motel coffee."

The college boys made no secret about their competition regarding who would take Avery home. Little did they know, none of them stood a chance.

Avery picked them off for private dances one by one. They didn't tip great, but the cost of the dances added up.

Liam periodically disappeared with one or two of the guys—usually to the bathroom, where Avery knew exactly what was happening. Each time Liam left the table Avery felt a twinge of jealousy. She wished she could have a bump from Liam's stash.

Finally, after a few rounds of lap dances, Avery scooted around the vinyl booth so she could sit next to Liam.

"These frat boys must have tiny bladders," she said as she snuggled her rear against Liam's hip.

Liam shot her a confused look.

"All that time they're spending in the bathroom," she said, waiting for Liam to get the joke.

"You're so funny," said Liam with a fake laugh. "Maybe they're in there comparing peckers."

Avery scowled. "Could be. How'd you stack up? I bet Savannah State puts you to shame. Look at that big ol' boy." Avery pointed with her lips at the kid wearing the sweatshirt. "I bet he's packing heat."

"Nobody ever accused you of being polite, did they?"

"Pffft. Says the boy paying naked women to sit on his lap."

"You see me paying for anything?" said Liam, talking cocky with his head full of uppers.

"Come to think of it, no, I don't. Let's fix that." Avery held out her open palm.

Liam laughed. "You're crazy."

Avery flipped her fingers in a hand-it-over motion.

"If I'm paying you something I'm getting a lap dance out of it."

Avery rolled her eyes. "You and I both know you brought these boys here because I'm working, and you knew I would show them a good time. How much blow have they bought tonight while I'm keeping them entertained?"

Liam sulked. "That doesn't mean I owe you anything."

"Fine. Bye." Avery stood up quickly.

"Wait," Liam pleaded. "Come on. Gimme one dance. I'll tip you good." He glanced down at Avery's chest while he spoke.

Avery thought about it. "Plus some powder."

"Fine with me. Come to the bathroom real quick."

"I can't. They'd fire my ass if I went in the men's room with a customer. Put the bag in your shirt pocket and I'll do some bumps during your dance."

Liam raised his eyebrows. He let Avery lead him back to one of the private rooms.

Unlike the dance Avery had given to Mack a few days earlier, with Liam's dance she simply went through the motions. Like she had with the college boys, she removed her clothing and writhed her body to the music, but she made no effort to engage emotionally in the act.

Most of her customers couldn't tell the difference whether she meant it or faked it. They were too drunk or stupid or indifferent to notice. All they cared about was that a beautiful naked woman rubbed her body against them for a few minutes.

"You know you've never actually given me a dance," Liam said a few seconds into Avery's routine.

Avery shrugged. "I don't usually grind on my friends for fun. Tends to make things a little awkward."

"But I'm more than just a friend?"

"Sure you are, sweetie." Avery leaned over with her breasts in Liam's face and kissed him on the cheek. As she did so, she deftly dipped a fingernail into the open baggie in Liam's shirt pocket and lifted it to her nose.

"Is this that good stuff?"

Liam smiled. "Yup."

"Perfect." Avery sniffed the powder from her finger. "Did you go back to McKearney's today?" she asked.

"Yeah. For a little refill, but I'm almost out again. Shit goes fast."

Avery had her back turned to Liam. She looked at him

over her shoulder. "I thought he was supposed to be selling it all to one buyer?"

"Something like that. Tomorrow, I think. Whatever is left over. I don't know how much he has. I'm gonna try and get another key tonight if he'll let me."

Chills ran down Avery's back as she remembered Mack's advice to keep Liam away from the bar.

"You're going back over there this late? Why not wait till tomorrow?"

Liam cocked his head sideways and looked at Avery. "What do you care?"

Avery turned her face away from Liam so he wouldn't see her look of concern. "I mean, I don't. Whatever. I was just hoping you and your college boys would stay here all night. You know, keep giving me money."

Liam scrunched his eyes. He studied Avery's facial expressions. After a few seconds, he sat up straight on the couch.

"You know something, don't you?"

"What? No. What do you mean?"

Liam spun Avery around to face him. "Bullshit. I know you. What's going on tonight? Where's your boy from the bar? The clean-cut motherfucker." Liam tightened his grip on Avery's arm. "Did you tell him something about me?"

Avery jerked her arm free from Liam's grasp. "Chill out. You're too coked up." She used her body language to relax Liam. "Don't be so suspicious."

Liam watched her out the side of his eye, searching for any clues of a betrayal. Eventually, he lowered his back to the couch slowly.

"If you told that dude something and I get in trouble

for it…you know Rafe Lucas doesn't play. He'll kill me. For real. Don't bullshit me."

"I'm not!" said Avery. "Just stay here with me tonight. Let's do some blow and have fun. I'll get the bartender to send over a bottle of champagne to impress your little boyfriends."

Liam stayed quiet during the rest of the dance. He seemed pacified but not entirely convinced.

Turning Avery's words over in his mind, Liam plied her with cocaine and got her chattering about the college guys again. He told her which ones in the bunch were virgins, and which were most likely to cough up extra cash. He wanted to keep her distracted.

When the song ended, Liam peeled off a handful of bills from the giant stack in his pocket and offered them to Avery. She took the money without counting it, knowing by the stack's sight and weight that Liam had paid her more than the going rate for a lap dance.

A few minutes later, when Liam felt sure Avery was preoccupied with other customers, he slipped out of the club. He got in his car, a baby blue 1991 Honda CR-X hatchback. From the glovebox he removed a Nokia cell phone and pressed a button so the backlit numbers illuminated with green light. The device always made Liam smile with delight. He liked using the cell phone in public because it made him feel important.

Liam pushed the soft buttons, inputting the phone number of the back office at McKearney's. He stuck a finger in his exposed ear to block the thumping bass sound that echoed across the parking lot from the club.

"Yeah?" said Rafe Lucas's gruff voice.

"Hey, it's Liam."

The phone crackled as Rafe exhaled through his nose. "I told you, nothing more until later this week. What you got today was the last of it for a while."

"I know. It's not about that. I got something for *you*."

"For me? I'm listening," said Rafe suspiciously.

"I think somebody's gonna—I got reason to believe that—" Liam realized he had no proof of anything. For that matter, he wasn't even sure exactly what he was warning Rafe about. "Somebody might be gonna hit you tonight."

"What do you mean?" Rafe asked with growing concern. He had already been on high alert. Any information that supported his paranoia pushed him closer to the edge.

"There's a new guy in town. He was at your bar last night. I don't trust him."

"Who?"

"Clean-cut guy. Doesn't say much. He was with a, uh, with a girl I know."

"I don't remember him. You think he's trouble?"

"Yeah, maybe so."

"Maybe?"

"I don't know, Rafe, I just got a bad feeling. Something ain't right. I think that dude is up to something." Liam played it careful about his source, not wanting to implicate Avery. "Somebody said he knows more than he should. I don't trust him."

"Who's somebody?"

Liam hesitated. "Just somebody I know. It's a reliable source. All I'm saying is, if you have anything at the bar, I'd get it out of there. Keep an eye out. It could be nothing, but I wanted to give you a heads up. You know, since we're friends and all." Liam added the last line to ingratiate himself as much as possible.

Rafe did not respond.

"You still there?" said Liam.

"Yeah, just thinking. It's probably nothing." Rafe seemed distracted as he spoke. "Anyway, I don't really have anything at the bar," he lied. "That batch is almost gone. Probably nothing to worry about."

Liam rolled his eyes, seeing through Rafe's line. "Whatever, bro. Just trying to help."

"That's fine. Yeah, I appreciate it. I do. Thanks for calling," Rafe said and then he hung up the phone.

"Dick," said Liam. He returned his cell phone to the glovebox, did a bump, and then went back in the club.

As soon as Rafe Lucas hung up with Liam, he dialed Bull's number. Rafe walked around his desk, stretching the phone cord taut. He extended his leg and closed the office door with his foot.

Bull answered in two rings. "Yes, sir?" His large fingers accidentally mashed a few buttons on the cell phone Rafe had given him, resulting in a series of loud beeps. "Sorry, haven't got the hang of this thing yet," he said in between beeps.

Rafe grimaced. "You still outside?"

"Bout a block down. All clear here."

"Don't worry about that anymore. We need to move again. I need you back here now."

"Huh?"

"We're taking it back to the warehouse. Somebody blew our cover here at the bar."

"Right now?"

"Yes. I'm calling Jerry and Steve soon as I get off with you. Back the truck right up to the door and start moving fast. I want the load out of here by midnight."

Rafe looked at his watch. That only gave them twenty minutes. It would be pushing it, but he wanted to light a fire under Bull's ass.

"Okay, I'm coming," said Bull.

Rafe hung up and immediately called Jerry's number, hoping Jerry would answer the phone and not his wife.

"Who in hell is calling my house at this hour?" said an angry Billie Musen into Rafe's ear.

Rafe hung his head. "Put Jerry on, please."

"I asked you a question."

"Mrs. Musen, I don't have time for this right now. I need to talk to Jerry."

"Are you the one dropped him off the other morning, sick as a dog?"

Rafe cursed under his breath. He heard the box truck beeping in the alley as Bull backed it up. "I don't know anything about that, ma'am. Jerry and I are business associates. I'm the one who pays your rent payment. Put Jerry on."

"According to the landlord, ain't nobody paying our rent right now, so it sounds to me like you're full of shit."

"Jesus Christ."

"He don't have nothing to do with it. Anyways Jerry's in bed. You leave off of him, he's got enough to worry about right now. He's going out tomorrow to get a job, whether he knows it or not."

Bull knocked on the office door and let himself in.

Rafe pointed at the stack of kilos and mouthed the words, "Load it up."

Bull began to make quick trips to the back door where he stacked the product in the box truck.

"Mrs. Musen, I'm not going to ask nicely again. If Jerry's in bed, wake him up and put him on the phone."

"I don't know who you think you're talking to but—"

"Billie, who's on the goddamn phone?" said Jerry's voice in the background, sounding groggy and irritated.

"Go back to bed," said Billie.

"Give it here," said Jerry.

"Quit! I'm hanging up!" shouted Billie.

"The hell you are."

"You gonna wake up the kids!"

Rafe pulled the phone away from his ear while Jerry and his wife scuffled and shouted obscenities at each other. Finally, Jerry got control of the receiver.

"This is Jerry," he said, panting from exertion.

"Jerry, I need you at the bar right now," said Rafe.

"Aw, man, I'm asleep. Can't it wait till tomorrow?"

Rafe gritted his teeth. "Get your ass here or you can kiss your cut goodbye."

"Hold up, now. You can't do that," Jerry protested.

"If we don't get the product out of the bar tonight, none of us will have a cut. This is serious, Jerry, or I wouldn't be calling you."

Jerry's tone sobered. "Really? Alright, I'm coming."

"Hurry. Bull is already working on it," said Rafe. "Do

you have a piece?"

Jerry swallowed. "Yeah, I got one."

"Bring it."

Rafe hung up the phone. He quickly called Steve—a much smoother conversation—and then he joined Bull at the task of loading the truck.

Jerry pulled his boots on over his bleached, white tube socks. He sat in a wooden chair in the kitchen and listened to his wife harangue him. Billie raised her whispered voice as loud as she could without waking the kids.

"You said you were done with all the late night running around," said Billie. "Your kids are in there sleeping. Are they gonna wake up again tomorrow to their daddy puking in the toilet all morning? Your little girl had to pee outside this morning cause her daddy couldn't get his head out of the toilet seat long enough for her to do a tinkle. *Outside*. Doesn't that shame you?"

Jerry pulled his pant legs down over his leather cowboy boots. "Yes," he said.

"Well, it oughta. I'm ashamed for you. It's unfit behavior for a grown man."

Jerry put his hands on his denimed thighs and looked at his wife. "Heat me up some coffee, will ya?" He nodded at the glass carafe on the counter that contained half a pot of black sludge leftover from the morning's brew.

Billie poured the coffee into a saucepan and set it on a stove burner. She switched on the burner without missing a beat. "And think about me, Jerry. I don't know what you're out there doing, but I know it ain't working a normal job.

It's almost midnight, for godsake. Where you going to work at this hour?" She took a coffee mug from the cabinet and slammed it on the counter next to the glowing stove coil. "How do I know you aren't arrested or dead somewhere on the side of the road? I'm lying in bed worrying all night. Think about it, Jerry."

"Honey, I can't reason with you when you're like this. It's gonna be alright. I have to go protect something belongs to us. I'll be back later. Tomorrow night at this time it'll all be over. Just hold on a little bit longer, will you?"

"Protect what? We don't have nothing worth protecting."

Billie poured the steaming coffee from the pan into the coffee mug. She sniffed the liquid, made a face, and set the mug in front of Jerry.

"Nothing you need to worry about. It's a deal I'm working on."

"Nothing to worry about, he says," muttered Billie. "I can't do nothing *but* worry anymore."

Jerry sipped the coffee. The burnt, acidic flavor of the black sludge caused his throat to tighten when he swallowed. He blew across the mug to cool the liquid and then chugged it as fast as possible.

"Don't wait up for me, honey. I'll be back as soon as I can."

Jerry stood up. He walked over to his wife, reaching out his arms in the dim light of the stovetop bulb.

Billie allowed her husband's arms to encircle her. She leaned into his chest when he pulled her close. Jerry kissed the top of his wife's head. He set the empty coffee mug in the sink.

Jerry opened the kitchen door. He took one more look back at his wife and smiled at her. Billie watched him leave, her eyes tired, her shoulders stooped with worry and exhaustion.

Jerry unlocked the rotten shed in the backyard. When he pulled the door open it felt as though he might yank the entire dilapidated structure to the ground. The wood groaned under the weight of itself.

Jerry felt along the inner wall of the shed. He squinted in the moonlight until he found his shotgun. He loaded as many shells as the weapon would hold and then stuffed a handful of extras in his pocket.

Jerry closed the door without bothering to replace the padlock. There was nothing left in the shed worth stealing.

Sitting in his Chevrolet pickup truck with the moon glowing above his steering wheel, Jerry laid his shotgun across the passenger seat. He prayed the engine would start.

The truck fired on the first try, for once. Jerry shifted the lever to drive. He felt the truck lurch under the depressed brake pedal.

He had never shot a man before. He wondered what it felt like.

16

"Ready to do this?" Mack raised his eyebrows, questioning Andy from across the motel room.

"Ready as I'm gonna be."

The two men checked their weapons once more and holstered them, donning loose jackets to cover the bulging handguns.

"We'll take the van since it's a rental with a fake name," said Mack. "I don't want anything in the vicinity that can be traced back to either of us."

"Man, I've resisted the pressure to get a minivan for years because I thought it would make me boring, and here I go—the most exciting night I've had in years—riding in a minivan!"

Mack chuckled. "Remember, we're hoping for *no* excitement tonight."

"Right. That's what I meant." Andy opened the van's door. He stood looking over the roof at Mack's eyes. "Maybe just a little excitement, though, eh?"

Mack shook his head. He slid into the driver's seat and shut the door. "Get in," he said across the center console.

Andy sighed and took his seat.

The engine started and the dashboard lights came on. The clock read 12:04.

A sudden thought struck Mack.

"Hang on a second," he said, climbing out of the van.

"You getting cold feet?" chided Andy.

The van's headlights shone on Mack as he re-entered the motel room. He went straight for the tracking device and switched it on.

It took a few seconds for the machine to power up. Mack ran through the plan again in his mind while he waited: sit at the bar, order one drink, sip it for an hour, case the back office. When all is clear, give the signal. Then he and Andy would get out of there.

The tracking device beeped when the screen loaded. Mack studied the display carefully, examining the green dot on the rudimentary map. The stash had not moved. The overhead map still located the tracking beacon near the back of the bar, although it seemed to be closer to the alley than Mack remembered. Must be something a little off in the GPS, he figured. The dot wasn't more than a fraction of an inch from where he remembered it.

Satisfied that nothing had changed, and that Rafe Lucas had not caught wind of the plan, Mack turned off the tracker. He headed back out to the minivan where Andy waited impatiently to start their operation.

Jerry parked his truck on the street. He walked up the dark alley next to the bar. When he rounded the corner, he saw Bull, Steve, and Lucas already in a flurry of activity. The men carried the wrapped kilos, rushing from the back door to the box truck, barely bothering to conceal their cargo.

"Y'all better be glad I ain't the po-lice coming around this corner," announced Jerry. "You're asking for it carrying that shit wide open like that."

"Bout time you showed up," growled Bull.

"Moose, go in there and get those last few keys. We're almost done," said Rafe Lucas.

"What's all the rush about?"

"Steve will fill you in on the way back," said Rafe before disappearing into the bar.

Jerry followed Lucas to the office. "Lucas, tell me what's going on," he said. "You know, I got as much riding on this deal as you do."

Lucas laughed in Jerry's face. "Are you dimwitted? All this coke is mine, Jerry. Every bit of it. You're getting a cut because I'm giving you one. You better get that through your thick skull. If I decide to keep your cut, then you're shit out of luck. You aren't in charge here."

Jerry stared at Lucas without answering. He gritted his teeth but did not look away.

"That's what I thought," said Lucas. He handed the last two keys to Jerry. "Now get out there and drive the truck back to the warehouse with Steve. Steve's gonna drive his car and bring you both back here once you dump the truck. Back it up against the warehouse door, and then you two get your asses back here as fast as you can. We got somebody thinks we're pushovers coming to visit us tonight. We're gonna let 'em know we aren't."

Jerry nodded. His face burned with anger at Rafe's lecture. He broke his stare from Rafe's forehead and frowned.

Jerry took the last two kilos and loaded them in the truck. A few minutes later, he was following Steve's Trans Am, rolling over the bridge toward the island.

What Mack didn't know when he checked the tracking device from his motel room was that the beacon had been loaded into the back of the box truck along with all the remaining kilos of cocaine.

Seconds after Mack turned off the screen, Jerry drove the truck out of the alley next to McKearney's and turned right on the river road.

Steve in his Trans Am and Jerry in the white box truck passed the motel parking lot while Mack and Andy waited for a Buick to pull out of the parking spot that blocked the Dodge Caravan's exit.

Five minutes later, Mack parked the van on the street across from the bar. He and Andy shuffled across the dark street in silence, heading into the bar at 12:15 a.m.

In the office, Lucas laid out every weapon he owned on his desk—three handguns, two shotguns, an assortment of knives, and a Louisville Slugger. Next to each gun he piled additional ammo.

Bull entered the office carrying a thick, rolled blanket. He laid the blanket on the desk and unrolled the flap to expose an Uzi submachine gun.

Lucas whistled. "Nice." He surveyed their stock of weapons. "We're gonna teach the bastards a lesson, aren't we?"

Bull nodded.

"Hope those two dimwits hustle back here," said Lucas. "We got more guns than we have hands."

Bull unsheathed one of the hunting knifes. Feeling the blade with his fingertip, he nodded approvingly.

"How many customers are out there?" said Lucas.

"Seven or eight at the tables, couple guys at the bar."

"Good. Not too many then. I'd like to close early and get them out of here, but I don't want to tip anybody off to anything." Lucas gripped the baseball bat. He took a few mock swings. "We close at two. I can have Alonzo do last call at 1:30."

"When's the hit supposed to come?"

"Don't know. That's why we need Jerry and Steve to get their asses back here. What I want you to do is sit at a table where you can see the front door and wait. I'm gonna put Steve in the alley and Jerry hiding in the bathroom by the office."

Bull nodded assent. He re-wrapped his Uzi in the blanket and placed it in an empty liquor box. He added the box to a stack of beer cases and used a hand truck to wheel the stack up front. Bull deposited the boxes next to the bar.

"Rafe said to restock your beer," Bull grunted at Alonzo.

Alonzo looked at him quizzically. "He thinks I don't know that?" Alonzo glanced at the stack of boxes. "Man, how many O'Doul's you think I sell in a day?"

"Don't shoot the messenger," said Bull. He scanned the bar. When no one was looking, he lifted the top box from the stack and quickly set it on the floor. He used his foot to slide the box over against the wall by a table in the corner of the room.

"You might as well wheel that stack on back 'cause I can't use any of that crap," said Alonzo.

Bull ignored him, instead taking a seat at the corner table where he had deposited his Uzi box.

"There's not enough pay in Savannah to deal with the dumb bullshit that goes on around here," muttered Alonzo. He draped a hand towel over his shoulder and strolled down the bar to greet the two new customers who had just joined him.

"Evenin', gentlemen. What are we drinking tonight?"

Mack and Andy both nodded at Alonzo.

"Hey, I remember you," said Alonzo. "You the one with the hottie, came in last night, was it?"

Mack smiled, his face turning red. He cringed a little, not expecting to be recognized so easily. "Yeah," he said.

"Ain't nothing to be embarrassed about. That girl was alright, man. Where's she at tonight?"

"She, uh, I'm just in town for work. I don't know her very well," Mack stammered.

Alonzo grinned. "Oh, I see what you're saying. Listen, no judgment here, my man. You do your thing."

Andy squinted his eyes at Mack, suspiciously. "Couple Buds sounds good to me," he said. "How bout you, Don Juan?" He jabbed Mack's ribcage with his fist.

"Yeah. Couple Buds, please."

"Coming right up," said Alonzo. He spun on his heel and knelt to reach in the beer cooler under the bar.

Andy continued to stare at Mack through squinted eyes. "Well, you gonna tell me, or do I have to ask?"

Mack shrugged. "Tell you what?"

"Brother, you might as well drop that act. Who's the broad?"

Mack's face broke into another smile. He tried to crouch down into his jacket to hide his red cheeks.

"Oh shit, you like this girl, don't you?" prodded Andy.

"I don't know."

"You do! You son of a gun. Where'd you meet her?"

Mack hesitated.

"Just tell me and get it over with."

"You met her, too."

Andy knitted his brow, trying to remember.

"From the club."

A look of surprise spread across Andy's face. "You mean a stripper?"

"I think they prefer to be called dancers."

Andy burst out laughing. "Oh my god, Abbott, you're dating a stripper?"

"Stop being so loud," said Mack. "Remember why we're here."

Andy forced the smile off his face. He lowered his voice. "Which girl is it? The one with the big ass?"

Mack frowned. "I guess that would be one way to refer to her."

Andy poked Mack again with his fist. "My fault, Abbott, I didn't mean to trash-talk your girlfriend."

"She's not my girlfriend."

"Hey, you're the one who took her out to a bar last night. How'm I supposed to classify that?"

Mack didn't answer.

"You get lucky? Wait, did you take her back to that sleazy motel room?"

"That's about enough of that," said Mack.

"You dog."

Alonzo placed the Budweiser bottles in front of Mack and Andy. "Just the beers for now, guys?"

"Yes, thanks," said Mack. He tossed a twenty on the bar. "You can keep it."

"Thank you kindly," said Alonzo. "Just holler if you need anything else." He palmed the cash and strolled to the other end of the bar.

"What's her name?" said Andy, ignoring Mack's request to drop the subject.

"Avery."

"Interesting name." Andy took a swig of beer. "Joking aside, she was by far the diamond in that rough. You got the good one."

"Thanks, I think."

"Don't be so cynical, Abbott. Loosen up a little. Have you some fun. So what, you bagged a hot stripper. I'd give anything to be able to do that again."

"Fair enough," said Mack. His thoughts turned to Avery now that her name had been invoked. He wondered what she was doing. Probably working, he figured. They had not spoken since she left the motel room that morning. Mack wondered if he would ever see her again. He would have to get out of town quickly once the hit went through. Hanging around Savannah would be too risky—especially now that the bartender could ID him. As for Avery, maybe Mack could catch her on his way out of town. He hoped he could. He wanted to see her again.

"There you go again," said Andy. "Brooding. You're too damn serious, man."

Mack snapped out of his daydream. He swallowed a gulp of Budweiser. "Maybe so," he said.

The radio blasted REO Speedwagon's "Ridin' the Storm Out" as humid night air blew across Jerry's face through the open passenger window of Steve's Trans Am.

Steve thumped his palms on the steering wheel, moving his hands along with the drums. He hammered the gas pedal. The Trans Am shot over the bridge back to downtown Savannah. The city lights loomed in the distance.

Jerry leaned over and hollered to Steve over the wind and music. "What are you gonna do with your share?"

Steve cocked his ear toward Jerry.

"I said, what are you gonna do with the money?" Jerry repeated, louder this time.

Steve turned the volume down a notch. "That's easy," he said, also shouting to be heard. "It's my 'fuck you' money."

"Fuck who?"

"I don't know, anybody, I guess. Anybody tries to tell me what to do from here on," said Steve. "I got a pile of cash, I can just tell em fuck you."

Jerry nodded slowly. "Can't argue with that."

Steve reached for the volume knob to turn it back up. Jerry caught him just in time, saying, "Me, I got bigger plans."

"Yeah? Like what?"

"I got a wife and two kids at home, for starters," Jerry said. A twinge of guilt washed over him as he pondered his dire financial state. He envied Steve's carefree situation. No attachments, no responsibilities. "Yeah, I'm gonna get us a better house. Better than the shithole we're in now. I'm tired of dealing with asshole landlords."

Steve kept his finger on the volume knob, waiting for Jerry to finish talking. His left hand drummed the steering wheel.

"My little girl is smart, too," said Jerry. "She's gonna go to college someday. The way I figure is, if I put money away for her now, one day I can pay for her school."

"Real heartwarming story, Moose," Steve said sarcastically. "Get your mind ready. We're almost back to the bar." He let his finger roll across the dial and REO Speedwagon shot back to a non-conversational volume. The dashboard clock read 12:43 a.m.

Rafe Lucas strolled into the main room of the bar. He glanced at Bull. He spotted the cardboard box that contained the Uzi at Bull's feet. Bull nodded almost imperceptibly at Lucas.

Working hard to play it cool, Lucas leaned an elbow on the bar. His eyes swept across the dim room, pausing momentarily on each of the few remaining patrons. Lucas tried to assess the threat level of each person in the bar. He looked for any signs of a pending attack.

Alonzo walked over to Lucas's corner of the bar, thinking his boss was summoning him. "You still here?" he asked.

The sound of Alonzo's voice startled Lucas. He jerked his head toward the bartender. "Huh? Oh yeah, just doing some bookkeeping."

Alonzo raised his chin in acknowledgement.

"Listen," said Lucas, "we might close up a little early tonight. Kind of dead in here."

"Fine by me. Just say the word."

Over Alonzo's shoulder, Lucas suddenly spotted Mack at the bar. The muscles in his back tightened. He recognized the guy. Was he the one Liam had tipped him off about? Clean-cut, quiet guy. It had to be him.

"What time you want to close?" asked Alonzo.

"I'll let you know." Lucas's voice trailed off when he heard the rear door open. Jerry and Steve had returned. He had to get them in position. If this guy sitting at the bar was his mark, the ambush could happen any minute.

In the club's backstage bathroom, Avery sat in a stall with the door closed. The black lace garter where she kept her cash was stretched to the brim with dollar bills. The thick wad expanded the elastic band so full that it dug into her thigh and left a mark on her skin.

Too much cash wasn't the worst problem to have. Liam's college friends were paying for dance after dance. And his cocaine stash had kept Avery flying high all night.

As she sat on the toilet seat counting her money, Avery's thoughts drifted to the man with whom she had spent the previous night. She knew something was going down that night at McKearney's. Judging by Mack's phone conversation that she had overheard while pretending to sleep, she could tell the plan was serious. Mack was plotting something, or at least his employer was plotting something.

Avery wondered how much Mack would be involved. She wondered if he would be in danger.

The thought of him getting hurt nagged at Avery. Mack had been nice to her. He treated her well, and he didn't seem to care about her profession. Plus, he was handsome and good in bed, which didn't hurt. She hoped he would be safe.

When her count reached $500, Avery stopped. She peeled off the bills. She folded them tightly and zipped them into a secret compartment in one of her hollow platform shoes.

The bathroom door creaked open. Avery heard high heels clicking on the tile floor. The voices of two women echoed around the fluorescent room. Avery listened through the stall as they talked about customers who tipped well, customers who tipped poorly, money, drugs, complaints about Leonard and the DJ—the usual strip club chatter for all the dancers at The Fuzzy Peach.

Avery counted the rest of her cash. She folded it in half and tucked it back in her garter. Avery rubbed the swollen indentation on her thigh, relieved to have some of the pressure taken off the tight elastic.

A craving for another bump sent a wave of panic through Avery's body. She felt the chill start in her scalp and spread down her neck and back. She hoped Liam was still out there.

Avery sat quietly, wishing the girls would leave her alone with her thoughts. She tried to remember what Liam had said about the cocaine supply at McKearney's. More coke than he had ever seen, or something like that. How much would that be? Tens of thousands of dollars' worth, certainly. A hundred thousand? A million? Avery wondered how much Mack's cut would be for whatever it was he was doing. For all she knew, Mack could be rich by the end of the night.

That is, unless Liam had tipped off the bar's owner about Mack. She shuddered when she remembered the nasty creep from last night who had tried to grope her in the back office. What was his name? Lucas? Why should Avery care what happens to that guy? Especially when a man she cared about—a potentially rich man she cared about—was on the other end of the deal.

Avery flushed the toilet. She unlocked the stall, said a quick hello to the two girls at the sink, and shuffled back out on the floor to find Liam.

"Did you tell him?" Avery demanded when she caught up with Liam. She stood at his table, hand on her waist, her hip cocked to the side. She stared down at the scrawny dealer, waiting for an answer.

Liam glanced nervously around the table, not wanting to appear weak in front of the guys. He didn't want to seem like the kind of man who would let a woman—a stripper—talk to him that way.

"Tell who, what?" he said, deepening his voice to project dominance.

Avery wasn't intimidated by Liam's display. "You know exactly what I'm talking about."

Liam slid around the vinyl booth. He stood up and took a few steps away from the table.

"I'll be right back," Liam said to the group as he left the

table. "Somebody get us a bottle of champagne."

Liam motioned for Avery to follow him, which she did.

"The only reason I said anything about the bar was so you'd stay away from there tonight," said Avery. "I didn't want you to get hurt or in trouble."

"And I appreciate that."

"But if you told anybody else what I said then you might be messing things up even worse." Avery's eyes darted around the neon room. A spinning disco ball reflected dancing spots across her bare shoulders.

"Why'm I supposed to give a shit what happens to your little boyfriend? Is that what you're worried about?"

Avery took a deep breath and exhaled, trying to calm herself down, aware that Leonard would be pissed if he caught her hassling a customer.

"He's not my boyfriend. He's just, just a friend. He's cool. I already told you that. Anyway, it's not only him. Other people might be involved…other people might get hurt." She added the last part so her warning would carry more weight.

Liam watched Avery, trying to discern how much she really knew. "Rafe Lucas is my meal ticket," he said. "And, in case you haven't figured it out, he's the one keeping you tits deep in this killer powder. I don't see why you'd want to go and mess that up."

Avery didn't respond.

"This clean-cut dude has you all twisted up, thinking he gives a shit about you. All he wants is the score on the other end of whatever scam he's running. He don't care about you any more than the information he can squeeze from you."

Another craving washed over Avery. Close to an hour since her last bump. She wanted more. The addiction clouded her perception, confused her ability to think rationally. She disagreed with Liam, but what if he was right? Was Mack just using her for information?

"You're wrong," Avery said.

Liam laughed. "Oh, am I? We'll see about that, I guess, won't we? See who still has your back tomorrow."

Avery shook her head, trying to convince herself of the truth as much as she was trying to convince Liam. She squinted her eyes cynically.

Without another word, Avery left Liam standing alone under the spinning disco ball. He called after her, asking if she wanted to visit the private room again, but she ignored him. She slipped behind the bar, took the phone off the hook, and dialed the number for Mack's pager. If he called back and realized it was The Fuzzy Peach, he would know the page had come from her.

Rafe Lucas greeted Jerry and Steve at the back door. He ushered them into his office quickly so no one would see them standing around.

Once inside the office, Lucas paced the floor, formulating a plan.

"We don't know when they're coming or how many there are. All we know is that they're coming." Rafe finally said, still pacing. He stopped long enough to glare at Jerry, who stood in front of the desk, slouching and staring at the floor.

"Jerry, are you listening?"

Jerry straightened up. He seemed to snap out of a daydream. "Huh? Yeah."

"Damn it, Jerry, pay attention. Or else you might get a bullet between the eyes." Lucas touched his own forehead with a thick index finger for emphasis. "I know that wife of yours hates your guts, but I don't think she wants to see you dead yet, far as I know."

Jerry pressed his lips together in a scowl. "Come on, now, Lucas. Don't talk about her like that."

"I just call 'em like I see 'em."

Jerry continued to scowl in Lucas's direction.

Lucas stared him down. "Did you bring a piece?"

"I got a shotgun in the truck."

"Not going to do you much good out there, is it?"

Jerry didn't answer.

"Go get your fucking weapon, Juice. After that, I want you to go in the men's room and lock the door."

"In the bathroom?"

"That's what I said. Wait in there till you hear something, then come out shooting."

"Why do I gotta be in the bathroom?" protested Jerry.

"Cause I said so. Anyway, you'll be right at home in there with the other turds."

Steve broke out laughing.

"What's so funny?" asked Lucas.

Steve wiped the smile from his face.

"Take this .357 and go stand in the alley behind the dumpster," Lucas said to Steve. "Make sure you can see the back door. Anybody comes back there, take 'em out. You hear any gunfire inside, come in and back us up."

Steve nodded.

Lucas handed Steve the .357. Steve hefted the large handgun, admiring its size.

"Alright then," said Lucas, relaxing a little now that the plan had been established. "Now for the good news. If we get hit and pull it off, I'll double your payout. I know you didn't sign on thinking we'd be ambushed. Sometimes that's the cost of doing business in this line. But I will make it worth your while."

Lucas stood directly in front of the two men.

"They don't know that we know they're coming. That's good for us. They think they got the element of surprise, but they don't. We do."

Jerry swallowed hard enough for the other men to hear his Adam's apple bob in his dry throat.

"Bull is out front at a table. We've got the whole place covered. We're ready for 'em."

"Hey, Rafe?" said Jerry.

"What, Jerry?"

"What do I do if somebody needs to piss?"

Lucas squinted at Jerry. "If *what?*"

"You said wait in the bathroom with the door locked. What if somebody needs to piss while I'm in there?"

"Jesus, Jerry, figure it out, will ya? I got to do everything for you?"

"No," Jerry mumbled.

"Hustle up, then. Get in position."

Jerry and Steve shuffled out of the office. Steve tucked the Magnum in his waistband when he got outside.

Jerry watched as Steve took his post in the shadows near the dumpster. Jerry zipped up his jacket as he walked to his pickup truck to retrieve the shotgun. A breeze coming off the Savannah River had introduced a slight chill to the night air.

Mack's pager buzzed on his right hip. The sudden vibration nearly scared him off his bar stool. A wave of nerves flushed his chest and made the back of his neck tingle. He clenched his jaw to suppress the shock. Taking his pager from his belt he glanced at the screen. He didn't recognize the number. The area code was local. Whomever it was would have to wait.

The clock behind the bar read 12:55. Five minutes until go time. Mack clipped the pager back on his hip. He stared at the clock, counting the seconds, waiting to make his move.

17

Jerry held the shotgun against his leg as he entered the back door of the bar. He took two quick steps across the dark hallway and ducked into the men's room.

The bathroom smelled of urine, like no one bothered to aim for the toilet. Jerry glanced in the stall. He saw the rim of porcelain stained brown from years of poor maintenance. One of the lightbulbs flickered in its socket, periodically cutting the light in the room to half its usual brightness.

"Put me in the effing bathroom," Jerry muttered. "Least they could do is mop the piss off the floor once in a while."

Jerry flipped the deadbolt above the door handle. The thumb turn spun freely with no resistance. Jerry turned it again. The deadbolt did not engage. He pulled the handle to check the lock. The door swung inward unimpeded.

"Damn it," Jerry growled. He closed the door and spun the deadbolt twice more, lifting and pressing the lever, hoping to make the lock function properly.

"Piece of shit."

Jerry spat on the brown tile floor. He smeared the expectorate with the toe of his boot.

Jerry glanced around the bathroom, searching for something he could use to brace the door. He found nothing but a broken plunger and a thin metal trash can.

He began to sweat, realizing he was standing in the bathroom with a shotgun and no way to secure the door. Someone might come in at any moment. How could he possibly explain himself?

Placing one of his boots against the door, Jerry stretched his arm toward the sink, hoping he could reach the surface that supported his weapon while still bracing the door. He could not.

His only option was to stand against the door with its broken lock. Hold it closed with his shoulder while cradling the shotgun in his other arm.

Jerry lunged for the shotgun, snatching it off the sink, and then threw his shoulder back on the door, expecting someone to push it open any minute.

All of Lucas's talk about an ambush had Jerry jumpy. He pressed an ear to the door and listened. He heard nothing but the faint sound of clinking glass and low conversation.

"Couple more minutes, right?" said Andy. "Easiest hundred grand I ever earned." He finished the last swallow of his beer. "What do we do? Just get up and walk out?"

Mack studied the few remaining patrons in the bar. Something seemed off.

"You see that guy over there in the corner? Don't look

directly at him," Mack said.

Andy turned casually, like he was stretching. "Yeah, I see him."

"I recognize that guy. Saw him here last night by the back office."

"Does he work here?"

"He look like a waiter to you?"

Andy shook his head. "Not really."

"He's muscle, works for the owner. I'm sure of it. What I don't know is why he's been sitting out here casing the joint for the last half hour."

"Maybe he doubles as the bouncer. The place is about to close, isn't it? I'd say he's just getting ready to lock up, go home for the night."

Mack thought for a minute. "Maybe," he finally said.

What specifically was Mack looking for on behalf of his employer? What would qualify as something suspicious enough to call off the ambush?

"It's probably nothing," said Andy. "Why, are you worried about him?"

"Not sure yet." Mack continued watching Bull at the corner table, studying him for any sign of alarm.

Andy's empty beer bottle thumped on the wooden bar.

"Anyway, I got to piss something fierce before we head out," he announced. "Want me to walk past him and have a sniff?"

Mack looked at his watch. The digital face read 12:58. "You can't wait til we get back to the motel?"

"Man, I'm about to bust a gut. It's the nerves. Remember how I got that way on missions? Had to make sure I pissed it all out before we started."

Mack did remember that quirk of Andy's. "Hurry up," he said. "Two minutes until we red line."

"Alright then. I'm gonna go make a *yellow* line real quick. Be right back." Andy cracked a smile and jabbed Mack in the shoulder as he passed him on the way to the bathroom.

Mack's beeper buzzed again. The screen displayed the same phone number as before. Two pages from the same number this late on a Monday night? It was enough to arouse Mack's suspicion. The only person with a Savannah area code who knew his pager number was Avery. It had to be her. Did she know something? Was she trying to warn him?

The digits on Mack's watch rolled over to 1:00 a.m. It was go time. Despite his concern, he could not risk the few minutes it would take to return Avery's call. By then, the bar could be under attack for all Mack knew. He had to give the signal and get Andy out of there. He would call Avery from the motel room in a few minutes. Maybe he could even brag a little about his success.

Mack stood up from the bar stool. He stretched his back to make it seem like he was preparing to leave for the night. As casually as possible, he strolled over to the front window. He did his best to appear innocent, as though he was waiting for his friend to finish in the bathroom and nothing more.

When he reached the front window, Mack squinted into the darkness. He searched the road for something—for what, he didn't know. A black SUV full of armed men, a SWAT team jumping from a helicopter, an army of Ninjas with swords? Mack realized just how little he knew about his employer, or about the plan that he would soon put in motion.

Andy gritted his teeth to hold back the urine. His bladder screamed at him to empty it. With one hand on his belt, Andy pressed the door of the men's room. It did not give.

"Oh, man. You got to be kidding me," said Andy. He pressed harder on the door. This time he felt it give a couple inches and then slam back.

"What the hell?" said Andy, his voice getting more urgent. "Somebody in there?" Andy called through the door. He knocked. "I need to go!"

Andy heard boots scuffling on the tile floor. A body pressed against the other side of the door. Someone was bracing the entry closed.

"Listen, pal, I just need to use the can real quick. In and out, then you can get back to whatever it is you're doing in there."

When no response came, Andy pressed hard on the door. Yet again, he felt it give and then slam back under the weight of his opposition.

"Son of a bitch," Andy growled. "You ain't gonna move, I'm gonna move ya."

Andy stepped back from the door. He raised his right leg and slammed the bottom of his boot against the bathroom door.

Inside the bathroom, Jerry stumbled and fell backward. The force of Andy's kick smashed the door open and sent Jerry sliding on his butt across the cold damp tile.

"Goddamnit!" shouted Jerry. "We're under attack!"

He swung the shotgun up quickly, failing to fully cradle it against his shoulder. He pulled the trigger. The recoil knocked him back even further into the bathroom. The shotgun bucked and missed wide left, blowing a hole in the open bathroom door.

"Holy—" Andy didn't finish his sentence. He rolled to his right toward the bar. As he spun, he drew his SIG Sauer and fired back into the bathroom.

"Mack, we got a live one!" Andy shouted, knowing Mack was already well-aware of the gunfire. As he yelled, Andy dropped back, gun drawn, hoping to meet Mack at the front door and escape. Andy's heart pounded in his chest. He kept the pistol trained on the bathroom door, waiting for Jerry to appear in the hallway.

The instant Bull heard the shotgun blast, he leaned over and picked up his Uzi. He knelt in his corner of the bar and flipped over the table for cover.

Mack spun away from the front window. He drew the Beretta and aimed it up the hallway in the direction of the gunfire. In the dim light, he saw Andy creeping backward toward him, gun drawn. Smoke and shrapnel from the wooden door filled the back of the hallway.

"Andy, come this way. Front door. I've got your back," said Mack. He shouted to be heard over the screams of patrons in the bar, who were scattering and ducking to avoid the melee.

Andy took a few steps backward until he could see around the corner of the hallway into the main room. He snuck a quick glance in both directions, and then snapped his head back to face the hallway where he knew the shooter was still hiding.

"We all clear?" Andy yelled over his shoulder.

"Let's get out of here!" answered Mack, who already had one hand on the front door.

Inside the bathroom, Jerry held the shotgun flat against his chest. He crept toward the bathroom door which hung limply on its hinges, blown half apart, swaying in the smoky hallway. Where the hell is everyone else, Jerry wondered. Bull and Steve hadn't even shown their faces yet. Surely, this was the ambush they were waiting for.

"Steve!" Jerry yelled from the bathroom. "Steve, get your ass in here!" He leaned against the door frame. The barrel of the shotgun trembled in his shaking hands.

Andy took one more step backward, unknowingly exposing himself to Bull's line of sight behind the overturned table. Bull wasted no time. He popped up on his knees and raised the Uzi.

The flash of movement caught Andy's eye. He dove out of the way just as Bull sprayed a wave of bullets across the room.

Andy raised his pistol and squeezed off a few shots in Bull's direction as he skidded across the polished concrete floor. Mack joined in the shootout, also firing his pistol toward Bull's table.

Bull stopped shooting. He ducked back out of sight, waiting for another opportunity. He wondered if Jerry was hit.

The room became eerily quiet for a few seconds until Alonzo's voice pierced the silence.

"I quit this job! You hear me? I quit!" he yelled from somewhere behind the bar. His voice was muffled, his chin tucked to his chest in a tight crouch.

No one responded to Alonzo's announcement.

Mack fired a few more shots into Bull's corner. The bullets ricocheted off the wall above Bull, sending plaster bits skittering over the tabletops.

Andy crawled toward the door. The butt of his handgun echoed on the concrete floor each time it contacted the hard surface.

Steve eased open the back door. He slipped silently into the hallway. Through the hazy smoke Steve spotted Andy's figure crawling on his hands and knees toward the front door. He raised his .357, aimed it at Andy, and pulled the trigger.

Andy lurched forward. He fell on his face and chest when the bullet hit him in the shoulder. He pressed himself up with his right hand. Blood smeared the floor where he had fallen.

"That stung like a bitch," Andy said through gritted teeth.

Mack unloaded the rest of his clip into the back hallway. He leaned over and grabbed Andy by the arm. "Get up!" he said, dragging Andy's entire bodyweight toward the exit while simultaneously pushing the door open.

Andy stood up in the open doorway. He stumbled until his feet caught up to Mack's firm grip.

"Give me your gun," said Mack. He holstered his empty Beretta. Taking Andy's SIG Sauer, Mack fired a few rounds through the open door back into the bar.

"Can you run?" he asked Andy.

"Yeah."

Andy shuffled his feet. He forced his mind to

overcome the pain in his shoulder. The two men ran in a full sprint across the street to the van.

Mack started the engine while Andy climbed in the side door. He pulled the door closed with his right hand, grimacing in pain and quickly clutching his left shoulder.

As the van screeched away from the curb, Rafe Lucas appeared in the doorway of McKearney's, holding a long-barreled hunting rifle. He took aim at the van. He watched through the scope as the taillights disappeared up the road.

"Don't fuck with me," Lucas growled into the stock of the rifle. He lowered the barrel slowly. He continued to stare in the van's direction long after the vehicle had vanished from sight.

"They gone?" asked Steve over Lucas's shoulder.

"Yeah, they're gone."

"You think they'll be back?"

"Not tonight. One of 'em got hit."

"I knew I hit him. Couldn't see from the smoke but I was pretty sure he went down."

"He went down alright," said Bull, who had just joined the two men outside. "His blood is smeared all over the floor in there."

"Good," said Lucas. "Hope that bastard bleeds out."

"What do you want to do about the customers?" asked Bull. "We got a panic forming inside."

Rafe Lucas shook his head rapidly to return to reality. "How many are in there?"

"Not many. Four or five. Plus your bartender. All that shooting, they're gonna need handling."

"Where the hell is Jerry?"

"Still in the bathroom last I saw him."

"Good-for-nothing sonofabitch. Was he the first one to shoot?"

"Sounded like it to me," said Bull. "First blast was a shotgun, I know that much. Then the other guy started shooting."

"That's what I thought," said Lucas. "Are we even sure that was the ambush? How can we know, if it was Jerry who shot first?"

Lucas spat on the sidewalk. He stared down at the tiny speck of white spittle on the dirty concrete.

"Go in there and get Jerry while I deal with the customers."

Jerry paced the office erratically, gesturing with the barrel of his shotgun.

"Both of them guys packing heat, shooting the place up, I'm telling you they were ready for something. Only reason I shot first is because they hadn't shot *yet*," said Jerry when Lucas confronted him. His voice was still shaky. "Way I see it, I just beat them to it."

"Jerry, quit waving that damn thing around," said Lucas. "Now what exactly did the guy say to you?"

Jerry leaned his shotgun against the wall. He closed his eyes, trying to remember the sequence of events.

"He kicked the door in, is what happened. Knocked me on my ass. And here I am lying on the floor of the bathroom holding a shotgun. What am I supposed to do?"

"Was his weapon out when he came in?"

Jerry pondered the question. "Yeah, I think so. He came in with the intention of shooting me. That's how I remember it."

Lucas shook his head. "Jerry, if you just shot up my bar for no reason…" Lucas stared at the floor, frowning. "And what about the guy that Steve hit—if he turns out to be Joe Shmoe Customer, then I'm fucked. You know that?"

"I'm telling you, that was our guy," said Jerry. "He ain't going to file a police report."

"He better not, for your sake. Cause if he does, it's your ass," said Lucas. "For that matter, we ain't filing a police report either. I can't have the cops poking around. So if it turns out our little bullet boy presses charges it sure ain't gonna look good for us."

"What about the customers? Won't they expect police to show up?"

"The customers are fine. Don't worry about them. I told them it was an attempted robbery and sent 'em all home. They're shaken up but they'll be okay."

Jerry, Steve, and Bull stayed quiet. They waited for Lucas to continue. The air in the room felt heavy with a mix of shock and pride.

Lucas looked at his watch. "We got less than twenty-four hours before the deal closes, at which point we all become wealthy men. We just got to make it one more day." He looked around the room at each of the men. "You all did good. You hear me? Good work. It's all gonna be worth your while we make it just a few more hours."

"What do we do now?" asked Bull.

"I want you to call the hospital and see if any gunshot wound that matches our guy checks in tonight. Steve, you drive back to the warehouse. Make sure it's all clear. You see anything, you call us immediately."

"What about me?" said Jerry. "I got to get home 'fore my wife kills me."

Lucas glared at Jerry. "We wouldn't want that, would we?" said Lucas. "Go out there and clean the place up. When you get done, I don't want to see any blood on my floor. Nobody's going home tonight till I say so."

The back wheels of the Dodge Caravan fishtailed as Mack jammed the gas pedal. He watched in his rearview mirror to see if they were being followed. Far back in the distance, the front door of McKearney's lay open. A small figure stood on the sidewalk in the light that spilled from the open door. Mack recognized the man as the owner of the bar.

"Stay down," Mack said to Andy, who lay sprawled across the back row of the van.

"Couldn't sit up if I had to," said Andy.

The van passed under a streetlight. In the mirror's reflection Andy's face—twisted with pain—temporarily flashed with light and then disappeared again in shadow.

Mack noticed a black SUV with dark tinted windows parked against the curb about a hundred yards up from the bar. As the van zipped past the SUV on the dark street Mack gazed out the window, trying to see inside. The windows were too dark to see anything. Mack couldn't tell if the SUV was occupied. Might that be his guy? Even if it was the man who hired him, it would be too risky for Mack to stop. He wondered if his employer would proceed now that their cover was blown.

"What the hell happened back there?" said Andy from

the back seat. A fit of coughing cut his speech short. Andy fought to regain control of his breathing.

"Somebody tipped them off is what happened."

"You think?"

"How else could they be so ready? A guy was hiding in the bathroom with a shotgun for chrissakes."

"Yeah. I hate to say it, but it seems like they knew we were coming."

Mack grunted. His thoughts flashed to Avery. He hoped she had not sold them out. He remembered the pages he had received moments before the shooting started. Could it have been Avery trying to warn him?

The van approached the motel. Mack slowed to turn into the parking lot but changed his mind. He sped up, passing by the motel.

Andy tried to speak but another bout of coughing overwhelmed him.

"You okay?" said Mack.

Andy took a deep breath. He exhaled slowly. "Fine," he said. "But I still need to pee. My bladder hurts worse than the gunshot."

Mack smiled. Andy always could keep the mood light. He felt around the driver's seat until his hand gripped a foam coffee cup. He passed it back to Andy.

"Brother, I bet I can fill this thing five times."

"Yeah, well, dump it out the window then I guess."

Andy groaned.

"Either that or piss your pants. At this point, I'd say my security deposit is long gone. What's a little urine added to all the blood stains?"

Andy smiled through the pain. After a few seconds, he

asked, "How far's the hospital?"

"Bout two hundred miles."

"Two hundred miles?" Andy repeated incredulously. "They don't have a hospital in Savannah?"

"You know as well as I do what happens if we check you into a Savannah hospital with a gunshot wound," said Mack. "First off, we can't file a police report. Second, I guarantee those guys will be watching for you. They don't understand that you and I are just the hired help. As far as they're concerned, we are the ones who came to take their stash away."

"Yeah, I was afraid of that."

"At least in Atlanta we're out of their reach. Bigger city, easier to blend in, easier to bullshit the situation," said Mack. He took the on-ramp to I-16 and accelerated to match the speed of traffic. "Can you hold out for three more hours?"

"I don't reckon I have a choice, do I?"

Mack flicked his eyes up to the rearview. He studied Andy, his body slumped in the backseat, his breathing shallow and labored.

Andy met Mack's eyes in the mirror. He forced a smile. "Drive fast."

18

Jerry knelt on his hands and knees. He scrubbed the blood from the floor of McKearney's with a wire brush. He dipped the brush into a bucket of soapy water to his right, and then he sloshed the sudsy brush back and forth across the concrete floor.

"Dude must have a hole in him the size of a baseball to bleed that much," Jerry mumbled into the red puddle below him.

"Did you see what Steve got him with?" said Bull's voice over Jerry's shoulder. Bull sat at the bar with a phone book open to the yellow pages, the telephone pressed to his ear.

"No, I was on my ass in the bathroom."

"A goddamn hand cannon," said Bull. "Three-fifty-seven. That'll knock anybody down." Bull traced a phone number in the book with his finger and then started to dial. "You didn't hear that thing echo in the hallway?"

"All I heard was some dumbass spraying the whole bar with a machine gun. And he didn't hit a damn thing with it either." Jerry looked over his shoulder to see if Bull had heard him.

Bull raised his index finger in Jerry's direction, requesting silence. Jerry returned to his scrubbing.

"Hello, I'm sorry to bother you at this late hour," Bull said into the phone, "but I got a ninety-year-old mother lives in an apartment near downtown—" Bull stopped to listen. "Yes, she sure is. You got that right. Anyhow, she woke me up just now saying she thought she heard something sounded like gunshots down near the river. Now, between you and me, her hearing ain't too good anymore and, frankly, her mind ain't either." Bull laughed to lighten his tone. "I'm sure what she heard was a car backfire or raccoons in her trashcans. But she won't leave me alone until I check it out and tell her everything's okay. Would you be so kind as to confirm for me that nobody has been shot downtown tonight, so I can call her back and tell her to go to sleep?"

Bull stopped talking. He raised his eyebrows at Jerry while he listened to the response to his question.

Jerry shook his head and muttered a curse under his breath.

"No, I understand that. Thing is, I didn't want to call the police because then they might have to send someone downtown to investigate, and, knowing my mother, that would be putting them on a wild goose chase. I'd hate to make an officer do that on her behalf, 'specially at this hour."

Bull got quiet and listened. The only sound in the bar was Jerry's wire brush slowly scrubbing against the concrete.

"Uh-huh," Bull said. "Right. So, you're saying nobody

has come in your hospital tonight with a gunshot wound?" Bull nodded slowly. "Okay, well, I knew mom was hearing things. Like I say, we've been through this before. Listen, I appreciate your time and your helping me out. Mom'll be happy to hear none of her neighbors was shot tonight." Bull laughed again to make his statement seem more innocent. "You have a good night, too. Thanks, again."

Bull slammed the phone down on the cradle. "As much blood as was on that floor, that sumbitch is dead if he ain't in the hospital. Where the hell did they go?"

"Maybe he *is* dead," said Jerry. "Hell, I hope he is." Jerry tossed his scrub brush into the soapy water. The dark liquid—tinted red with blood—sloshed against the rim of the metal bucket. "I'll tell you one thing right now. I'm done with this crap. This spot is cleaner than the rest of the damn floor."

Bull raised his chin, pretending to examine the spot Jerry had been scrubbing. "Rafe said you ain't done till it's all gone."

"Why can't Alonzo do this? He's the only one actually on the damn payroll here."

"Who?"

"Alonzo. The goddamn bartender," said Jerry. "You ever been here before?"

Bull frowned. "I don't pay attention to the help."

"That's part of your problem."

"Oh yeah? And what problem is that?"

Jerry shook his head. He wiped his blood-soaked hands on his jeans.

"Where is that guy anyway?" said Bull, still holding the phone in his hand. "What's his name? Alonzo did you say?"

"I haven't seen him since the ambush. He probably left to report your ass to the cops for trying to kill him with an Uzi."

"He better not be if he knows what's good for him."

Jerry didn't answer. He rested his hands on his thighs, pausing the work to give his back a break.

"Did you hear what I told you?" growled Bull. "Lucas said don't stop till every drop of blood is cleaned up."

"Yeah, well, I've heard about enough from him tonight. If I scrub anymore there'll be a more obvious spot from where the top layer of wax is rubbed off."

Bull frowned. "Go ask him. He's in the office."

"I'm not asking shit. And, in case you forgot, you ain't my boss." Jerry stood up. "I'm done here for tonight. My wife is liable to call the police if I don't show up soon."

"Then she's even dumber than she looks."

Jerry raised up, puffing out his chest. He took two steps toward Bull with his fist clenched.

Bull rested his hand on the Uzi, which lay next to the open phone book on the bar top. He tapped the barrel of the weapon with his index finger.

Jerry stopped advancing. He watched Bull's hand fidget with the Uzi. He scowled and gritted his teeth.

Bull grinned sadistically.

"If you or Lucas has a problem y'all can both kiss my ass," said Jerry.

He pivoted on his heel and stormed out the front door of the bar, leaving the bloody pail and brush on the floor alongside the wet spot where he had been scrubbing.

"Good riddance," said Bull. He picked up the telephone again and dialed another hospital. He forced his mouth into a fake smile while he waited for a nurse to answer.

Despite the windfall Avery had collected from the college boys, her mind weighed heavily as closing time approached at The Fuzzy Peach. She had paged Mack three times without hearing a word from him. Now, a little after two a.m., Avery gathered her belongings from her locker. She slipped her wad of cash—nearly two grand—into the pocket of her thin cotton jacket.

According to Leonard's rules, the girls were not supposed to return to the floor once they had changed into their street clothes, but Avery didn't care. She shouldered the backpack that contained her high heels and work outfit.

Pulling aside the curtain, Avery shot past the stage, hoping to avoid Leonard's watchful eyes. She caught the bartender taking out the trash and followed him through the open door that led to the dumpster.

"Did you get any calls for me?"

"Same answer I gave you last time," said the bartender. "No calls tonight except for the usual drunk assholes asking the usual dumb questions."

"Hmm," said Avery, biting her lower lip. She watched the bartender swing the heavy trash bag up into the dumpster. A trail of foul-smelling liquid leaked from a rip in the black plastic. Avery stepped back to avoid being splashed by the oozing fluid.

"Surely there's plenty of what you're looking for backstage," said the bartender. He assumed Avery had been waiting for a call from a drug dealer. "What's the point of calling in reinforcements at this hour?" He clapped his hands together and then wiped the dampness from the leaking trash bag on his pants.

"That dumpster is nasty," said Avery.

"Don't I know it. You do any good tonight? That table of college guys was all over your ass."

"Not bad," said Avery. "Don't worry, I'll tip you out before I leave," she added.

The bartender raised his hands, smiling good-naturedly. "Hey, I'm not nagging you."

"I know. I always take care of you."

"Yes, you do. You're one of the good ones," said the bartender. "No matter what everyone else says." He laughed at his own joke.

Avery didn't even hear him. Her mind was elsewhere.

"Yo, you look like you need a couple nights off," said the bartender. "Take a break for a little while, why don't you?"

"Huh? Oh yeah, I think maybe I will," said Avery. She ducked under the bartender's arm as he held the door open for her. "I'm leaving here in a minute. Be sure and tell me if I get a call, will you?"

The bartender locked the deadbolt on the steel door with a firm twist of his thumb. "Will do. Think about what I said, though. Everybody needs a vacation once in a while."

Avery knew the bartender meant more than just taking time off from work. Her drug use had been getting a little too regular lately. People were starting to notice.

"Okay," she said. She counted out a hundred dollars in ones, twos, and fives. She handed the tip to the bartender.

"Thanks for always looking out for me," she said.

Liam and his crew had gathered near the front door of the club, preparing to leave. Avery thought she heard Leonard calling her name from somewhere behind her, but she ignored the voice. Instead, she cut across the floor and caught Liam just before he exited.

"Hey, babe. I thought you left," said Liam. His eyes were glassy and heavy from the alcohol, but the cocaine kept his senses heightened. Balancing the downers with the uppers kept his voice clear and straight. He almost sounded sober, if not for the speedy tone and rapid chattering.

"I'm about to."

"Want to come party with us? We're going back to the house to get wild."

Avery shook her head. "I have to go. I'm worn out."

Liam smiled slyly. "I've got the fix for that."

"I don't want any more tonight."

"First time I've heard that one out of you."

Avery looked at the floor. "Yeah, I guess," she said. "I'm thinking I might take a break."

"Right. Sure. You do that." Liam mocked her earnest statement.

"I'm serious."

"Fine then. Do yo thang, girl."

Avery frowned. "Have you heard anything from, what's his name, the bar owner guy?"

"Rafe?"

"Yeah, him."

Liam knitted his brow in a flash of anger. "I knew you were up to something. What are you plotting with old boy?"

"I'm not!" said Avery. "I just wondered."

"You been doing a lot of 'just wondering' lately."

Avery looked away. "I gotta go before my boss catches me out here in street clothes."

"Door's right there. I'm not stopping you." Liam extended his palm, beckoning Avery to leave before him.

Avery took a step forward. She leaned over and lowered her voice. "You have anything that'll help me sleep? I'm afraid I'll be up all night. I feel so tired, but my mind won't stop running."

"Oh, so you do need your ol' buddy Liam for something, eh?"

"Stop it. You know I care about you, whether or not you're dealing to me."

Liam's face softened a little. "Yeah, I guess," he said. He reached in his pocket and produced a small blue pill. He handed it to Avery. "Here's a Xanny. Take it with a glass of bourbon and you'll be out pretty quick."

Avery palmed the pill. "Thanks," she said, giving Liam a quick peck on the cheek.

"Don't drink too much with it," said Liam. "I'm serious. It'll knock you on your ass."

Avery nodded. She smiled at Liam and then slipped past him. She got the attention of one of the bouncers, who escorted her through the dark parking lot to her car, where she took a couple deep breaths and then drove the two miles back to her apartment, praying the whole way for no flashing lights in her rearview mirror.

Jerry shut off the truck's headlights before turning into his driveway. He eased the pickup along the weed-eaten gravel path, cringing with each popping rock. He hoped the noise of his arrival would not wake Billie.

He got out slowly, leaving his shotgun lying across the seat in the truck. Every sound—the creaking door, the rusty shocks, the flapping seatbelt—might as well have been a gunshot echoing against the house's paint-chipped wood siding.

The neighbor's hound gave a single half-hearted bark from somewhere under the deck.

"Shhh, it's okay, girl," whispered Jerry. He shuffled over to the small concrete landing outside the kitchen door and sat down.

The moon bathed the backyard in pale light. Jerry slipped off his boots by bracing a toe on each of the hard leather heels.

For a few seconds, he sat still on the porch. His white socks glowed against the dark concrete step below him. The intruder at the bar had shot at him. More than once. Jerry had lain helpless on the bathroom floor while a man shot at him. And he himself had aimed his gun at another man and pulled the trigger with the intent to kill that man.

For years, Jerry had felt his life slipping downward. Since the factory had closed a few years back, leaving Jerry an unemployed forklift operator, his life had gotten steadily worse. Another good-paying blue-collar job was hard to come by. He had tried for a while. Eventually, the rent payment became intolerable. Jerry had to do what he had to do. At least that's what he told himself in that moment as he stared into the darkness of the backyard.

But what about Billie? She hadn't asked for this life. She

deserved a better man than Jerry had become. He had become the kind of man who could not take care of his own family. And now, the kind of man who was willing to kill or be killed, all for a few hundred pounds of white powder. Tonight had been a new low for Jerry. He felt it deep down within him as he sat in the moonlight.

"Tomorrow night and it's over," Jerry spoke into the cool night air, as much a rehearsal for what he would say to Billie as it was a reassurance to his own restless mind.

Jerry stood up. He placed a hand on the rusted metal handle and clicked the button that released the latch of the screen door.

Before he even stepped inside Jerry saw the silhouette of his wife at the kitchen table. The dim stove light behind the chair illuminated Billie's shoulders and cast a streaking shadow across her face.

Jerry held up the palm of his hand. "Billie, don't start. Please don't start. It's been a hell of a night, and I can't take another hard word. I'm at the end of my abilities."

Billie didn't respond. She watched her husband cross the linoleum floor noiselessly in his socked feet and dip his hands in the water bucket on the sink. Billie said nothing while Jerry splashed cold water on his face and ran his hands over his hair, plastering his bangs back in a slick helmet over his skull.

Jerry sunk into a chair at the table next to Billie. The skin on his ashen face hung like an old dog's, almost dripping from his stubbled chin. He stared at the checkered tablecloth until his eyes blurred.

"You need a shave," said Billie. "You look like hell."

"I know," said Jerry.

"Did you get it?"

Jerry broke his gaze and looked up at his wife. "Get what?"

"Whatever you were after."

"Oh," Jerry said. "I guess so. For tonight at least."

"That's good, honey."

Billie scooted her chair closer to her husband. She put her hand on Jerry's leg and waited.

Jerry looked into his wife's eyes. He tried to tell her "one more day" but a knot stuck in his throat. He could not coax the words past it. He leaned over until his head rested on Billie's chest. She put her arm around his shoulder. The two sat together in the quiet stillness waiting for dawn to come, praying it would bring with it a renewal of hope.

The Xanax kicked in by the time Avery pulled her Volkswagen Jetta into the parking lot of her apartment building. She sat in the driver's seat and allowed her eyes to unfocus. The soft light of the emergency bulb on the side of the building feathered into rolling waves across the hood of the Jetta. The narcotic dragged on Avery's speeding brain and slowed her reactions. She felt her chin droop slightly. She realized she had been breathing through her mouth. Her sinuses were wrecked from the long night of cocaine use. A dull throb swelled behind her eyes.

Avery's body felt exhausted. Climbing the stairs to her apartment seemed nearly impossible. The full weight of the past few days crashed over her, pressing her shoulders into the cloth seat of the Jetta.

A powerful thirst finally drove Avery into motion. She opened the car door and climbed out. Like always when returning late from the club, Avery carried her keys tightly in her fist with a key protruding between each finger like claws, just in case. She had never had someone follow her home from work, but she knew other girls who had been attacked late at night. The walk from her car to her apartment at three a.m. always made her nervous—even when she wasn't strung out on drugs.

Avery stopped at the top of the staircase and glanced back over her shoulder. The apartment complex was silent. The only sound was the key ring jingling in her hand. She unlocked the door, slipped inside, and quickly turned the deadbolt behind her. She pressed her forehead to the door and looked through the peep hole. Not a soul in sight. The lights in the parking lot twinkled in the peep hole's convex lens.

Avery tossed her bag on the floor by the door. She exhaled a long sigh and stepped out of her shoes, leaning a hand against the wall for balance. She kept her palm lightly touching the wall as she walked into the kitchen where she turned on the faucet. She tilted her head to the sink and drank for several seconds until her thirst was quenched. Then she allowed the water to run over her face. The cool water soothed Avery's inflamed sinuses. Dark drips of eye liner splashed in the metal sink.

With her face still wet, Avery poured a glass of bourbon. She wanted sleep to come as soon as possible, so she drank the bourbon down and poured another glass. She carried the drink over to the couch, pausing midway to take a sip. She set the glass on the coffee table.

Avery returned to the kitchen and picked up the phone. Her vision began to get cloudy. The digits on the handset danced and swirled before her eyes. She dialed the number for Mack's pager. When she heard the beep, she punched in her own callback number.

No longer able to stand on her wobbly legs, Avery stumbled back to the couch. She took another drink from the bourbon glass.

She reached over the arm of the couch and plugged in a string of Christmas lights that criss-crossed the ceiling. The subtle blues, greens, and reds comforted Avery. The lights cast a warm, numbing glow over the dark room.

Avery stared at her reflection in the black television screen across the room. She took another sip of bourbon and closed her eyes.

19

An hour before sunrise the Dodge Caravan hit the loading zone outside of the Atlanta hospital's emergency room at forty-five miles per hour. Mack slammed on the brakes. The van squealed to an abrupt stop.

Andy had gone mostly silent in the back seat. Mack tried to keep him talking but his responses had dwindled to little more than an occasional grunt or soft groan.

Mack climbed over the driver's seat into the back row of the van. He pulled open the sliding door with one hand while lifting Andy with the other.

"Help!" Mack shouted through the open door.

The van's screeching entrance had elicited the attention of a few hospital orderlies. The nurse-on-duty poked her head inside the van.

"What's going on?" she asked.

"He's hurt bad. Lost a lot of blood," said Mack. He decided not to mention the gunshot wound.

"Can he walk?"

"No."

The nurse turned to the nearest orderly. "Get a gurney,"

she said. "Tell Dr. Clark we need to prep for surgery."

The orderly nodded and disappeared.

"Do you know his blood type?" the nurse asked Mack.

Mack did not. He looked at Andy.

"Do you know it?" he asked.

Andy's eyes barely opened. His pupils rolled down to acknowledge Mack's question. "O," he whispered. His pupils disappeared again behind the lids.

"That's good news," said the nurse.

The orderly returned pushing the gurney with a partner. They carefully transferred Andy's limp body to the bed and began pushing it into the hospital.

The nurse walked alongside the rolling gurney, checking Andy's vitals. Mack followed close behind.

"What happened to him?" asked the nurse. She placed a blood pressure cuff on Andy's arm and began pumping it up.

Mack glanced around quickly before answering. "He, uh, he got shot."

The nurse looked at Mack. She took a stethoscope out of one ear. "Shot?"

"Yeah."

"Why didn't you say so? When did this happen?"

"I, well, I'm not sure exactly. I think it's been a while. A couple hours."

The nurse cut Mack's shirt open with a pair of scissors. She peeled the bloody shirt back from his chest. "There is a lot of blood on his clothes. More than an hour ago you say?"

"Yeah, I think so."

The nurse shook her head. "The bullet must not have

hit the brachial or he would be dead by now." She gingerly lifted Andy's shoulder off the bed. He complied, wincing in pain.

"I see two holes—front and back. At least the bullet isn't still inside him."

Mack nodded.

The nurse gestured to a carpeted enclave with vinyl-cushioned benches and several houseplants.

"The waiting room is right there. He's going to surgery immediately. We'll keep you updated."

Mack slowed his pace. He took a few more steps before stopping just past the entrance to the waiting area. He watched the gurney roll down the white hallway toward the operating room.

Mack headed for a phone hanging on the wall across from the waiting room. He took a scrap of torn paper from his pocket. He read the scribbled phone number and braced himself for the call he had to make.

He lifted the receiver and dialed. The phone rang five times before a sleepy female voice answered.

"Hello?"

"Olivia, this is Mack. You know, Andy's friend?"

Mack paused for a second, giving her time to wake up.

"I'm at the hospital in East Atlanta. With Andy. You should get here as soon as you can."

In a deep sleep, Jerry dreamed of a tall mountain. He climbed the mountain, but the trail never seemed to end. Every crest appeared to be the last, but the mountain's peak did not arrive. Another switchback in the trail waited for him at each turn. The mountain got steeper and steeper until eventually the pitch of the ground beneath him became almost vertical. Jerry's body tilted backwards. He leaned forward to keep from falling. The trail got steeper still. The ground under his feet separated from the terrain on each side. The trail rolled backward like a conveyor belt. Jerry dug in his heels and leaned into the moving sidewalk beneath him. His legs felt like rubber. Eventually, he could no longer keep up with the conveyor belt. Jerry wobbled and then flipped backward like a turtle on its shell. He waited for the ground to catch him. But the ground never came. The mountain became a cliff. Jerry reached desperately for the rock face, but his hands grabbed only air. He fell back into the abyss behind him.

Jerry jumped, flailing his arms. His searching fingers clutched the kitchen table, inadvertently pulling the checkered tablecloth toward him. The salt and pepper shakers flipped and rolled off the table. The shakers smashed on the linoleum floor. Glass shattered and spread around Jerry's feet.

Startled and confused, Jerry opened his eyes.

Morning sun filled the kitchen. Jerry's back and neck felt stiff from sleeping in the wooden chair. He leaned over to pick up the broken glass. His butt had gone numb. Jerry tried to move his legs but felt nothing in his lower half except stabbing pins and needles.

He waited for the blood to recirculate to his extremities. Jerry gave his thighs a few light thumps with his fists, trying to encourage them to respond.

The house was silent. From his seat, Jerry could see down the hallway. The bedroom doors were both closed.

He looked at the clock that hung on the kitchen wall next to a hand-painted sign that read "Shut up and Eat."

"Hey, Billie," said Jerry. His voice cracked. He smacked his lips a few times to restore moisture to his tongue. "Billie, you in there?"

Jerry stood up. His legs still tingled. He limped into the living room. His wife lay on the couch with a blanket pulled over her head.

"Billie, you awake? I slept in the kitchen."

"Huh?" said his wife from under the blanket.

"I must've been out. I didn't even hear Maddie leave for school."

Billie threw the blanket back from her face. "Huh?" she said again.

"I said, she got out to the bus without waking me up. Did you feed her breakfast with me in there sleeping at the table?"

"What time is it?" Billie's eyes opened wide.

"After nine."

"Shit!" said Billie. She jumped up from the couch and immediately fell on her face when her legs tangled in the blanket. "We're late!"

Jerry, still groggy from the night before, took a second to grasp the situation. He watched his wife run past him and open the door to his daughter's bedroom.

"Maddie, honey, time to get up," Billie said from within the room. Her voice was soft and coaxing, nothing like her body language a moment before. "We overslept."

Jerry heard his daughter's voice. Maddie asked if they were late, and then tried to convince her mom to let her stay home.

"Daddy's gonna give you a ride to school today, sweetie. How does that sound?"

"Daddy is?"

"Yes, he is. He wants to drop you off himself. Right out front."

"Can we go to McDonald's?"

Jerry smiled at his daughter's request. An Egg McMuffin sounded pretty good to Jerry. He hadn't eaten anything since dinner the day before.

"If you get up and get dressed right now, we'll see," said Billie.

"Yes, we will," Jerry said from the hallway. "You want a hashbrown, honey?"

"Yeah!" exclaimed Maddie.

Jerry heard her little feet land on the floor as she jumped out of bed.

"Do like your momma said then. Brush your teeth and come out to the truck."

While Jerry waited for his daughter to get dressed, he used the neighbor's hose to refill the kitchen bucket with fresh water. The hose water smelled strongly of plastic. Jerry swished it around in the bucket and then took it in the bathroom. He filled the toilet tank so it could be flushed and then set the bucket with the remaining water in the sink basin for face-washing and tooth-brushing. One more day of this crap, Jerry thought.

Jerry knelt on the kitchen floor. He carefully picked shards of glass out of the scattered piles of salt and pepper. He heard the soft voices of his wife and daughter in the bathroom. Maddie talking with a mouthful of toothbrush, asking her mom about where all the turkeys live and how come we eat them for Thanksgiving. Billie said something Jerry couldn't make out. Then, he heard his daughter spit toothpaste into the dry sink.

"Now we splash some water in there to rinse it down," said Maddie.

"That's right," said Billie. "Sit down here and tinkle before you get dressed."

The plastic toilet seat bounced on the porcelain ring. Jerry waited for the toilet to flush but it never came. Maddie ran out of the bathroom wearing nothing but a t-shirt.

"Why don't you put on your purple dress?" said Billie from the bathroom. With the door still wide open Jerry heard the distinct sound of adult urine trickling into the bowl. The toilet did flush this time and Billie walked out. Saving water by doubling up. She followed her daughter to the bedroom to help her get dressed, then went to check on the sleeping baby.

Jerry stood up with a cupped palm full of glass. He carefully dumped the shards into the trash can. With a broom and dustpan, he swept up the remaining mess.

A flash of purple rushed from Maddie's bedroom through the dining room.

"Hold on, lil' bit," Jerry said. "Put your shoes on before you come in here. There's glass on the floor."

Maddie froze in the doorway. "Something broke?" she said.

"Something broke," answered Jerry. He made another pass with the broom and dustpan.

Maddie sat down on the carpeted dining room floor and pulled on her Velcro shoes.

"Daddy, you're supposed to make a hand turkey for me. Remember?"

"I remember."

"Thanksgivings is soon."

"I know it is. This Thursday."

"When is Thursday?"

"Not tomorrow, but the day after that."

Maddie thought for a few seconds. "Did you catch us a turkey?" she asked.

Jerry smiled. "I tried to last night, but he got away."

"Are you gonna try again?"

"I am. I know where he is now. I'll catch him tonight."

"Okay," said Maddie, satisfied that her dad had things under control. "Can we still get a hashbrown?"

"Who told you we were getting a hashbrown?" said Jerry with a teasing smile.

"Daddy!" exclaimed Maddie. "You did!"

"I did?"

"You just now did!"

"Oh, well, if I said so, then I guess we have to." Jerry winked at his daughter. "Go give your momma a kiss and come get in the truck."

Maddie ran into her mother's arms. Billie picked her up and hugged her tightly. Over Maddie's shoulder, Billie and Jerry locked eyes. Neither spoke but they shared a moment of understanding.

Jerry swung open the screen door. He shuffled down the concrete steps. His hand slid along the rusted iron railing. He opened the passenger door of the pickup truck for his daughter.

The shotgun lay across the seat exactly where he had

left it only a few hours before. Jerry heard the screen door slam. He quickly lifted the shotgun—gripping it by the barrel—and lowered it down to the floorboard behind the seat.

"Hop on up here, tiny," he said to his daughter. He watched as she climbed into the truck one limb at a time. She had recently declared that she wanted no help with this task, admonishing her parents that she could get in the truck and fasten the seatbelt all by herself.

"Are you situated?" Jerry asked, once the girl was seated.

Maddie nodded, ignoring her dad's teasing.

"What are we doing again, I forget?" said Jerry.

The girl sighed dramatically. "Hashbrown and then school, daddy. Pay attention!"

"Geez, I don't know where I'd be without you keeping me straight."

"Geez!" echoed an exasperated Maddie.

Jerry shut the door. He caught a glimpse of his disheveled reflection in the passenger window and decided to stick with the drive thru.

Sitting in the hospital waiting room, Mack saw Olivia rush through the double doors. She walked fast, her head tilted forward with purpose, her shoes squeaked slightly on the polished floor. Olivia's eyes darted past the waiting area. They locked on the information desk, which she approached like a linebacker sacking a quarterback.

Mack stood up. He dreaded the interaction he knew was coming.

"Olivia," he called her name from a few feet away. He stepped back and braced himself.

Olivia turned her attention to the man whom she had met only once, a few days earlier at the Atlanta Zoo.

"I knew this was a bad idea," she said. "I just knew it."

"I'm sorry." Mack made no effort to placate her. Olivia was too smart to be fooled regarding the nature of the accident.

Olivia shook her head. "He's a dad. You know that, right? You met our son."

Mack hung his head. "We shouldn't have done it. I thought it would be easy money for your family." Mack spoke to the thin carpet beneath his feet, to the faded geometric pattern worn into the fabric by thousands of pacing loved ones. "It wasn't supposed to happen that way."

"You mean the way where my husband ends up shot, lying in an emergency room in the middle of the night? The way where I, his wife, have to find a babysitter at six a.m. and try to explain to our son why his Daddy is sick?" Olivia traced the toe of her shoe along the edge of the carpet. "Yeah, I'd say you're right. It wasn't supposed to happen that way."

Mack felt Olivia's eyes staring a hole in the top of his head. He lifted his face. Over Olivia's shoulder, an orange and red sunrise painted the parking lot outside the emergency room doors.

Mack stared into the sunrise until his eyes blurred and unfocused. "I'm going to make it up to him," he said. "To you."

Olivia shook her head again. "I think you've done

enough. I'd rather you stay away from Andy. Stay away from all of us. He's better off without the influence of the Navy hanging around, trying to pull him back into old habits. That life is behind him."

"I understand," Mack mumbled.

Olivia sighed. "Where is he now?"

"In surgery. They think he's gonna be okay. He lost a lot of blood, but they say he is stabilizing."

"That's good."

Neither of the two spoke for a few seconds. A distant beeping echoed down the bustling hallway. The intercom announced a message in the coded jargon spoken by the hospital personnel.

"Can I see him?" asked Olivia.

Mack shrugged and pointed to a nurse's station. "They haven't let me yet. He's probably almost out of surgery by now. I'm sure you'll have more influence as his wife."

Olivia turned away from Mack. She stepped off the carpet toward the nurse's station. Turning back over her shoulder, she said, "Thanks for bringing him here. And for calling me."

"I meant what I said about making it up to you."

Whether or not Olivia heard him, Mack could not tell. She gave no response, nor did she acknowledge him again.

Mack closed his eyes. When he opened them, Olivia was nowhere in sight.

The lack of sleep hit Mack hard now that his adrenaline had faded. He wanted to post up in the waiting room and doze for several hours, to be there waiting when Andy came out of surgery. But he had work to do. There was no time for sleep.

20

With a head full of Xanax and bourbon, Avery had also fallen into a tortured sleep. She dreamed she was back at the club, sitting in the bathroom stall counting her money. Leonard stood outside the stall door calling her name and pounding repeatedly with his fist on the light pink plastic wall. His thick, hairy knuckles rattled the door on its metal hinges. The stall shook like an outhouse in a tornado, vibrating and humming. Avery tried to tell Leonard to leave her alone. She pleaded that she had earned all her money, and he couldn't have it. But when she opened her mouth all that came out was a bubble. The bubble inflated like a balloon between her lips. It sealed shut and then floated away. She tried again to yell. More bubbles escaped from her open mouth. They filled the stall and floated up through the open top. The bathroom flooded with shimmering bubbles.

The pounding noise continued in her dream. Bubbles popped all around Avery. As they exploded, dark red liquid splattered on the stall walls. The liquid splashed on her face and on her dress. In her dream, she wore the same dress she had donned for prom ten years earlier. She tried frantically to wipe the red liquid from her dress, but the fluid smeared and oozed over her like blood from a picked scab.

"You can't have it!" Avery yelled.

She opened her eyes. She lay on the couch in her apartment. Daylight filtered through the curtained windows behind her. The dawn dampened the glow from the Christmas lights that had remained on all night.

The knocking resumed.

"What?" Avery whined, still curled in a ball on her couch. "Go away!"

"Avery!" said a man's muffled voice.

Avery sat up quickly. She found her footing and shuffled over to the door. She looked through the peephole. Opening the door a crack, she peered out from under the chain lock.

"What are you doing here?"

"Good to see you, too," said Mack.

Avery hesitated. She wasn't sure if she could trust him. What had happened the night before? Could he be in trouble?

"How did you know where…how did you find me?"

"It wasn't easy."

Avery squinted through the crack in the door, making it clear she did not yet feel safe.

"You told me your apartment complex," said Mack. "I drove through the lot until I found your Jetta. After that, I started knocking on doors until you answered."

"Are you fucking serious?"

Mack nodded.

"Pounding on doors like that? How many of my neighbors did you scare to death before you got to me?"

"More than a couple."

"Are you psycho?"

"Not that I know of."

"What do you want?"

"To come in, for starters. Judging by the late-night calls I received from you, I think you are well-aware of how my night went."

Avery looked away. She stared back into the apartment. "Why didn't you call me back?"

"Well, I was a little tied up, you know, with all the people shooting at me."

Avery's eyes widened. "Somebody shot you?"

"Not me but they got my friend."

"Oh my god. Are you okay? I was trying to warn you."

"That's what I hoped you would say," said Mack. "Now, can I please come inside? I've got some mean dudes in this town pretty mad at me right now, and I would rather not stand around in broad daylight."

Avery's face disappeared behind the door. She slipped off the chain lock and swung the door open. "Yeah, get on in here," she said. She stepped to the side and held the door open for Mack to enter.

Mack stepped cautiously into the apartment. He, too, harbored some suspicion, not entirely confident that Avery wasn't working with his opposition.

"So this is your place, huh?" Mack said. He glanced around the apartment. His eyes paused on the darkened windows and the illuminated string of Christmas lights.

"It's no Victory motel but it'll have to do."

Mack smiled. "Something wrong with my motel room?"

"I'm still waiting for the bed bugs to show up. I thought about burning my clothes when I got home, but I really like those panties."

"The ones with the butterfly?"

Avery looked surprised. "I'm shocked you remember considering how fast you took them off."

"I notice things."

"Like women's underwear."

"Yeah, like women's underwear."

Avery watched Mack. He stood in the middle of her apartment, his hands in his pockets. He shifted his weight from side to side.

"Sit down and quit hovering," she said. "There's nobody hiding in the closet, if that's what you're worried about."

Mack raised his eyebrows. He picked up a wrinkled blanket from the couch, folded it in half, and tossed it on the wide arm of the sofa. He sat down and relaxed into the soft cushion with a slight sigh.

"Anyways, they're probably as pissed at me as they are at you right now," said Avery.

"Oh, I highly doubt that. Unless you shot up their bar, too."

Avery tucked her legs under her waist and lowered herself on the couch next to Mack. She studied his face for a few seconds.

"You really shot somebody?"

"I don't think we hit anyone. They started it."

"Damn. That's some shit right there."

"That's one way to put it."

"I didn't realize you were, like, a gangster or whatever."

Mack chuckled. "Don't get too excited." He looked at Avery. He reached out his hand and rested it on her leg, waiting to see how she would react.

Avery nudged herself closer to Mack, responding to his touch. "I was worried about you," she said.

"I missed you, too. Did you think I forgot about you?"

"Wouldn't be the first time a guy has done that."

Mack nodded slowly. He put his arm around Avery's shoulder and pulled her against him. "I wanted to see you again."

Avery leaned into Mack's arm. She fell against his chest. For a few moments, the two sat quietly in the colorful glow of the Christmas lights, their chests rising and falling against each other.

Avery put her hand on Mack's thigh and pressed herself up. She looked in his eyes, almost inviting a kiss, before asking, "where did you sleep last night?"

"I didn't."

"That explains why you look like hell."

"Ouch," said Mack, feigning consternation. "That, and maybe getting shot at."

"Oh, right. That, too."

For a second, Mack held Avery's gaze. He noticed her tired eyes, puffy cheeks, runny nose. "I look like hell, eh? You aren't exactly having your best day either," he said with a smile, teasing her.

"Hey!" Avery slapped Mack's shoulder.

"I meant to say you look great. You always look great."

"That's more like it."

Mack smiled. "I have some things I need to do today. But before I do anything I should rest for a few hours. Can I crash here?"

"I think we can arrange that. But there's something I need you to do first."

"What's that?"

"Come back here in the bedroom and I'll show you."

Jerry pulled up to the entryway of his daughter's school. While the diesel engine idled, he scribbled a quick note on the back of his Egg McMuffin wrapper asking the teacher to excuse Maddie's tardiness.

Maddie took the note and stuffed it in her backpack.

"Finish your hashbrown," said Jerry.

Maddie took another bite of the fried potato patty and set it on the dashboard.

"Are you done?"

The girl fiddled with her seatbelt. "Yeah," she said into her lap.

Jerry grabbed the hashbrown and finished it in one bite.

"Hey, you," said Jerry.

Maddie continued fidgeting.

Jerry tickled his daughter's ribs. "I'm talking to you."

Maddie giggled and squirmed out of her dad's reach.

"Daddy's working tonight. I won't be home till late."

His daughter looked up with big eyes.

"You mind your momma, okay?"

"Okay."

"Is there school tomorrow?" Jerry couldn't remember what days the kids were out for Thanksgiving.

Maddie shrugged.

"Lemme see your hand," said Jerry.

He took his daughter's tiny hand in his own calloused palm. He examined her hand for a few seconds, making exaggerated motions with his eyes and mouth, saying, "very interesting" and "yes, I think this will be perfect."

"Perfect for what, Daddy?"

"Perfect for making hand turkeys. Look at the shape of your fingers—I've never seen anything quite like it."

"You're being silly."

"Am I?"

"Yes!"

"Remember what I said about those turkeys?"

"Mm-hm."

"We'll make 'em tomorrow."

Maddie smiled. She opened the door and slowly slid off the bench seat until her feet landed on the curb.

"I love you," said Jerry.

"Love you, too."

The girl put her hand on the truck door and leaned with all her weight. The door swung closed but didn't latch.

Jerry waved at Maddie through the window. He watched his daughter walk up to the school. A teacher greeted her at the door. The teacher waved to Jerry, and he responded in kind.

Once Maddie entered the school Jerry leaned over and pulled the truck door closed so it latched. He sat still for a few seconds, listening to the truck's engine, smelling the diesel exhaust. The radio played Waylon Jennings.

Jerry drove around absentmindedly for half an hour. He didn't want to go home but he had nowhere else to go.

At ten-thirty he found himself on the east side of Savannah near the storage warehouse. He decided to drive past and check on the stash.

Coming up to the turn on Highway 80 Jerry reached his arm over the back of the truck's seat. Keeping a hand on the steering wheel he braced his feet on the floorboard and lifted his butt off the seat until his fingers reached the barrel of the shotgun. He carefully lifted the gun and placed it across his lap as he made the turn.

Jerry slowed the truck to a crawl. He cruised past the warehouse with his face pressed to the window, squinting to see across the parking lot.

The box truck was still parked exactly how he and Steve had left it the night before. Backed all the way up to the loading dock so no one could get the rear door open without opening the dock.

The building looked empty. Even if Lucas was in there, Jerry was not in the mood to deal with him just yet. He goosed the accelerator and passed the warehouse.

At the highway, instead of turning left back to Savannah, Jerry flipped on his right blinker and headed for the island.

"What do you figure that Jetta's worth?" Mack asked Avery from the kitchen. She was still lying in bed. He raised his voice to reach her.

Mack held a steaming glass coffee pot in one hand. He wore a pair of blue jeans with no shirt. He poured the coffee into two mugs. The heat from the caffeinated liquid radiated out to his bare chest.

"Huh?" said Avery from the bedroom.

"Your Jetta. What's it worth?"

Mack took a mug in each hand and carried them into the bedroom.

A dim lamp by the bed illuminated Avery's features. Her hair spilled across the pillow. Her naked body lay in full repose, surrounded by soft blankets.

"You look good bringing me coffee in bed. You should do it every morning."

"Are you proposing to me?"

Mack handed one of the mugs to Avery. He lowered himself on the bed next to her, carefully balancing the full cup of liquid in his left hand.

"Yeah. Proposing that you make me coffee every day."

Mack took a sip and swallowed. "A coffee wench?"

"Now you're getting it."

Mack set his mug on the nightstand and rolled over to Avery. He slid his arm under the pillow, behind her back. Pulling his face toward her, he nuzzled into her neck, kissing it softly.

"Mmm. You can do that every day, too," said Avery.

"Part of my duties as your wench."

"Exactly."

Mack spoke quietly. His lips grazed Avery's ear lobe. "I'm serious about the car. What do you want for it?"

"Why?"

"Cause I might want to buy it from you."

Avery shifted her weight, turning her neck to see Mack's face. "You want to buy my car from me?"

"I might."

"That's my only car. What am I supposed to drive?"

"I'll give you a good price for it."

"Like how good?" Avery decided to play along with the game.

"What do you think it's worth?"

"I don't have any idea. It's a 1989 Volkswagen Jetta. Probably not that much. Five grand?"

Mack thought for a few seconds. He sipped his coffee.

"Would you take fifty thousand for it?"

Avery's eyes widened. "Are you out of your mind?"

"That's a question for another day."

"You're gonna give me fifty grand for an eight-year-old Jetta?"

"Yeah."

"Sold."

"There's just one catch."

"Oh, right. I should have known."

"I don't have the cash yet. You have to trust me. I'm getting it tonight. But I need the car in order to get it."

Avery rolled her eyes. "That's some B.S. right there. You sound like one of the johns at the club. Give me a lap dance and I'll pay you tomorrow."

"I'm serious though."

"They always are."

Avery rolled over and faced the wall. Mack put his hand on her hip and lightly stroked her thigh.

"I can't drive the van anymore. It's too risky. I think they'll recognize it from last night."

"Right up the road there's a place that'll finance you a car no money down," said Avery, her voice muffled by the pillow. "Their commercials are all over the radio."

"I don't know how connected these drug dealers are.

They might have people looking for me all over town," said Mack. "Anyway, the less hassle the better. You've got a car right here."

"Why do I feel like you're going to get in my car and leave town, never to be heard from again?"

"I could."

Avery bent her knee and kicked Mack's leg with her heel. "That wasn't the right answer!"

"Just being honest."

"Yeah, well you're not doing a very good job of selling me on this deal."

"Fifty thousand dollars," Mack whispered over Avery's shoulder.

"Mm-hm. Now you're speaking my language again."

Mack smiled, his lips pressed against Avery's nape.

"When do I get the money?"

"Late tonight."

"But you need the car now?"

"Not for a few hours. Once it gets dark."

Avery lay silent for a few moments. Mack watched her shoulders rise and fall with each breath.

"Fifty for the car. What do I get for letting you hide out in my apartment all day?"

"The pleasure of my company."

Mack earned himself another heel to the shin, but this time Avery left her leg draped across his calf.

"I'll think about it," said Avery. "In the meantime, how bout topping off my coffee, wench."

Jerry stopped at a beach supply shop on Tybee Island. He

rolled down the window and took a deep breath of the salty air. He parked the truck in the gravel lot. Before getting out, he covered the shotgun with an old t-shirt.

A chime sounded when Jerry opened the door of the beach shop. He stepped inside. The place felt humid and stuffy. Thin, green turf carpeted the floor. Sand gritted under Jerry's boots. Racks of cheap tourist souvenirs cluttered the counters and aisles. Sand dollar earrings, bright neon t-shirts, party paraphernalia, key chains with clichéd phrases like "Island Time" and "The Beach is my Happy Place."

Jerry browsed around the shop, waiting for a clerk to appear. He flipped through the children's section looking for something he could buy Maddie. He came to a row of cubbies containing polystyrene foam boogie boards.

"Hello?" said Jerry. "Anybody work here?"

He heard nothing in response. Jerry pressed his thumb into one of the boards until the foam dented. He did the same thing to the next board on the rack.

"Piece of shit," he muttered.

Jerry tried on a few pairs of sunglasses, looking at his reflection in the tiny mirror above the spinning rack. The third pair he tried had large aviator-style lenses with an amber tint that got lighter toward the bottom. Jerry scowled into the mirror and quoted a few lines from the movie Scarface. He checked the price tag on the sunglasses.

"Hey, I want to buy these sunglasses. You back there taking a shit or what?" he said, raising his voice toward an open door at the back of the shop.

The cash register sat on the counter to Jerry's left. An old, vintage model. The kind where you press a button, and the drawer snaps open like a clown's jaw in a carnival game. Jerry slid a finger under the register and lifted to see if it was attached to the counter. No resistance. The cash register stood lopsided on its three remaining legs.

Jerry considered the shotgun in his truck. He could bring it in and rob this place easily. Hell, he didn't even need the gun. Just pick up the cash register and walk out. He hesitated for a few moments, his hand supporting the weight of the machine. He lowered the leg back to the counter.

Jerry snapped the tag off the sunglasses. He took another look at himself in the mirror, and then walked out with the sunglasses on his face.

The beach was mostly empty. A few fishermen, a handful of couples, a jogger running barefoot at the edge of the water. Tuesday before Thanksgiving. Not much of a tourist day.

Jerry walked out on the beach, about halfway down to the water. He sat in the sand. With his western snap-button shirt, blue jeans, and cowboy boots he didn't exactly fit the picture of a typical beach comber.

A fisherman stood waist deep in the surf. He cast his rod and reeled in the line quickly to avoid getting his lure caught in the current.

Jerry sat in the sand, his eyes covered by the new pair of sunglasses. He watched the man fish for several minutes.

The sun felt warm but not hot. Jerry leaned back on an elbow in the sand. He scanned the beach for anything interesting—a couple of college girls from SCAD would be nice.

"Watch yourself. It'll suck you right in."

Jerry turned to see an older man squatting on his heels a few feet to his left.

Jerry shrugged. "Sometimes I wish it would."

The old man gave no response. He dug a shell from the sand with his finger. He lifted the mollusk to his face and spat on it, then shined it with his thumb.

"I was you," said the old man. "Yes, I was. At one time I was." The man stared forward while he spoke, as though mesmerized by the crashing waves.

"You don't know anything about me, old man."

The man laughed. A sudden staccato burst of sound.

"You can tell yourself that. Sure, you can. We can tell ourselves anything we want, can't we?"

Jerry dug the heel of his boot into the sand, rocking it back and forth until he had made an indentation in the ground like a stirrup that cupped his heel.

"Can't we?" repeated the old man.

"Yeah, I guess. Whatever."

"Oh, whatever. Whatever, whatever." The man said the word like he had never heard it before, turning it over in his mouth, tasting it as it left his lips.

"Did you need something?" said Jerry, getting perturbed.

"No, but you do."

"What do I need?" said Jerry. "And don't tell me Jesus or I'll throw you in the ocean."

The old man laughed hysterically. After a few seconds he caught his breath. "That one won't help you," he said, becoming serious. "Waste of your time and mine."

Jerry began to feel a little uneasy. "I better be getting back to work soon," he said, sitting up. He dusted the sand off his elbow.

"You're doing something big tonight," said the old man. "Aren't you?"

Jerry studied the man's face.

"You don't need to answer me," said the man. "I already know you are."

"What if I am?"

"What if you are."

"That's what I just asked."

The man snickered, making a high-pitched sound in the back of his throat.

Jerry shifted his weight away from the man. The laugh unsettled him.

"What do I need?" Jerry asked.

"What do you need?"

"Are you asking or telling?"

"You tell me."

Jerry shook his head. "You ain't right in the head, are you?"

The old man shrugged. He scratched his heavily stubbled face.

Jerry continued, "You said I need something."

"You expect me to tell you everything?"

"You're just a crazy old man."

"You can tell yourself that."

"You already said that one. Somebody needs to flip over your record."

"Sure, sure."

Jerry gritted his teeth, his temper rising. "You don't

know anything."

"Only what you told me."

Jerry stood up. He looked down at the old man still squatting on his heels in the sand. The man stared into the ocean. He made no attempt to move, his body caught in Jerry's shadow.

"I didn't tell you anything." Jerry spat the words with contempt. He had an urge to kick the man over. "You're just a little shriveled up old man."

The high-pitched snicker came again. The noise grated on Jerry's nerves.

"He's standing on your shadow," muttered the old man.

"What did you say? Who is?"

"He is. Look at it now. He's standing on it." The old man's voice rose with excitement. He pounded the sand below Jerry's shadow, then executed a quick shuffling jig in the sand. "I was you. I got him off my shadow. He's standing on it. You can never be free when he's standing on you."

Jerry took a step back. "You got it backwards, old man. You're the one in the dark. See? The shadow is on top of you, not the other way around."

"Sure, sure. You can tell yourself that."

"God, you're an annoying little bastard, ain't you?"

"Oh, him again."

"I've heard about enough from you," said Jerry.

The old man laughed yet again. He stood up slowly in a half crouch. He held one hand to his lower back, carefully maintaining his position within Jerry's shadow as he rose. Suddenly, the old man snapped upright and sprinted away with surprising speed. He ran until he disappeared over the sand dunes.

Jerry watched the old man's figure until it became indistinguishable from the scrub brush that divided the sand from the road.

"Crazy old codger," he said.

At Jerry's feet lay the spiraling shell the old man had spit-shined to a polish while they spoke. Jerry bent over and picked up the shell. He examined it for a second and then slid it in his pocket.

21

Rafe Lucas sat at his usual table in the front window of the bar, sipping espresso, rehashing the events of the previous night, when he heard a knock at the front door.

"What is it now?" he muttered. He leaned against the window to see the front patio from his chair.

The knock came again.

Lucas sighed. He finished his espresso and stood up, taking his time to walk over to the entrance. He turned the deadbolt and swung open the door.

"We're not open yet," Lucas said before he had eyes on the visitor. He squinted in the morning sun. When his pupils adjusted to the light, he realized the guest was a uniformed police officer. The officer stood square-shouldered in the door frame with his hand resting on his nightstick.

"Oh. Morning, officer." Lucas changed his tone. He forced himself to smile. "Little early for a drink, isn't it?" he joked.

The officer didn't smile back. He looked closely at the shattered edge of the door jamb, examining the wood that had been marred by bullets the night before.

"What happened here?" asked the officer.

"That? Oh, we had an issue with a keg exploding last night," said Lucas. "You ever seen one of those things blow? They send shrapnel all over the place."

The officer raised his eyebrows. "Can't say that I have."

"Yeah, well, it doesn't happen often but when it does it makes a real mess." Lucas played the 'aw shucks' angle, exaggerating his southern accent like he was some kind of country bumpkin lost in the big city. "Can I get you an espresso—I mean, a coffee or something, officer?"

"I'm good, thanks."

"Just let me know," said Rafe, still standing in the doorway. He stretched to block the officer's view of the bar. "Like I said, when that keg exploded last night, we had to close up early. Sent everyone home. You never know about those things. You get a bad batch, you might have more'n one blow on you. Figured it best to get everyone out and safe."

The officer sniffed and made a sound in the back of his throat that sounded like "hm."

"Well, if there's nothing else, officer, I'm in the process of cleaning up so I can open today."

The officer looked past Lucas's shoulder. Lucas shifted his weight slightly to block the view.

"Reason I'm here is somebody reported gunshots last night," said the officer.

"Gunshots?"

"Didn't call it in till this morning, though. Just a few minutes ago," said the officer. "Kind of curious, isn't it?"

"Yes, sir. Very curious, considering I have no idea about

any gunshots." Lucas pretended to ponder for a second, and then added, "Unless they're thinking the exploding keg was a gunshot? That must have been it. It really did sound like a gun going off. I could see that."

The officer eyeballed Lucas, unconvinced. "Multiple gunshots is what they said."

"Now that I think about it, shrapnel went flying all over the bar. It probably did sound like multiple gunshots. It was a miracle nobody got hurt."

"How many customers were in here?"

"It was late. Not too many. They were all intoxicated, too, so it would be hard to trust their account of anything. We evacuated 'em pretty quick to keep them safe. No telling whatall they might've thought."

"You know serving a drink to an intoxicated person is against the law?"

"Oh, of course. Yes, we know that. I think they were right on the line. You know how that goes. We're a bar. We have to make our money somehow."

The officer nodded slowly.

"I should mention we support you guys every year," continued Lucas. "I need to get my donation check into the fraternal order. I always do every year around this time. The holidays, you know. We couldn't do what we do without the men in blue. We sure appreciate you. Always make a nice donation."

"I'm not here to pass the plate."

"Oh, of course, I know that. Just wanted to tell you, since you're here and all, that we appreciate you." Lucas's face twisted into another fake smile.

"So you're telling me there was no gunfire here last

night? Nothing out of the ordinary?"

"Nothing other than that bad keg. You want, you can talk to my bartender. He should be here in a few hours if you want to stop back by."

"I may do that."

"You'd be welcome. Come in later after your shift and you got a free pint on the house."

The officer ran his hand over the bullet holes in the door frame. "Okay then. Have a good day. We'll see you again soon," he said.

"You, too. Hope all your calls today are as easy as this one." Lucas laughed and waved goodbye as he closed the door. He locked the deadbolt and leaned his back against the door. His heart pounded in his chest.

"Jesus, I can't wait to unload this shit tonight and be done with it," he breathed with a shaky voice.

Jerry stopped by the bar on his way home from the island to check in with Lucas. When he saw the police car parked out front he froze and waited, wondering if the cops were on to them.

Sitting in his truck across the street from the bar, Jerry watched the police officer leave and get in his cruiser. Jerry held the shotgun across his lap. He waited tensely for any sign that something had gone wrong. When Lucas closed the door of McKearney's, Jerry relaxed his grip on the stock of his weapon.

The cruiser idled at the curb for several minutes, a mere two car lengths away from Jerry's truck. Inside the vehicle the officer seemed to be waiting for something. Twice he lifted the two-way radio and spoke into it. Sweat rolled down the back of Jerry's neck. His heart thumped.

After what seemed like an eternity, the police car finally nudged forward and drove on up Bay Street.

Jerry slid the shotgun off his lap. He got out of the truck and headed for the alley beside McKearney's. He walked around to the back door where he knocked three times.

Jerry waited for Lucas to answer. In the light of day, the back alley wasn't much to look at it. Grease-stained concrete, a downspout leaking some kind of greenish sludge, a couple of filthy brown dumpsters. A horn honked on the road out front.

The sound of locks turning. Then the heavy steel door swung open. Jerry jumped back to avoid being hit by the swinging door.

Lucas saw Jerry and nodded. Without a word of greeting, he turned and walked back into the bar, leaving the door open.

"Lock that up, will ya?" Lucas called over his shoulder.

Jerry entered the bar. He stopped to close the door and lock it. Lucas had already resumed his seat in the front window when Jerry joined him inside.

"What'd that cop want?" said Jerry. He stood in the middle of the bar, talking loudly. The heels of his cowboy boots skidded and clicked across the polished concrete floor.

"You see him?" answered Lucas. He stared out the window at two women who were carrying shopping bags.

"I was out front in the truck about to come in when I noticed him."

"What do you make of it?"

"I don't know. What did he say?"

"Said somebody called in about gunshots just now."

"Just now?"

"That's what he said."

"What'd they wait till just now for if they were gonna call?"

Lucas didn't answer.

"What did you tell him?" said Jerry.

"Told him a fucking keg exploded."

Jerry joined Lucas at the table. The wooden chair creaked when he sat down. "He buy it?"

"Hard to say. Seemed to."

"He left. I guess that's something."

Lucas, still staring at the women with the bags, said, "I guess. I don't like it much."

Jerry cracked his knuckles. He stretched his arms above his head. "You got any coffee?"

"Espresso."

Jerry pursed his lips. He nodded toward the bar. "That coffee maker work?"

"I think Alonzo uses it."

Jerry got up. He went behind the bar and fumbled around until he found a coffee filter and a big jar of Folger's. Once the pot started gurgling, he turned his attention back to Lucas.

"What's the plan? For tonight?"

Lucas blinked. He broke his gaze away from the window and turned to face Jerry.

"Plan is to get this goddamn blow sold. I'm about tired of fooling with it."

"No argument here."

"The buyers said they'd come to the warehouse at nightfall."

"Nightfall? What is this, a Western?"

"Hell, Juice, I don't know. Sooner the better far as I'm concerned."

Jerry poured a cup of the coffee. "That sumbitch Bull gonna be there? He's the one shot the whole place up last night with that stupid Uzi. That's your gunfire call right there."

Lucas frowned. "You aren't one to talk. Blasting that shotgun like you did. I was right across the hallway for godsake."

Jerry shrugged. "We got 'em, didn't we?"

"We did." Lucas sounded proud.

Jerry took another drink of coffee and swallowed hard. "When the hell is nightfall anyway?"

"I guess about seven this time of year."

"What's that, like nine hours from now?"

"I hope you don't do the tutoring in your house."

Jerry scoffed. "I left my watch at home."

"It's almost noon now," Lucas said, pointing at the clock above the bar.

"I wasn't that far off."

"Bout as close as you are with a shotgun."

Jerry felt his face getting hot. He set down the empty coffee mug. "This coffee tastes like piss," he said.

"Yeah? Who made it?"

"Shit. How old is it?"

"Nevermind that," Lucas growled. "Be at the warehouse early tonight. Load up that shotgun and be ready for trouble.”

For the third time in a day Mack tried to call his employer. He let the phone ring a dozen times but got no answer. He wanted to discuss the botched ambush of the night before. So far, he had not received any pages, and he had not been able to get his client on the phone.

Mack began to suspect his client had abandoned the job. Frankly, he didn't blame the guy for giving up after the prior night's setback. The element of surprise had been compromised. Mack himself would just as soon get out of town and never look back. Any further action would be more dangerous now that the adversary had seen their hand. If his client wanted to abort the mission, well, that would be fine.

But the matter of payment remained. The client owed Mack money for his time, and for the risk he had assumed. Mack had put in four days' worth of surveillance. He had been involved in a shootout that had almost killed his friend. No question some amount of compensation was due to him, even if the job was cut short. Mack wanted to get the guy on the phone to negotiate a partial payment.

“Still nothing?” asked Avery when Mack hung up.

Mack shook his head. From his seat at the dining table, he watched Avery execute a half-hearted yoga stretch in the living room.

“Who is this guy anyway?” said Avery with her head pointed at the floor. Her body looked like a triangle, hips hinged in mid-air, palms and feet touching the floor. Her chest slightly muffled her voice.

"That's the thing about this kind of work—you usually don't know anything about your clients. You just do what they ask and take their money when it's done."

Avery turned her neck. She looked up from under her armpit, still holding the yoga pose. "Uh, yeah, I know a little something about that game."

Mack gave a slight laugh, exhaling through his nose. "Oh, I guess you do."

Avery dropped her knees to the carpet. "Where's he live? In Savannah?"

"I honestly don't know. On the phone, it always sounds like there are other people in the background. It's hard to say. He's never told me anything. Not even his name."

"You kinda put yourself in a bad spot there, didn't you? Doing the work without cash in your hand, no way to get a hold of the guy or even identify him? That's just asking to get screwed."

Mack stared at the linoleum beneath his chair. Yellow and brown geometric patterns with scuffs and a couple of dark burn marks. The linoleum probably hadn't been replaced since the 1970s.

"Yeah," he mumbled.

"I'm not trying to add insult to injury," Avery said. She finished her exercise. She padded barefoot across the carpet and joined Mack on the linoleum. Stopping at Mack's chair, she placed her hand on his shoulder and squeezed.

"That feels good," said Mack.

Avery put her other hand on Mack's neck and began kneading the tight muscles in his back.

"What are you gonna do?"

Mack closed his eyes. He relaxed his shoulders into

Avery's grip.

"If it was just me, I'd blow this whole thing off and skip town. Water under the bridge."

"Yeah?"

"But I got Andy involved. He's lying in a hospital bed right now. I did that to him. What about his wife? And his kid? I shouldn't have put him in that position."

"There's no sense worrying about that now. It's over. Like you said, water under the bridge."

Mack sighed. "I made a promise. I can't just hang him out to dry."

Avery continued to squeeze and release Mack's shoulder muscles. Mazzy Star's "Fade into You" came on the stereo in the living room.

"I love this song," Avery whispered.

The two listened to the acoustic guitar and tambourine, blended with the ethereal voice of Hope Sandoval.

Neither Mack nor Avery spoke for a while. Mack's eyes unfixed. He gazed at the patterned linoleum beneath his feet. Avery swayed slightly to the music. She mouthed the lyrics softly over Mack's head.

"I need to go back to the motel," said Mack.

"Won't it be dangerous there?" said Avery. "Don't you think they figured out where you were staying by now?"

"Maybe," Mack said. "But I left something in the room that I need. I have to go get it."

"Are you taking the Jetta?"

"Can I?"

"Keys are in the little green bowl by the door."

*

The front door of McKearney's remained locked at three o'clock in the afternoon. Alonzo had not shown up for work. Lucas hadn't really expected to see the bartender, but he thought maybe there was a chance.

Alonzo had been working for Lucas more than five years. He had seen a lot of sketchy stuff. And he had let it all slide in exchange for a good paycheck, plus the occasional "bonus." However, the events of the previous night had pushed Alonzo past his limit.

Lucas poured himself a shot of Jameson. He took it down with a quick jerk of his head. He slapped the empty shot glass on the bar and smacked his lips, making an "ahhh" sound that echoed in the empty bar. He glared at the pockmarked plaster and the chipped paint on the wall where Bull had sprayed the Uzi.

The bullet marks kind of blended with the aged walls and exposed brick. Maybe Lucas could get away with leaving it. Going for a rustic, unfinished vibe. Kind of an edgier motif.

Lucas leaned forward on the bar. He drummed his fingers on the wood. He fidgeted with a stack of cocktail napkins. Suddenly, in a quick flash of motion, he grabbed the fifth of Jameson, and headed for the back door.

Lucas's Range Rover waited in the alley. He propped the bar's steel door with a brick, and then he swung open the rear cargo door of the SUV.

Lucas took a slug of whiskey straight from the fifth. He set the uncorked bottle on the rear bumper of the Range

Rover.

Lucas disappeared back into the bar. He returned shortly, his arms laden with the weapons from the office. He dumped the guns into the Range Rover's cargo area. He took another pull from the whiskey and stepped back to admire his firepower.

On the way to the warehouse, Lucas took a detour on Liberty Street. He stopped in front of a historic home that had been divided up into unique apartments. Alonzo's place.

Lucas knew which unit belonged to Alonzo. He parked the Range Rover out front.

While climbing the stairs of the wraparound wooden porch, Lucas thought he saw a flash of movement in one of Alonzo's windows. He gritted his teeth and knocked on the door.

A cat hopped up on the porch. It flicked its tail and purred at Lucas. The animal cautiously approached, playing coy, waiting to see if Lucas would bend over and acknowledge it.

Lucas knocked again. When the cat reached striking distance, Lucas gave it a swift shove with the side of his loafer. The cat skidded a few feet across the porch until its claws caught the wood. It jumped off the porch and disappeared in the bushes.

"Hey, 'Lonzo. I know you're in there," shouted Lucas. He pounded on the door a third time.

Finally, the curtain slid sideways, and Alonzo peered out.

"Let me in," said Lucas. "We need to talk."

"You can talk from right there. I can hear you," said Alonzo through the glass.

"Come on, man. How long we worked together? Let me come inside. I don't care about you skipping out today. I decided to stay closed anyway."

Alonzo studied Lucas through the small windowpane on the door. After a few seconds, he opened the inner door. He flipped the switch on the screen door to lock it.

Lucas laughed. "Buddy, if I was gonna get you, that screen wouldn't help you much."

"It's fine how it is."

Lucas shrugged. "Suit yourself."

"I don't work for you anymore. I thought about it, and I decided this morning."

"Hate to hear that. 'Specially considering I'm paying out big bonuses to all employees tomorrow."

Alonzo winced. "You just trying to mess with me."

"Guess you'll never know," said Lucas. "Since you're quitting."

"Guess not."

"You really want to quit?"

"Man, I almost got killed last night. That dumb son-of-a-bitch could have shot every person in the bar with, what the hell even was that thing, some kind of machine gun."

"Nobody was hurt."

"Bullshit. One of those guys got shot. I saw the blood on the floor."

"Yeah, well, serves him right. They started it. We were just defending ourselves."

"I don't doubt they showed up because of some stupid

shit you got going on. You think I don't know what you're doing back in that office?"

Lucas clenched his jaw. He looked away, off in the direction the cat had run.

"See, that right there is what we need to talk about. You know I've always taken care of you."

Alonzo looked skeptically at Lucas.

"Every time I've put an envelope in your hand, you've accepted it, haven't you?"

Alonzo still gave no response.

"That's what I thought. Where do you think that money comes from?" Lucas didn't wait for an answer. "Someone might even say you are complicit in my business. Police might even say that."

"Police?"

"I'm just saying, if word ever got out about what happened at the bar last night, it wouldn't be hard to show how the bartender was as involved as anybody else."

"That's not true and you know it."

Lucas raised his hands. "Hey, I'm just saying. The line is blurry."

Alonzo shook his head. "Nah, man. You ain't pulling me down into your bullshit. This has gone too far."

Lucas grimaced. "Damn," he said slowly. "I was really hoping you wouldn't say that."

In one motion, Lucas pulled a small pistol from his pocket. He squeezed off three quick rounds. Two hit Alonzo in the chest, and the third passed right through his throat.

Alonzo fell to the floor with terror in his eyes. He clutched at the blood spurting from the hole in his neck.

He gagged on the blood, trying to shout for help. No sound came from his mouth except for gurgling gasps like he was drowning.

Through the three bullet holes in the screen door Lucas watched Alonzo die. The struggle ended in a matter of seconds.

Lucas stepped away from the door. He darted down the stairs, pocketing the pistol as he ran. He jumped in the Range Rover and gave it some gas. He was gone before the neighbors realized what happened.

22

Mack made a few passes of the motel before turning into the parking lot. He cruised the road, looking for suspicious vehicles in the area or anything else that might indicate that his room was under surveillance.

He parked the Jetta in a spot about a hundred feet from the door of his room and waited. Andy's Tahoe had not moved from the parking space where they left it the night before.

Mack stuck his hand in his pocket. He palmed the Tahoe's keys and jingled them softly. The plan was to move the weapons from Andy's truck into the trunk of the Jetta. The Tahoe's guns combined with the firepower Mack had taken from the Caravan added up to a small arsenal.

For half an hour Mack sat patiently in the Jetta. He observed the comings and goings of motel guests. Any car that entered or exited the lot, Mack studied its passengers. He watched carefully for the men from the bar.

Nothing seemed particularly out of the ordinary. Just a few business travelers, some couples, one family. No strange men in parked cars, other than himself. The place seemed safe as far as Mack could tell.

Mack gripped the Beretta. His thumb flicked off the safety. He got out of the Jetta and paused yet again to case the parking lot. Keeping both hands in his pockets—one on the motel key and one on the pistol—Mack strolled across the lot to his room.

The door to the adjacent room stood slightly ajar, its sliding lock jammed in the crack to keep the door open. Inside, a couple argued over the television channel. Mack smelled marijuana smoke escaping through the crack as he approached his own door.

He took the key from his pocket and inserted it in the handle, but the key would not turn. Mack pulled it out and re-inserted it. He jiggled the handle and tried again. Nothing. His key no longer worked. The lock had been changed.

"Well, shit," Mack said under his breath. He turned around and scouted out the main office. The arguing in the next room reached a crescendo. Mack followed the sidewalk away from the shouting and toward the office.

The motel office smelled moldy and damp. A small man wearing an absurd toupee that resembled roadkill parted a bead curtain with both hands and stepped through the clacking strings. He held a burning cigarette between his lips, the smoke from which wafted directly into his eyes, though he seemed to be unfazed by the irritant.

"Whaddaya need?" the man said. The cigarette bounced on his lower lip as he spoke. "Night or hour?"

"I've been staying here a few days. Room 139."

The man coughed without removing the cigarette from his mouth. "Bet your momma's real proud."

Mack frowned. "My key doesn't seem to be working."

"Why do you think that is?"

"Well, I'm not sure. That's why I'm in here telling you about it." Mack tossed his key on the counter.

The motel clerk rifled through a spiral notebook with yellowing pages. He stopped on a page and pointed to a line of illegible handwritten text.

"Just like I figured. Delinquent payer."

"Delinquent?"

"That's what I said. You don't pay, you get locked out."

"Hold on, now. Who said I didn't pay?"

The clerk looked at the clock on the wall. "Checkout was about six hours ago. Did you pay for another day?"

"Not yet. I had to—there were some extenuating circumstances."

"Ain't my problem."

Mack felt his blood rising. "You mean you change the locks in a matter of hours?"

"We got a guy. Round here we see a lot of deadbeats like you. Goes with the business."

Mack brushed off the clerk's insult. "Fine. What will it take to get me back into my room? I left something in there."

The clerk studied his notebook. "For starters, you'd have to pay for another night, like you should have done in the first place if you wanted to keep your stuff in the room. On top of that, we assess a fee for changing the locks."

"Another whole night so I can walk into the room for

thirty seconds?"

"Ninety-three dollars'll cover everything."

Mack shook his head. "Right there is your key back." He nodded at the counter where the key lay attached to a piece of hard red plastic with 139 stenciled in white letters. "You ought to be able to reuse the lock."

"Don't work like that."

Mack took a wad of cash from his pocket and peeled off $93. He handed it to the clerk.

The clerk counted the money slowly, saying aloud each bill as he came to it. He put the cash into a leather pouch.

The room keys hung on a board behind the desk. The clerk located the new key for Room 139 and handed it over to Mack. "You got it for the night if you want it."

"I'll be back in two minutes," Mack grumbled.

When Mack returned to the locked motel door the couple's arguing in the adjacent room had changed to loud moaning accompanied by the disgusting sound of slapping skin. The bed creaked. The headboard banged repeatedly against the wall.

"Jesus, take it easy in there," Mack said as he unlocked his door.

The room looked exactly as it did when he and Andy had vacated it the night before. The beds were unmade. Discarded towels lay in a pile on the bathroom floor. Mack wondered why it was so important to change the locks when they had no intention of re-renting it. No doubt a money-making scheme for the motel.

Mack headed straight for the small table near the window where he had last used the tracking device. The table was empty, the tracker nowhere to be found.

Mack got on his knees and searched the floor of the motel room, looking under both beds. He checked the bathroom and the closet. The tracker was gone.

Mack stormed out of the room. The door slammed behind him, temporarily causing the lovebirds next door to pause in the act.

"Where is it?" Mack said the second he entered the motel office.

The clerk looked up from his notebook. "Where's what?"

"You know exactly what I'm talking about."

The clerk smirked. He pointed to a sign on the wall above his head. He recited the words without even looking at the sign.

"All abandoned items are property of the motel."

Mack seethed with anger. "You can't do that!"

"Says who?"

"You steal from your guests? Is that how this place does business?"

"Whoa, excuse me, sir. We do not *steal* anything from anyone."

"You took my tracker from the room."

"Is that what that thing is? We were wondering."

"So you do know what I'm talking about."

"Our housekeeping staff sweeps the room after checkout time. Any items left behind are confiscated. Complain if you want, but you agreed to it when you signed the rental contract."

"That device is worth a lot of money."

"Lucky me then, I guess."

Mack shook his head. He wanted to knock the guy out

and reclaim his property. For a second, he considered the Beretta in his pocket but decided against it. The last thing he needed was more attention in this town. The clerk had him against a wall.

"Everything's about money to you it seems like," said Mack. "What do you want for the tracker?"

The clerk pondered Mack's question. "It's not for sale," he finally said.

"Not for sale," Mack repeated. He took the wad of cash from his pocket. He showed it to the clerk. "Come on, what do you want for it?"

"Guy carrying that much cash is up to something, that's what I think. Tracking device? What is it you're tracking?"

"Don't worry about that. It's important enough for me to pay for it. Now how much?"

"I already told ya. Not for sale."

Mack again considered pulling his pistol on the guy.

"You're telling me there is no amount of money that will get you to return my stolen—or as you say, *confiscated*—property to me?"

"Don't think so. But I'll rent it to you."

"For how much?"

"One thousand dollars a minute."

Mack gasped. The clerk's statement was so ludicrous that he actually laughed out loud. "You're out of your mind."

"That's my price. Take it or leave it."

Any other circumstances and Mack would have gone around the counter, knocked the annoying clerk on his butt, and taken back what belonged to him. But he had to swallow his pride for a few more hours. If the guy called the police, it would mess up Mack's whole plan. Or worse, if word got out to the smugglers that some guy matching his description was running a tracking device of some kind in town, it would certainly blow his cover.

Mack knew if he could locate the stash, it would be worth a lot more to him than a thousand dollars. He begrudgingly counted out the money and laid it on the counter.

The clerk's eyes lit up like a child on Christmas morning. "You really do want this thing, don't you?" he said, rubbing his palms together.

Mack scowled at the clerk without answering. He waited while the guy disappeared into the back room.

A few seconds later, the tracker sat on the counter. The clerk gripped the machine tightly in both hands.

Mack reached for the device.

The clerk pulled it away, shaking his head. "Unh-uh, I hold it. You tell me what to do."

Mack had already resigned to the clerk's eccentric and obnoxious demands. He all but anticipated this final humiliating blow.

"Flip the switch on the side."

The clerk flipped the switch and the screen lit up. "Ooooh," he cooed. "Now what?"

"Hold it up so I can see it."

"The clerk obeyed.

"Okay, see that little green dot? Use the arrow keys to zoom in on it." Mack watched as the clerk fumbled with the buttons. "Hold on. Stop there."

Mack studied the screen with its rudimentary map. He recognized the location of the beacon—exactly where he had first deployed the device. The stash was back at the warehouse where it all started. Mack felt relief knowing the drugs—and the money—were still in town.

"What are we looking at here?" said the clerk.

"Keep it steady for a few seconds."

"The little green dot, what does it mean?"

Mack ignored the question. He watched the marker blink on and off. It never moved from its location.

"You can shut it off. That's all I need to know."

"Already? What did you see?"

Mack shrugged. "What do you care? You got your extortion money."

The clerk snickered. "I can't believe you paid that much to use this hunk of junk for one minute."

Mack glared at the guy.

"What's this thing worth anyway?" asked the clerk. "Say if somebody was going to sell it? What would you put the street value at for a machine like this one?"

"It's not worth a damn thing without the corresponding piece that causes the little green dot to show up on the screen. You'd need to have both parts. And believe me, you'll never get your hands on that other piece."

"How do you know? Maybe I'll turn it on and do what you did, get there before you do."

"Good luck with that. You don't even know what you're looking at."

The clerk sneered. "You come back and see me when you need another look at your little green dot. The price goes up for the second minute."

Mack barely heard the guy. He left the office, letting the door slam behind him.

Within a few minutes, Mack had transferred the duffle bag full of guns and ammunition from the Tahoe to the back seat of the Jetta.

Dusk shrouded the city when Mack pulled out of the motel parking lot. He turned toward the island.

23

"Bout time you showed up," Bull growled when Jerry climbed the stairs of the loading dock.

Jerry ignored the comment. He walked over to the large warehouse door. He clicked the latch open and slid the creaking door up on its metal track. The box truck was still backed up a foot from the dock where he and Steve had left it.

"You guys gonna stand around with your thumbs up your butts or are we unloading this truck?" said Jerry over his shoulder to Bull and Steve. "Lot of good you did getting here early if all you did was stand around."

"Rafe didn't say unload it," said Steve.

"Is he here?" said Jerry.

Neither man answered.

"That's what I thought. You want to be standing around doing nothing when he shows up, be my guest. But I'm getting started. Show some initiative, why don't you."

Bull rolled his eyes. He and Steve followed Jerry into the back of the truck. They got to work carrying bricks of cocaine into the warehouse.

"Lucas told me he's taking your share to fix all your stupid bullet holes in his bar," said Jerry to Bull. He hopped across the small gap between the tailgate and the dock. He smiled, knowing his comment would piss Bull off.

"Bullshit."

"Is that your full name? Bull Shit?"

"Don't fuck around about my money," said Bull.

"Hey, I'm just the messenger. Don't shoot me. Although it doesn't seem like you could hit me if you tried."

Bull threw down the kilo he was holding. When the package hit the floor of the truck it broke, sending a cloud of powder into the air. He took three steps toward Jerry with his fists raised.

"What the hell is going on in here?" shouted Rafe Lucas.

Bull froze when he realized his boss had entered the warehouse.

Lucas continued, "Bull, you idiot. If you wreck one of those keys, it's twenty grand out of your ass. You hear me?"

Bull hung his head. "Jerry said you was—"

"Don't worry about what Jerry said. Get down there and scrape up every last crumb of white powder. And tape the key back up like it was."

Lucas threw a tape gun at Bull, hitting him in the chest.

Bull caught the tape gun. He got on his hands and knees and began scraping up the cocaine. The powder covered his hands. Cocaine dust swirled in the air. All three of the men in the truck breathed it as they worked.

"Anyway, who told you guys to unload the truck?" said Rafe, still barking orders at the men.

No one answered.

"Did I tell you to unload it?"

"No," said Steve.

"Do you know why I didn't tell you to unload it?"

The men recognized the question was rhetorical. They waited for Lucas to continue.

"I didn't tell you to unload the truck because we ain't unloading the fucking truck!"

Bull's glare could have burned a hole in the side of Jerry's head.

"Guy wants three mil worth of blow, says he'll throw in an extra fifty K for the truck," said Lucas. "What do I care? Makes it easier that way. They give us the cash, we hand 'em the keys to the truck." Lucas brushed his hands together like he was dusting them off. "Easy as can be. They drive off into the sunset. Done in five minutes. Then we divvy up the cash and go our separate ways."

"Three million," Jerry breathed quietly. It was the first time Lucas had put a definitive price on the job. More money than Jerry had imagined. According to their agreement, Jerry would get ten percent for his part in arranging the deal and seeing it through. That worked out to $300,000. Jerry swallowed hard, thinking about what he would do with more than a quarter million in cash.

"Juice, quit daydreaming and help those two put everything back," snapped Lucas. "Stack it all up on the pallet nice and neat. Wrap the whole thing in plastic. Then get your asses out of there. Shouldn't be long now."

Mack wondered if all strippers drove cars with tinted

windows. It made sense—after a long night of getting ogled all they'd want to do is hide out behind dark glass. Not to mention some of the creeps who hung out in the lot hoping to catch a glimpse of an exotic dancer in the wild. Either way, Mack appreciated the Jetta's dark tint job. It made his own work easier.

The sun had just slipped below the horizon when Mack pulled off the highway. He turned toward the warehouse.

The humid air blowing off the ocean retained its salty moisture. The refracting sunset tinted the sky an eery pink hue, covering the world in a thin layer of electric neon.

Mack parked the Jetta a hundred yards past the warehouse behind a strip of other vehicles. He didn't want to take a chance of spooking his marks. He knew they would be paranoid after the events of the previous night.

Mack pulled one of the canvas duffle bags from the back of the car. He dropped it the passenger seat. He unzipped the bag and rifled through the contents. Several guns, a few knives, a pair of bulletproof vests. Mack slipped one of the vests over his shoulders and secured it with Velcro straps.

The second duffle bag held the item Mack hoped he would find: a high-powered scope. He raised it to his eye, and adjusted the cylinder until the lens came into focus. He inched down in his seat for discretion.

Mack swept the scope across the sparse road until he found the chainlink fence that surrounded his target. Another adjustment of the focal lens, and he had a visual of the warehouse parking lot. The box truck backed up to the loading dock door. He guessed the drugs would still be inside the truck.

The scope showed no movement in the lot. The door at the top of the stairs stood slightly ajar, the only indication that the building was occupied.

A safety lamp across the street from the warehouse flickered and came to life, bathing the lot in fluorescent light.

Mack counted the parked cars near the warehouse. A Range Rover, an old pickup truck, and a Trans Am. That meant at least three guys, probably more.

A mound of decaying trash lay smeared in the gravel near the rear wheel of the pickup. Mack recognized it as the ruined remains of the pizza from the other night, the last time he had staked out this warehouse. That night had been exciting, like the beginning of something new. Tonight felt more like an ending, a final act. One more item to check off his list before Mack could leave this town behind.

Once the daylight disappeared, Mack slipped out of the Jetta. He jogged back about twenty feet until he came to another vehicle. A Buick sedan with a flat tire. Using the screwdriver blade on his pocketknife, Mack loosened the screws on the Buick's license plate. The plate popped off with a clink. He carried it back to the Jetta where he switched out the license plate that was registered to Avery. Just in case anything went wrong, Mack didn't want someone to look up the registration of the Jetta. He took a few running steps and chucked the Jetta's old license plate like a discus. The thin metal plate soared through the air. It skidded and landed in a pile of refuse along the side of the road.

Satisfied that his tracks were covered, Mack got back in the car and continued his surveillance.

*

"Bull, I want you outside," Lucas barked. "Stand at the bottom of the stairs and wait for them to show up. Jerry, you and Steve stay in here. Nobody talks unless I tell them to. You got that?"

The three men nodded.

"Keep your weapons out and keep the safeties off. I don't expect any trouble from our buyers—they're professionals. But we don't know if our friends from last night will show up again." Lucas paused, making eye contact with each of his men. "They do, then kill 'em."

Steve nodded. He shifted his hips and clenched his jaw. He stuffed a fist in his pocket. Lucas watched as Steve conspicuously gripped his groin and shivered like a kindergartner.

Lucas frowned. "You got something you need to tell us?"

"Gotta take a leak is all."

"I can see that. Why don't you hit the can like a grown ass man. Quit shifting around like you're on the playground about to piss your diaper."

A twisted smile spread across Bull's face. He slung the strap of his Uzi over his shoulder. He popped out the clip, checked it, and reinserted it with a palm slap.

"Hey pal, watch out when you go in there," Bull said to Steve. "Jerry might be lying on the floor trying to blow your dick off."

Steve and Bull both laughed.

Jerry scowled down at his boots. He took a position near the rear of the warehouse with his shotgun gripped tightly in both hands.

"That's enough," growled Lucas. "Quit flirting with each other and do your jobs."

The toilet flushed in the small bathroom. Steve came out, exhaling a sigh of relief. He found a post in the opposite corner from Jerry. He spotted an old radio on the shelf behind him and started fidgeting with the buttons.

"Anybody care if I put on some tunes?"

No one answered.

"Too quiet in here. I'm gonna try and find us some Speedwagon while we wait. Maybe some Dio."

Steve turned on the stereo. He scrolled the knob through static, searching for a station.

"Hey Juice, you like Dio?"

"I guess."

"He guesses," Steve muttered. "Either you like 'em or you don't."

The radio crackled and hit a clear station playing The Cranberries.

"Nah, I don't like any of this new crap," said Steve.

He kept scrolling. The next station Steve found caused him to cheer and fist pump when he heard Winger's "Easy Come Easy Go."

"That'll get your blood flowing right there," Steve said to Jerry, who squinted and nodded to appease him.

"Quit fooling with the goddamn radio," said Lucas. "Leave it where it is."

"Fine by me," Steve whispered into his sleeve.

From his position in the back of the warehouse, Jerry saw the top of Bull's head rise just above the landing outside. The gel in Bull's flat top shimmered in the fluorescent light. The rest of the parking lot was dark and quiet.

The men waited.

About an hour passed with Mack observing the warehouse. He recognized the stocky henchman posted at the bottom of the stairs. And he also recognized the Uzi strapped to the henchman's shoulder. Mack hoped he would not have to tangle with that weapon again. One close call with a machine gun was enough.

A little after 8:00 p.m. a pair of headlights flashed at the end of the empty access road.

Mack slid down in his seat. He watched the car approach the warehouse. The vehicle turned slowly into the parking lot. Mack focused his scope on the car. A shiny black Mercedes SUV with windows so dark they reflected the streetlight like a mirror.

The Mercedes drove slowly through the gate in the chainlink fence. The driver parked the vehicle near the box truck. Three doors opened at the same time. Men dressed in all-black tactical clothing with tall black lace-up boots exited. Three in all—the driver plus two men from the backseat. They all carried submachine guns.

A few seconds later, the front passenger door opened. Out stepped a middle-aged man wearing a dark red suit with a black turtleneck. His permed hair spiraled over his ears and hung almost to his shoulders. A thick gold chain lay over his turtleneck and rested on his broad chest. Several of the man's fingers were adorned with matching gold rings.

Mack studied the men's square, hard faces. He guessed them to be Russian or some other Eastern European nationality. He watched as their eyes cautiously scanned the fenced lot. The men proceeded up the stairs, nodding at the guard with the Uzi as they passed him.

Jerry saw the Mercedes' headlights enter the parking lot. He stiffened when Lucas jumped up from the desk. Lucas practically floated across the concrete floor to greet the buyers at the top of the stairs.

Jerry glanced at Steve, who assumed a similar, stoic posture. They were now officially on duty.

Jerry slid the fingers of his right hand in the pocket of his tight blue jeans. He felt the smooth seashell he had collected earlier from the beach. He rubbed his index finger over the polished surface. The sleek hardness of the shell calmed his nerves. He recalled the old man's words regarding his shadow. The bum's cackling laughter still echoed in Jerry's mind.

There could be no mistaking which of the new arrivals was in charge. The guy in the red suit did all the talking. He wore yellow-tinted sunglasses with gold frames that glinted under the warehouse's fluorescent lights.

Jerry leaned forward. He strained to hear the conversation between this new man and his own boss. Most of the words were inaudible at the distance that separated them. The guy in the suit had a thick accent that sounded Russian. Jerry couldn't tell for sure.

Lucas snapped his fingers. "Hey, Juice. Open this door for the man!" he shouted.

Jerry reacted to Lucas's voice as though he'd been shot. His nerves were ratcheted to high alert. He winced and stepped backward, quickly releasing the shell, and withdrawing his hand from his pocket. He collected himself and jogged to the front of the warehouse, shotgun in hand.

Lucas pointed at the rear door of the box truck. Jerry tried to unhook the latch, but he needed both hands to do it. He shifted the shotgun to the crook of his arm. The long weapon was too awkward for him to hold. For a few uncomfortable moments Jerry contemplated whether it would be better to ask for help or to relinquish his weapon.

"Set the goddamn thing down!" said Lucas. Then, turning to the buyer, he grumbled, "he ain't the sharpest knife in the drawer."

The man in the suit raised his eyebrows over the yellow lenses. He shifted his weight to the other leg and glanced around at his men.

Jerry leaned his shotgun against the wall. With both hands, he unclasped the latch and slid up the door with a crash of metal on metal. He stepped back and retrieved his shotgun.

The buyer nodded to one of his guys who jumped into action. He lowered his machine gun, letting it hang at his side on the shoulder strap. He hopped across the gap. The truck's shocks creaked and shuddered when the man landed on his heavy combat boots.

The man flipped out a pocketknife and flicked it open. He cut a hole in the plastic wrap about halfway down the stack. He stabbed the knife into one of the bricks of cocaine. The man withdrew a pile of white powder on the tip of his blade. He raised it to his nostril and sniffed hard. Within a few seconds, his eyes lit up. He swallowed the drainage in the back of his throat. He looked at his boss and nodded.

The boss spoke something in a different language. Jerry felt pretty sure now that the language was Russian. The henchman in the truck wiped the blade of his knife on his black cargo pants and closed it. He jumped back over to the warehouse floor, then pulled the truck door closed and locked it.

Another word from the boss, and a second henchman darted out of the warehouse. Jerry heard his boots clanging on the metal stairs outside. A car door opened and closed. The man returned carrying three large duffle bags. The combined weight of the bags slowed him down. He took the stairs one at a time. At the doorway, he turned sideways to clear the bags through the tight entry. He tossed them on the floor at Lucas's feet.

Lucas knelt and unzipped one of the bags. His eyes widened. A smile crept across his face. He lifted a stack of bundled cash and fanned through it.

Jerry, still standing near the door, saw the contents of the bag reflected in the Russian's yellow sunglasses. He swallowed hard. He wiped his palms on his jeans, one at a time, switching his grip on the shotgun.

Lucas dug through the bag. He checked multiple bundles and tossed them back into the folds of the canvas bag. He moved on to the other two bags, spot-checking random bundles of cash from each.

"Three million," said Lucas to no one in particular. He stood up and handed the truck keys to the Russian.

"Looks like you're the new owner of a 1992 GMC Vandura 3500."

The Russian took the keys without a word or a smile. He tossed them to one of his men. The driver left the warehouse, followed closely by a second man. They shuffled down the stairs. The truck rocked from side to side as each man climbed aboard. Seconds later, the engine fired. The truck nudged forward a few feet and stopped with the engine still running.

"Pleasure doing business with you," said Lucas.

The Russian nodded. He signaled to the last of his men, and the two of them left the warehouse together.

Jerry watched through the open garage door as the two men walked past Bull at the bottom of the landing. They got back in the Mercedes.

"Weren't much for conversation, were they?" said Jerry.

Lucas shrugged. "Money talks," he said. "I speak that language and that's all that matters."

"Heard that."

The Mercedes backed out of the parking spot. Its headlights illuminated the driver in the box truck as it passed by. The truck fell in line behind the SUV. Thirty seconds later both cars were gone from sight, just as quickly as they had come.

"Did we get it?" Bull hollered up through the open warehouse door.

"What the hell do you think?" said Lucas. He tossed a bundle of cash down to Bull.

Bull caught the bundle in one hand. He flicked the cash like a Blackjack dealer. "Three million dollars?" he said, his voice pitched with excitement.

Lucas smiled. "Yep."

Bull fist-pumped the air. He raised the money to his nose and sniffed. "Smells damn good."

"Wait till you see it all in the bag," said Lucas. "But before you come in, do a lap out there and check the parking lot. Then get on up here and let's divide this shit up."

"Hell yeah," shouted Steve. He left his post at the back of the warehouse to join the other men. He had taken a dozen steps when the radio behind him switched songs. Hootie and the Blowfish's "Hold My Hand" began reverberating throughout the empty warehouse.

"Oh, hell no," said Steve. "We ain't counting our money to this bullshit." He spun on his heels and headed back toward the radio.

Mack watched as the two black-clad men climbed in the box truck. The headlights switched on when the engine started.

"Guess they took the deal," he whispered. He still held the sighting scope to his eye. He searched the dock for the cash.

When the truck followed the Mercedes out of the lot Mack barely paid attention to the vehicles. He had no interest in their cargo. What he wanted sat just inside the door, perched on the edge of the open loading dock: three black duffle bags that held all the money.

Mack's plan was to catch the men off guard by hitting them immediately. He switched the interior light of the Jetta to the OFF position. He opened the door and slid out in the darkness. Once outside, he dragged the bag of weapons to the edge of the seat.

Mack stuffed a pistol in each pocket. He slung an AR-15 rifle over his shoulder. He whispered a quiet thank you to Andy for his elaborate gun collection.

The thought of Andy lying in an Atlanta hospital bed with his wife and child by his side renewed Mack's resolve. He had made a promise to Andy that he would earn enough money to change his family's future. Since Mack's employer had abandoned them with no way to collect on the contract, this was Plan B.

Mack closed the door of the Jetta with a soft click. He raised the AR-15. He took a deep breath and sprinted across the road. As he ran, Mack's mind switched into combat mode, courtesy of his time in the Navy. As far as Mack was concerned, shooting Andy had been an act of war.

Fluorescent lights from the open loading dock flooded the parking lot. Mack scanned the lot as he traversed it, straining to see into the dark shadows. He stopped short of the circle of light, about thirty feet from the open door. He raised the AR-15 to his shoulder and aimed it at the first man he saw.

"Stay where you are, or I'll put one right through you," Mack shouted.

Lucas froze. He lifted his hands to his sides and turned around slowly. He squinted down at the darkness until his eyes found Mack.

"You again?" said Lucas. "You're the guy from last night, aren't you? Hate to break it to you, but you just missed all the fun, pal. Your score left in that box truck."

Lucas nodded in the direction of the road.

"I don't care about that. I want what's in those bags."

Lucas scoffed. "Where's your buddy? He didn't make it? We got his ass, didn't we?" He smirked down at Mack. "I have a roomful of armed men up here. You make one move for those bags, and you're dead just like your friend from last night."

In the back of the lot, Bull watched as Mack took aim at Lucas. His palms poured sweat. He adjusted his grip on the Uzi. He slowly crept forward out of the shadows until he had Mack in range. He raised the Uzi and pulled the trigger. The weapon clicked but the trigger did not depress.

"Damn it!" he said, slapping the side of the machine gun. He pulled the trigger again and the barrel erupted in a spray of bullets.

The temporary hiccup gave Mack just enough time to duck behind a dumpster before the Uzi fire pierced the air.

With his back pressed against the cool metal dumpster, Mack gave up hope of negotiating a peaceful arrangement with these men. They had called his bluff. He edged around the side of the trash container and returned fire.

Bull had no cover. He stood exposed in the middle of the parking lot, holding down the trigger of his Uzi. The weapon sent ricocheting bullets scattering along the side of the dumpster.

Mack took a deep breath and exhaled. He rolled around the side of the trash container and took aim at Bull. He squeezed the trigger.

Bull dropped hard to the pavement, the Uzi at his side.

Above them, on the loading dock, Lucas panicked.

"Shoot him! Shoot him!" Lucas shouted at Jerry.

Jerry shouldered his shotgun, but he had no clear view of Mack behind the large trash can.

The deafening machine gun report subsided. The only sound in the warehouse was the radio, still playing "Hold My Hand." The music echoed through the warehouse and spilled into the parking lot where Mack remained hidden.

Steve, who had abandoned the radio when the gunfire began, ran to the side door. He braced himself against the cinder block wall, his pistol gripped tightly against his chest.

Steve poked his head around the door jamb and fired three shots into the darkness. The noise rippled around the room. Soon, the warehouse became silent again except for the music.

"What do we do?" Steve said to Lucas.

Lucas was busy gathering up the duffle bags. He slung one over his shoulder. When he tried to add a second bag, the first one slid off.

"Shoot that son of a bitch!" he yelled. "He's trying to take our money!"

Steve nodded. He again swung around the side of the door frame. This time, Mack was waiting for him. He caught Steve with a bullet in the shoulder. Steve spun around, crying out in pain. Blinded by adrenaline, Steve charged the staircase. He descended the steps, firing erratically toward the dumpster.

Mack lowered the rifle. He pulled a pistol from his pocket, and reached the weapon around the side of the trash can. He emptied the clip in the direction of the staircase. He paused and listened. Silence. When he peered around the side of the dumpster, he spotted Steve lying face down, his body crumpled on the metal stairs.

Tucking the empty pistol back in his pocket, Mack again raised the AR-15. He cautiously approached the stairs. He stuck the toe of his boot in Steve's ribs to check for life. The body rolled sideways on the step.

Mack paused on the landing. He listened for sounds from within the warehouse. The music from the stereo was louder now. Some pop song he recognized but couldn't place. Mack strained his ears, but he could not discern any sounds over the music. He peeked through the doorway, leading with the barrel of his rifle.

A blast from Jerry's shotgun sent a spray of buckshot inches from Mack's head. The gunfire echoed. The deafening noise rumbled throughout the metal-framed warehouse. Mack ducked back outside.

"Two down!" Mack shouted. "How many are left in there?"

"Ten inside, and ten more on the way!" said Lucas. "You got a death wish if you don't get out of here."

Mack scoffed. "I don't think I believe you. I think there's just two of you left in there. Two down, two to go. That's how I figure it. And if I counted right, there's three bags of cash. One for each of us, and we all three walk away from here."

Lucas laughed. "No chance in hell," he growled.

As Lucas spoke, he dropped to his knees. He carefully slid off the loading dock. With his feet on the ground, he crouched down, gaining a direct line of sight to Mack on the stairwell landing above.

Lucas raised his pistol and pulled the trigger. The bullet nailed Mack square in the chest, embedding in the bulletproof vest. Mack stumbled backward. He tripped and broke his fall on Steve's body. He quickly struggled to his feet. Lucas squeezed off another shot as Mack dove through the warehouse door. The second bullet grazed Mack's arm, ripping the flesh of his right bicep.

Mack hit the ground rolling. He somersaulted behind the desk just in time to avoid another shotgun blast from Jerry. Mack lay there behind the metal desk, panting for air. He touched his arm and felt the blood that trickled from the wound.

"Come on, man, don't make me kill you," said Jerry, his voice almost pleading.

"Jerry, now ain't the time to get soft. Execute that son of a bitch," said Lucas. His head showed above the loading dock as he stood in the parking lot below. Lucas grabbed one of the duffle bags and slid it off the dock. The bag landed with a thud on the pavement.

"Hold on, now, where are you going with that cash?" said Jerry. His eyes darted from the desk where Mack was hiding to Lucas's face at the ledge of the loading dock.

"Juice, don't worry about what I'm doing. Pay attention to the guy with the gun. I'll get the cash out of here, and we can meet up later."

Jerry glanced nervously at Lucas. "I don't like that idea. Divide it up here. That was the plan. It's two-on-one. We can take this guy out right now and split the cash."

Lucas stretched his arm for the second bag. His fingertips grazed the strap. He jumped and lunged forward, reaching for the bag, but he could not quite grasp it.

"Is Bull and Steve dead?" said Jerry. His voice grew more frantic.

"Fuck 'em," said Lucas. "More for me."

"You mean us."

"Yeah, whatever."

Jerry clenched his jaw. His eyes hardened. He swung the shotgun over to Lucas.

"Man, I've had just about enough of you. Leave that bag right where it is."

"Damn it, Juice, don't be stupid."

Lucas extended the barrel of his pistol so the tip barely reached the bag's handle. He started to pull the second duffle bag toward the edge of the dock. The metal gun barrel scraped along the concrete floor.

"I said leave it alone," said Jerry. He racked the shotgun and took aim at Lucas.

"Hold on, now. Jerry, take it easy," said Lucas, softening his tone. He let go of the bag and raised his hands slowly. "We're on the same side here. Don't do anything crazy. Remember, you got a guy over there trying to kill us both. We have to work together."

Mack listened to the two men talking from his post behind the desk. His right bicep stung ferociously from the bullet's damage. He cautiously peered around the edge of the desk.

Jerry stood still, looking down at Lucas. His shotgun was leveled at Lucas's head.

"You want to work together, how bout you toss the other bag back up here. Then, go around to the stairs and help me flush this guy."

"That's what I was trying to do."

"The hell you were. You were gonna take those bags and leave me standing here like an asshole."

Jerry used the toe of his boot to drag the second duffle

bag out of Lucas's reach. He kept the shotgun pointed at Lucas.

"What's stopping me from blowing your head off right now and taking all three bags for myself?" said Jerry. "For all I know that's what you planned to do all along."

"Jerry, you're talking crazy, man. When have I ever treated you bad?"

Jerry scoffed. "Every goddamn time you've seen me. And I'm tired of it."

Jerry raised the shotgun to his shoulder. He sighted the crosshairs between Lucas's eyes. Both men lost focus on the world around them.

The distraction was exactly what Mack had been waiting for. He popped up from behind the desk and took a quick shot at the man holding the shotgun.

"Yow!" Jerry shouted.

The shotgun clattered on the floor. Jerry raised his left hand to his face. Blood spurted from the knuckle where his index finger had once been.

"My finger's gone!" he said in a state of shock.

Mack charged at Jerry with the AR-15 ready. Jerry, now unarmed, dropped to his knees. He searched the floor of the warehouse for his missing finger. He mumbled to himself, on the verge of tears.

Mack covered the distance between them in seconds. He kicked the shotgun away toward the back of the warehouse. Turning to the open loading dock, Mack scanned the dark parking lot for Lucas. He spotted the man running up the road with one of the duffle bags slung over his shoulder.

Mack turned his focus back to Jerry.

"Hey, guy," said Mack, trying to get Jerry's attention.

"Where's my finger?" mumbled Jerry, still feeling around for the missing digit.

"You've got bigger issues than a missing finger."

Jerry stopped whining. He looked up at Mack.

"Don't kill me, man. I'm just a guy like you, trying to make some cash for my family. You want the money? There it is. We can split it," Jerry said hopefully. He nodded at the two remaining bags.

"Your buddy just left with some of it," said Mack. "How much is in those bags?"

"Supposed to be three million, but I don't know anything other than what they told me."

"A mil in each bag?"

"That'd be my guess."

Mack studied the man cowering on the floor at his feet. Blood poured from his mangled hand.

"Wrap that hand up in your shirt. You'll be okay if you don't bleed out."

"Okay?" said Jerry as he tore a piece of cloth from the tail of his shirt and tied it around his hand. "What part of this looks okay to you?"

Mack didn't answer.

"I got a little girl at home. Five years old. Maddie is her name. And a wife. They don't deserve what I've done to them." Jerry hung his head. "The city cut off our water last week. My daughter takes a bath in a bucket."

Jerry choked back tears. "You know how that feels, man? You got any kids?"

Mack shook his head. He lowered his rifle slightly.

"This deal was supposed to fix everything, get us back

on top. But now that's all over, I guess. Come to think of it, you might as well go ahead and kill me. My family would be better off without me."

Mack winced. "Don't say that. It's not right to talk about yourself that way, no matter who you are."

"At least they'd get the life insurance check."

Mack squatted down by one of the open duffle bags. He kept the rifle propped across his knee for easy access. With the palm of his hand, he swept through the bag of money.

"There's a million bucks in here, eh?" He lifted a stack of hundreds and tossed it lightly in the air. "What was your cut supposed to be?"

Jerry stared at the floor, squeezing the bloody cloth around his hand. "Ten percent."

"What's that, three hundred?

"Yeah."

"Assuming that prick didn't stiff you and leave you to die." Mack nodded in the direction that Lucas had run.

"Pretty much."

Mack thought about Andy. He remembered his family barely a week prior at the Atlanta Zoo, how excited the kid was, how happy they looked together.

"I got five hundred I promised to somebody. That's non-negotiable off the top," said Mack. "So the way I see it, that leaves one-point-five for you and me to figure out between us."

"What?" said Jerry, still in shock and unable to grasp Mack's suggestion.

"I'm not gonna kill you," said Mack. "I wouldn't have shot the other guys, either, if they didn't come at me first.

If I could have walked in here and taken half a million from one of those bags, and walked out without a shot I would've done it."

Jerry looked up. "You aren't?" he stammered.

Mack shook his head. "I don't like killing people. I try to avoid it. You wouldn't believe it if I told you the story of how I ended up here. It wasn't supposed to happen this way."

"Buddy, you said a mouthful."

Mack laughed. "We better not stick around here too long, though. Cops'll show up sooner or later with all the shooting we did."

Mack hesitated. He looked down at Jerry, studying the man's face to decide whether he could be trusted.

"If I put this rifle down, can I count on you to not try and shoot me?"

Jerry shook his head. "Man, I don't like killing people, either. I never have done it before. I just want to get my family back on track."

Mack leaned the rifle against the wall.

"I'll tell you what, I don't want to wait around for the police. I see a real simple solution. Two bags, two of us. What do you say?"

"You'd let me have a million dollars?" Jerry's eyes widened.

"Hell, it ain't my money," said Mack. "What about old dude though? He'll be pretty pissed off when he finds out his cash is gone, won't he?"

"He already got one of the bags," muttered Jerry. "Far as I'm concerned, he doesn't need to know anything."

"I shot your finger off and took all the cash? Is that

your story?" said Mack, raising his eyebrows. "That puts all the heat on me, doesn't it?"

Jerry shrugged. "You got a better plan?"

Mack thought for a few seconds. "No, I don't guess I do. In a couple hours I'll be many miles away from here. He's not gonna find me."

Mack picked up one of the duffle bags. He slid it across the floor. The bag skidded to a stop at Jerry's feet. Jerry bent over cautiously. He hoisted the bag up by its handle.

"Okay then," said Jerry.

Mack nodded, picking up the last bag. He retrieved the rifle. With both hands full, he slid off the loading dock. He turned back to Jerry. "Well, have a good life, I guess."

Jerry gave a wan smile. He raised his non-bleeding hand in farewell.

Mack sprinted across the dark parking lot. He didn't stop until he reached the Jetta. He tossed the weapons and the bag of cash in the backseat.

As Mack drove past the warehouse, he saw Jerry lift his duffle bag with his good hand and carefully load the cargo into a pickup truck.

24

"I didn't think I'd see you again," said Avery when she opened the door of her apartment a little before midnight.

"I told you I would come back. I owe you for the Jetta," said Mack, smiling. "Besides, I didn't want to leave town without seeing your pretty face again."

Avery groaned but her smile betrayed her true feelings. She looked over Mack's shoulder. She squinted and swept her eyes through the parking lot.

"Where is that Jetta anyway? I don't see it out there."

"Yeah, about that. It's at the motel. I had to leave it so I could pick up that black Tahoe." Mack pointed at Andy's truck.

Avery knitted her brow momentarily, and then shrugged. "The Jetta is your car now. Do whatever you want with it, I guess."

"Can I come in?"

Avery stepped aside and waved Mack through the door.

"You have any bourbon? I could use one."

"Sure, I have something good if we're celebrating?" Avery said her statement like a question, leading Mack to share his news, good or bad.

"That'll be perfect, thanks," said Mack. He took a seat at the kitchen table. He picked up a cigarette lighter and fidgeted with it while Avery poured two glasses of bourbon.

"It's Blanton's. You ever had that?"

"I don't think so."

"The bottle has a little horse on top. See?" Avery showed the bottle to Mack.

"Looks fancy."

"I told you, it's the good stuff."

Avery set the glass down in front of Mack.

He raised it to his lips and took a long sip. "Hm. Pretty good," he said.

The two remained silent for a few seconds until Avery could no longer take the suspense.

"So are we celebrating? Did you get the money?"

Mack smiled through tired eyes.

"I did."

Avery's face brightened. "All of it? How much?"

"Not all of it. But I got what I needed."

Avery hesitated. "And my fifty thousand?"

"I have it."

Mack reached in his jacket pocket. He withdrew a stack of bundled hundred-dollar bills. He laid the stack on the table.

Avery's eyes sparkled. She picked up the bundle of cash. "This is fifty thousand dollars? It doesn't look like that much."

"It never does. You can count it if you want."

"No, I didn't mean it like that. I've never held this much

money in my hand."

Mack finished off the bourbon. He set the empty glass on the wooden table with a hollow thud.

"Okay, here's what you need to do," he said, switching his tone to sound more confident than he felt. "Tomorrow, you report that Jetta as stolen. Call the police, have them do an official investigation and everything. Get a copy of the police report. When those bad guys come asking—and they will, cause your buddy the drug dealer is going to tell them you know something—when they come asking, you say you met me at the club, and I spent the night. When you woke up yesterday the Jetta was gone, and you never heard from me again. Show them the police report if you have to."

Avery listened. She started to respond, but Mack continued.

"You don't know my last name. You barely met me. You think maybe I might have overheard something about the drug deal that night at the bar when you were talking to, what's his name, Liam. That's your best guess. You didn't tell me anything, you don't know anything."

Mack paused to let his words sink in.

"Can you do all that?"

Avery nodded. "But they can't prove you did anything, can they?" she said. "It's not like they're going to the police. Maybe it will all blow over if we lay low for a while."

"I shot two men and took a duffle bag full of cash. It's not going to blow over."

"Holy shit. You did? Are they…dead?"

The look on Mack's face answered her question.

"I can't stay here," he said. "I need to leave tonight."

Avery shook her head slowly. "I was just starting to like

you," she said.

Mack felt the same way. He gritted his teeth to fight back the emotion that was welling up inside him.

"Me, too," he said. He watched Avery's face for a reaction. "You know, you could come with me. If you wanted to."

Avery dropped her eyes to the table. She sighed.

"It only works that way in the movies," she said after a long pause.

Mack frowned. "I have more money. We could go anywhere."

"You can't just do that. You know you can't. It's not fair to come in here and ask me to change everything for you, to accommodate your situation."

Avery stood up. She walked over to the counter. She stopped in front of the bottle of Blanton's. With an index finger she stroked the tiny metal horse on top of the cork.

"I have a life here. I don't want to give it up."

Mack flicked the cigarette lighter once and tossed it on the table. "I know," he said. "I just don't want to leave you."

Avery turned and faced Mack. She put her palms on the counter behind her and leaned until the edge contacted her lower back.

"Yeah, well, you were kind of growing on me, too," she said. "But you should have thought about that before you shot up a bunch of drug dealers and stole their money."

"I didn't have a choice."

Avery rolled her eyes.

"I promised that money to someone. It was the only way I could get it."

"To someone other than me? Did you buy yourself *two*

cars on credit?"

Mack smiled, acknowledging that he had made special deals with both Avery and Andy.

"Sort of."

Avery pursed her lips, thinking.

"Well, you kept your promise to me, I'll give you that."

"Yeah. And now I need to run to Atlanta so I can keep the second one."

"You're leaving town already?"

"I have to. The longer I stay here the more dangerous it gets for you and me both."

Avery frowned. "You aren't coming back, are you?"

Mack stared at the table.

"I didn't think so," Avery said.

Mack looked up at the woman with whom he had spent the past several days. "My offer stands. Page me in a couple weeks when things die down. I don't know where I'll be, but you can come join me wherever I am."

"We'll see."

Mack reached in his jacket pocket. He took out another stack of hundreds—he figured around twenty thousand dollars. He set the cash on the table.

"What's that for?" said Avery.

"I never tipped you for that lap dance. Best lap dance I ever had."

Avery's face cracked a smile. "I told you I was good."

"You did. And you were right."

Jerry pulled his pickup truck all the way to the back of the gravel driveway by the dilapidated shed. The dashboard clock said 11:03 when he turned off the key. The truck sputtered and died. Jerry took a deep breath and exhaled slowly. The truck's engine ticked arrhythmically as it cooled, the only sound in Jerry's backyard other than crickets.

Raising his left fist to catch the moonlight, Jerry examined the bloody cloth wrapped around his hand. The bleeding had mostly stopped. The t-shirt bandage felt crusty to the touch. His entire arm throbbed with pain all the way up to his shoulder.

Jerry reached across his body with his right hand and opened the door. He slid out, feeling the gravel under his boots. He grabbed the duffle bag and dragged it slowly toward the house. His entire body felt exhausted, like he could sleep for a week straight.

"Jerry?"

His wife's voice came from the living room when Jerry opened the kitchen door.

"Yeah, it's me," he said, surprising himself by the weak sound of his own voice.

"Daddy!" squealed Maddie as she ran around the corner and entered the kitchen. When she saw her dad's appearance—the exhausted eyes, the dirty clothes, the blood-soaked hand—she stopped cold a few feet from him. She hesitated, looking up at him, waiting for him to greet her and tell her he was okay.

"What are you doing up so late?" said Jerry. He forced a tired smile.

"There's no school tomorrow!"

"It's too late for little girls to be awake, school or no school."

"Mommy said I could."

"Did she now? And where is she?"

Just then, Billie Musen entered the kitchen. She took one look at her husband's bandaged hand and rushed over to him.

"What did you do?"

"It's not bad. I had an accident at work."

Billie studied her husband's face. "Not bad? It looks terrible. What did you do, lose a finger?" she asked, half-joking.

Jerry grimaced. "Yeah."

"What? Are you serious?"

"Fraid so."

"Oh my god, Jerry. You need to go to the hospital."

"I don't disagree with you, honey. I may need you to drive me, though."

"Daddy lost a finger? Where did it go?" Maddie asked her mother.

"A shark ate it," said Jerry.

"Don't you tell her that," said Billie.

"A shark?" said Maddie, a confused look in her eyes.

"He's just pulling your leg, sweetheart. We're going to take him to the doctor to fix him up."

Jerry dropped the duffle bag on the kitchen floor.

"Billie, why don't you help me unpack before we go." He winked at his wife and nudged the bag with his boot.

Billie lowered her eyebrows, questioning her husband nonverbally. She cautiously knelt before the bag and unzipped it a few inches. She looked inside and her eyes widened.

"Is this—? Did you—?"

"Yep," said Jerry, beaming.

"How much is it?"

"Way more than enough."

Billie smiled. She tried to find the right words to thank or congratulate or even chide her husband, but she came up empty. She just shook her head slowly. She hoisted the duffle bag and dragged it away to the bedroom.

"Put it in the special place, hon. We'll look at it when we get back from the hospital," Jerry called after his wife.

"Hey, Daddy," said Maddie, her voice almost a whisper. "Can I ask you a question?"

"You sure can. Come over here and give me a hug."

The girl approached her father. She hugged his right leg, careful to avoid the bloody hand.

"What did you want to ask, sweet pea?"

Maddie's big eyes stared up at her father.

"Can you still make a hand turkey without a finger?"

Jerry smiled. Emotion caught in the back of his throat. He felt tears forming in his eyes.

"I think we can figure it out," he said. "Good thing I have two hands."

He showed the girl his unmarred right hand.

She gripped two fingers of her father's dirty, bloodstreaked right hand, examining them closely. Once satisfied, she released his hand, announcing, "Yeah, it's a good thing."

25

Twenty-three hours after Mack left Atlanta, he returned to the hospital. He parked Andy's Tahoe in the visitor lot early on Wednesday morning.

Mack opened the truck's rear door. Using the cargo area as a table, he unpacked a bag of supplies he had picked up from a nearby drugstore. He used gauze and alcohol to clean the bullet wound on his shoulder. Luckily, the bullet had only grazed his flesh. He cut away the sleeve of his undershirt and wiped the cut dry. He treated and bandaged the wound, and then gingerly slipped his jacket back over his tender shoulder.

With his injury treated, Mack turned his attention to the duffle bag full of cash. He dragged the bag to the edge of the cargo area. He glanced over his shoulder to make sure no one was watching, and then he unzipped the bag.

Mack grabbed stacks of cash with both hands. He quickly transferred the money to a gift box he had procured at the same drugstore where he had bought the medical supplies.

Fifty stacks of hundred-dollar bills. Each stack

contained a hundred individual bills. Five hundred grand.

The cash barely fit in the box. Mack pressed the lid down hard to close it. For an added touch, he wrapped the box in wrapping paper—the only paper the store stocked this close to Christmas. Bright red paper that featured little reindeer with glowing noses.

When Mack finished wrapping Andy's "present" he tucked it under his arm. He stepped back and slammed the back door of the Tahoe.

The morning sky had just begun to lighten. Mack felt the lack of sleep catching up to him. He needed to get out of Georgia fast, to find some quiet motel off the interstate where he could take a shower and rest.

At least money would not be a problem for him. He would need lots of cash to buy the anonymity required to escape. Five hundred to Andy plus about seventy-five to Avery. That left him with somewhere around $400,000 in the duffle bag.

The nurse at the desk directed Mack to Andy's room. When he arrived, Mack poked his head into the dark chamber.

Andy lay sleeping on the bed. His arm held an IV. His upper body was wrapped in a white bandage from waist to neck. A machine next to his bed beeped methodically.

Mack took a few steps into the room. He spotted Olivia sitting in a chair near the bed. She watched Mack without speaking.

"How is he?" Mack whispered.

Olivia raised a finger to her lips. She stood up and joined Mack near the door.

"Sleeping. Surgery went well. They think he will be fine once everything heals." She spoke tersely, making it clear Mack's visit would be a short one.

"That's good news."

Mack raised the gift-wrapped package. He offered it to Olivia with both hands. "Got him a little something. To help with the recovery."

Olivia took the package. Her arms wobbled under the unexpected weight. "What's in here, rocks?" she asked.

"It's a surprise."

"I think we've had enough surprises for one day."

Mack shuffled his feet. "Listen, I need to run," he said. "I just want you to know again how sorry I am this happened."

"I know you are."

"When he gets healthy again, tell him to give me a call, will you?"

Olivia frowned. "I most certainly will not, but I'm sure he will anyway."

Mack thought he saw a slight smile cross the woman's face. He took the cue and smiled back. "He always was a rascal, wasn't he?"

Olivia shrugged. "I knew that when I married him."

"Well, take care of him, okay? Tell him how much I appreciate him."

"I will."

Mack turned to go but remembered one more thing he had to do. "Oh, the Tahoe," he said. "I brought it back. It's down in the visitor lot. I need to grab something out of the back real quick, and then I'll leave the keys for you at the front desk."

Mack left Olivia holding the package wrapped in Christmas paper. As he headed for the elevator he felt his pager buzz in his pocket. A phone number he didn't recognize. He got in the elevator and pushed the button to return to the ground floor.

Just as he stepped off the elevator, Mack's pager buzzed again. "Jesus, chill out already," he muttered, checking the pager screen again, expecting to see the same unknown number.

But this page came from a different caller, a number he very much recognized—the same caller with whom he had been communicating throughout the entire Savannah job. The phone number belonged to his mysterious employer. Mack had not heard from him since the shootout at McKearney's.

Mack stopped at a group of pay phones near the hospital's exit. He dropped a quarter in the slot and dialed the number displayed on his pager.

"What happened?" said the chilling voice without offering any other greeting.

Now accustomed to the cold tone of his former client, Mack responded in kind. "How bout you tell me, pal? Last time I checked we took heavy fire for you. And not only did you not show up, but you stiffed me on payment."

"We did not authorize you to use a partner."

"Well, you didn't *not* authorize one, either. Good thing I had him or else I'd probably be dead right now, no thanks to you."

"Did you expect we would walk into a fire fight in a public area? We were nearby. The opportunity never presented itself."

Mack frowned. He looked across the waiting room as a child pushed a toy truck around the carpeted floor.

"I don't suppose the opportunity to pay me presented itself either?"

The voice paused. Mack heard the man breathing. "The job was not completed."

"Yeah, that's what I figured you'd say."

"Where is the shipment?"

"You got some balls on you to ask me that question after you left me holding the bag."

"Perhaps an amended payment could be arranged in exchange for the current location of the shipment."

"I'm gonna pass on that offer."

"It's very important that we locate the package."

Mack smiled as a thought crossed his mind. "I'll tell you what, there's a little motel downtown off Bay Street. Go in there and talk to the front desk clerk—real pleasant little fella—tell him you need to see his tracking device. He'll fix you right up."

The voice started to respond but Mack didn't wait to hear it. He hung up the receiver. His quarter dropped into the bowels of the pay phone with a clink.

The kid with the toy truck made engine noises as he steered the truck at a ninety-degree angle directly up the side of a chair leg.

Mack scrolled through his pager to find the unrecognized number. Area code 606. He didn't know which state owned that code but knew it would be long distance. He jingled the change in his pockets, extracted three quarters and fed the pay phone's slot.

"This is Abbott," Mack said when a man answered the

line.

"Would that be Mack Abbott?"

The voice had a thick southern drawl. Mack hesitated to divulge too much information to a stranger.

"It would. Who's this?"

"Mr. Mack Abbott, my name is Jefferson. Riley J. Jefferson. Have you heard of me?"

"Can't say that I have."

Riley Jefferson laughed. "That's alright I reckon. Maybe I'm not as well known outside of coal country."

"Coal country?"

"That's right. Eastern Kentucky is where I'm calling you from. Right in the heart of coal country. Harlan County, Kentucky, to be exact."

"Harlan County?" Mack asked slowly, surprised by the coincidence between the location of this Mr. Jefferson and the name of the ship Mack had been stationed on in the Navy. The U.S.S. *Harlan County*.

"You heard me correctly. Beautiful country here. You ever visited?"

"No."

"Listen, Mr. Abbott, I'm not here to waste your time. Suffice to say, I am a man of considerable means. The coal business has afforded my family and I with a lifestyle beyond most men's wildest imagination. But it has also introduced a number of headaches. Seems to be those headaches are increasing in frequency for me these days. Now, I'm in need of a special kind of man. Some might call him a fixer."

"I'm listening."

Jefferson laughed again. "Good, good. This man would

need to be capable of solving all sorts of…problems. Anything that pops up, I need him to be able to deal with it, quickly and discreetly." Jefferson paused, letting his words sink in. "I have heard you may be just that type of man. The one I'm looking for."

Mack exhaled. "Mr. Jefferson, you caught me at a tough time. It has been a hell of a week."

"Please call me Riley. I'll tell you what, why don't you come to Kentucky as my guest for a while. Take a break, recover. Let me show you around. I want you to know money is no object to me. The man I'm looking for, I will pay him well. Very well."

"Kentucky, huh? I've been through Lexington on I-75. How far away is Harlan County from there?"

"Difference in miles? A couple hundred. Difference in everything else? They ain't even close. Where are you now?"

"Probably a day's drive."

"You'll make it just in time for Thanksgiving then. You won't believe the spread we put on the table for Thanksgiving around here. Come and join us."

Mack considered the offer. What did he have to lose? He needed to put miles between Georgia and wherever he slept that night. This man was offering him a place to rest and a free meal.

"If I did come, where in Harlan County would I find you?"

"You make it to Eastern Kentucky, then ask anybody on the street where my house is, they'll tell you. Everybody around here knows Riley J. Jefferson."

Mack thanked Jefferson and hung up the phone. He left

the hospital on foot and walked half a mile up the road to a small used car lot he had passed on the way into town. He would come back for the duffle bag once he secured transportation.

Inside the cramped trailer that served as the car lot's office, a salesman sat behind a desk covered in wrinkled papers. Cheap wood paneling lined the office walls.

The salesman raised his head and nodded at Mack. He sniffed his coffee mug and took the first sip of the steaming beverage.

"Morning," said the salesman. "What are you in the market for today?"

The coffee pot gurgled and steamed on the counter in the corner. The salesman smiled at the sound.

"A cup of that coffee for starters," said Mack. "Then I'd like to see your inventory. I'm looking for something reliable and fast. Something that can get me from here to Kentucky in as few stops as possible."

About the Author

Josh Boldt is a Southern crime and mystery author known for his realistic dialogue, regional flavor, and exploration of the Southern psyche. Boldt is the author of three novels: *Moneymaker*, *The False Favorite*, and *Slurry*. He lives in Lexington, Kentucky, where he's hard at work on his next novel.